PRAISE FOR THE
JEWELL COVE SERIES

"Oh, my silly heart, be still. This is a wonderful romance, packed with family drama, a sexy hero, an incredible old house. You'll fall in love from the very first page." —Debbie Macomber,
#1 *New York Times* bestselling author

"A wonderful, witty, and memorable book! Donna Alward's *The House on Blackberry Hill* is a heartwarming, delightful debut to an engaging new series. Readers will love discovering the richly layered stories and enticing secrets residing in Jewell Cove."
—*New York Times* bestselling author Shirley Jump

"A wonderful story with plenty of sizzle and the perfect hint of mystery. Donna Alward writes with emotion and heart." —RaeAnne Thayne,
New York Times bestselling author of
Christmas in Snowflake Canyon

"Donna Alward writes warm, memorable characters who spring to life on the page. Brimming with old family history, small-town secrets, and newfound passion, you'll want to pack up and move to Jewell Cove, Maine!" —Lily Everett

"A promising, creative, and deeply emotional homecoming journey that will captivate readers."
—*RT Book Reviews*

"Old family secrets, a bitter tragedy, and a restless spirit add mystery and an eerie touch to this compelling story that is steeped in small-town New England flavor so rich you can taste it and beautifully launches the author's new series." —*Library Journal*

"*The House on Blackberry Hill* was my first Donna Alward book and I loved it! The romance was sweet, the characters were quirky, and the town of Jewell Cove was amazing. It sounds so enchanting; I would love to live there!" —*Badass Book Reviews*

"A lovely contemporary romance with historical ties and a strong feeling of roots and family connections. Every once in a while I am lucky enough to find a book that has such wonderful atmosphere that it transports me from the world I know to the same place the characters are in. This is one of those books. The descriptions are perfect. I could smell the scent of blackberries in the air and feel the breeze upon my skin." —*Readful Things Blog*

Summer on Lovers' Island

Donna Alward

St. Martin's Paperbacks

This is a work of fiction. All of the characters, organizations, and events portrayed in this novel are either products of the author's imagination or are used fictitiously.

SUMMER ON LOVERS' ISLAND

Copyright © 2015 by Donna Alward.

For information address St. Martin's Press, 175 Fifth Avenue, New York, NY 10010.

ISBN: 978-1-250-04518-8

Printed in the United States of America

St. Martin's Paperbacks edition / May 2015

St. Martin's Paperbacks are published by St. Martin's Press, 175 Fifth Avenue, New York, NY 10010.

10 9 8 7 6 5 4 3 2 1

To Fenton Burke and Tish Thornton, and all the other teachers and professors who fed my appetite for literature and, most of all, believed in me.

CHAPTER 1

As punishments went, Lizzie Howard could have done a lot worse.

The "recommendation" was for her to get out of town for a few days, and she'd chosen to visit her best friend, Charlie, in Jewell Cove. The story Lizzie'd given Charlie was that they could spend the weekend celebrating Lizzie's thirtieth birthday. That sounded much better than the truth, which was that she was slinking away from Springfield with her tail tucked firmly between her legs.

Thirty. Her career was supposed to be taking off instead of stalled in its tracks. How the hell had this happened?

The wind was cool even for spring in New England as Lizzie's convertible wound around the scenic road that led to her best friend's house. Charlie lived with her husband, Dave, a few miles from town limits. Their home was nestled along a curve in the road, its cedar deck overlooking the shimmering waters of Penobscot Bay—the perfect retreat for Lizzie to clear her head.

With each mile separating her from Massachusetts, she could feel her tension ease a little. Maybe Maine wouldn't be so bad after all, she thought, pulling in the gravel driveway in front of the little cottage Charlie now called home. Gray shingle siding and white-trimmed dormer windows gave it a cozy, worn-in look. The trees and lilacs were budding, unfurling their new spring-green leaves to the sun, and at a small white picket gate hung a quaint little sign that read: Seashell Cottage.

Lizzie loved it immediately. It was like something off a postcard.

As she got out of her car, she realized that the walkway to the door was lined with shells and she let out a soft laugh. Her best friend was living in an idyllic world far away from the high-class Boston neighborhood where she'd been brought up.

Lizzie breathed in the sweet-scented air and smiled to herself, thinking of the shell-studded candles she had in her bag as a delayed housewarming present. Her only regret was that she hadn't come sooner. She hadn't actually seen her friend since Charlie and Dave's destination wedding on a Jamaican beach in January.

At least she wasn't completely out of touch where her best friend was concerned. Lizzie knew Charlie had always wanted a home like this. Nothing big or ostentatious, but a little corner of the world that she could call her own and an adoring husband across the breakfast table. A few babies with brown eyes and dimples to call her "Mama."

Lizzie wanted more. She'd been working her ass off in Springfield, determined to fill Ian Fortnam's shoes as Chief of Emergency Medicine. It was what her father wanted for her and she would do him proud even though he wasn't here to see it. The fact that Ian had been the one to ask her to take a leave of absence—a strong suggestion that Lizzie equated to a suspension—annoyed the hell out of her.

Ian insisted it was because he cared and the time off was for her own good, but she wasn't so sure. Yes, she'd screwed up, with devastating results. She'd admitted that. And she had been working too hard. She admitted that, too. But the biggest mistake she'd made was having an affair with Ian in the first place. They'd remained "friends" when it ended, as they both knew it would, but she hated that he was in a position to influence the career she'd worked so hard to build. Mixing her personal life with her professional one was a mistake she wouldn't repeat again. Ever.

So now here she was, standing in the dappled afternoon sunlight, miles from home and hospital. Lizzie shouldered her travel bag and blew out a breath, determined that she wouldn't be dragged down again. She'd make the most of the days ahead and recharge her batteries. This was only a weekend, after all. Didn't she deserve that much of a break?

When Lizzie returned to Springfield it would be time enough to fight to get her position back. This forced leave was utter nonsense. If there was a lawsuit, it would be settled, just as they always were. She was a good doctor. Everyone would move on. . . .

She was halfway up the shell-lined path when the screen door slammed open and Charlie was there, bouncing on her toes and with one hand on her slightly rounded belly. "You're here! You're finally here! At my house!"

"Yes, I'm here." Lizzie laughed, her dark thoughts banished by Charlie's enthusiastic greeting. "I promised, and here I am."

Charlie came down the stone steps and drew Lizzie into a hug. "Gosh, it's good to see you."

Lizzie felt Charlie's strong arms around her and closed her eyes. It wasn't one of those polite, restrained hugs full of pretension between casual friends and colleagues. This was big, hearty, and full of affection. After all the weeks of being so very alone, it felt wonderful. She could feel the firm baby bump against her own tummy and laughed, drawing back and framing the gentle roundness with her hands.

"My God, look at you. You're beautiful." Tears pricked Lizzie's eyelids and she laughed self-consciously. "And showing already."

Charlie laughed, too, wiping her eyes, then tucked her dark hair behind her ears. "Dave says future linebacker in the making. I'm not due until September."

"He could be right."

Lizzie straightened, looked at her best friend, and couldn't stop smiling. No unwanted pregnancy here, no angst or uncertainty. This was, Lizzie realized, exactly how it should be. "You're glowing, Charlie. God, I'm so happy for you."

Charlie sniffled and beamed even as she flapped her hands at her tears. "You see? This is why you needed to come! It's going to be good for you. You're skin and bones, Liz. I'm going to stuff you full of yumminess all weekend."

"Hey, I eat."

"Peanut butter doesn't count."

Lizzie couldn't help but laugh. Charlie was the closest thing to a sister she'd ever had, and they'd definitely gone through starving student days when peanut butter sandwiches kept them going, especially during long days of labs and hospital shifts. In an emergency they'd forgotten about the bread and just gone for a spoon.

"Come on in. Dave will be home later this afternoon and he promised to cook us dinner. We can sit on the deck and catch up."

Lizzie followed Charlie into the house. The inside was as charming as the outside, filled with sun-strewn windows whose light bounced off walls the color of the sand on the beach below. The flooring was wide plank hardwood, stained a gorgeous shade of oak. White country cupboards filled the walls in the kitchen and a stunning butcher block held a bowl of lilacs, bringing the fragrance in from outside.

"This is your room," Charlie said, opening a door. The walls were the same sandy taupe, but splashes of aqua at the windows and on the duvet brought it to life.

"It's beautiful, Charlie. Just beautiful."

"Get yourself settled, then come find me," Charlie offered, stepping out to give Lizzie a moment of privacy.

Lizzie put down her bag and went to the windows. The room overlooked the ocean, the sun glinting almost painfully off the constantly shifting surface. She knew why she was here and it had little to do with her birthday or even a suggested leave of absence. She was running from her grief and running from her problems, pure and simple.

A lone sail bobbed on the water, skimming parallel with the shoreline. She squared her shoulders. *Not running,* she corrected. *Regrouping.* There was a difference.

She found Charlie in the kitchen heating the kettle.

"Tea," Lizzie said with a smile. A plate held several cookies. "And shortbread. Did you read my mind?"

"It's not my shortbread, are you kidding? There's a bakery on Main that is amazing. I'll take you there tomorrow." She handed over a square and poured water into the mugs. "I still haven't learned to cook very well. Oh well. No one's perfect, right? Dave cooks and if all else fails there's takeout. Or frozen pizza."

Lizzie took a nibble of the cookie and sighed happily. "It's yummy."

"It's orange spice. Told you it was amazing. Jewell Cove has all sorts of treasures and I'm going to show you them tomorrow. We're going to hit all the shops along the waterfront."

"You wouldn't still happen to be trying to sell me on covering your mat leave, would you?"

Two weeks ago, just before Lizzie was ordered to take her "break," Charlie had called asking if she wanted to cover her maternity leave. Leaving Springfield right now wasn't an option, not when what Lizzie really needed to do was get her act together. She had a job, a reputation, at stake. Responsibilities. Like proving to Ian and the rest of the administration that she was worthy of the faith they'd placed in her. Proving to herself that she hadn't lost her edge. Physicians lost patients; it came with the job. They had to deal with it.

Besides, family medicine in a small town would bore her to death, even for a few months.

Charlie handed over the mug, a saucy grin lighting her lips. "Shamelessly. Is it working?"

Lizzie had to admit, the pretty drive and idyllic setting had already eased some of her tension. But this was a weekend, not months. And she figured she'd only last a few days in a small town before going stir-crazy. "Let's go outside," she suggested, changing the subject. "I need to hear the ocean."

They settled into Adirondack chairs and Lizzie closed her eyes, let the sun bathe her face as she listened to the shushing sound of the waves hitting the shore below and the gulls shrieking as they circled. The spring breeze was fresh and chilly; Lizzie pulled her knees in and rested her feet on the edge of the seat. Charlie said nothing. She always seemed to know when Lizzie needed quiet and when she needed to talk. After a few minutes Lizzie opened one eye and squinted to look at her friend. Charlie was taking a sip of tea, completely comfortable to just *be*. One hand rubbed the curve of her belly. Lizzie would bet any money that the action was one of sheer habit, and she took a moment to appreciate the picture that was Charlie, burgeoning with motherhood.

Lizzie didn't know exactly how to explain how she felt. Adrift, maybe. Definitely alone. Her mom and dad had been her guiding stars. Losing her mom to Alzheimer's bit by bit was terrible, and visiting her now was bittersweet, never knowing what state of mind Rosemary would be in. But losing her dad . . . they'd been so close. Going through the last months without his wisdom was horrible. She'd put every ounce of energy into work, and she didn't even have that now. She had no idea how to explain it all to her best friend, but she desperately wanted to.

"I needed this," she said simply. "So thank you."

Charlie reached over and took her hand. With anyone but Charlie it would have been awkward. But they'd been through a lot together, since the beginning when Lizzie had walked into her dorm room to find Charlie on one of the beds. The two made an unlikely pair, but from the first moment they'd been there for each other. Just like they were now.

"Everything's out of control, Charlie. Just everything." She swallowed against the lump in her throat. "For the first time in my life, I don't know what to do." She felt her lip wobble. "I don't know what to do," she whispered.

"Oh, honey," Charlie said, squeezing Lizzie's fingers. "I know it's been so hard. I should have been there for you more. . . . I'm really sorry about that. I suck as a friend."

"You had enough on your plate, with the pregnancy and planning the wedding and everything." Lizzie tried a watery smile. "And look at you. You were always so shy, so reserved. Dave's been so good for you. He really brought you out of your shell."

Charlie's gaze softened. "He is pretty wonderful. But that doesn't make it all right that I neglected you."

"Well, I'm here now. Just what the doctor ordered."

Charlie nodded. "Hey, don't worry. I know you. You're like a rubber ball; you always bounce back. You'll figure it out. I know you will." The confidence in her voice was clear.

But Lizzie shook her head. "I don't know this time. I don't know who I am, or what I want. . . . The one thing holding me together was work." She squeezed Charlie's fingers back before letting them go.

"You've been grieving so hard, Liz. I know it's been eating away at you. You're here now, and that's what matters. You did the right thing taking some time off."

Lizzie smiled but felt herself crumbling inside. How could she admit that her vacation wasn't voluntary? Charlie was under the impression that this weekend was just that—a weekend. Lizzie's smile wobbled and she took a deep breath, promising herself she wouldn't cry. "I wasn't ready to talk about it before. Didn't want to." She swallowed, hard. "Couldn't."

"But you want to now?"

She took a sip of tea, the hot brew restorative, warming her belly, giving her strength to say the painful words. "I'm falling apart, Charlie. Seriously falling apart." Her voice broke on the last syllable.

Charlie turned in her chair, tucking her legs beneath her. "What is it? Can I help? Are you sick?"

Lizzie shook her head. "Nothing that sleep won't cure. But I'm not sleeping. I've been working extra shifts just to keep busy and keep myself occupied." *Mistake number one.*

"And burning yourself out."

Bingo. "What else am I supposed to do?"

Charlie didn't answer but waited patiently. Lizzie thought that Charlie would make a very good mother. She was logical and tolerant and always thought things through. Marriage, too, had given her a new kind of serenity that Lizzie envied. Lizzie didn't have that kind of patience. She didn't wait for things; she went after them. Always moving forward and not backward. There were so many other things she wanted to do before having kids . . . if ever.

She struggled to speak past the tightness in her throat. This was so unlike her! She was a doctor, for God's sake. She handled tough decisions every day. She spoke to family members and delivered bad news and it wasn't easy, but she always kept it together. But it was different when it was her own life. Her own feelings. She couldn't look at Charlie or the sympathy she knew would be in her best friend's eyes. She looked out over the sparkling ocean and whispered, "I didn't know that when I lost him I'd lose everything. I haven't even brought myself to put the house on the market. I don't want it, but I can't bear the thought of someone else there. It's like it's waiting for him to come home and say it was all a mistake."

Charlie wisely stayed put in her chair. Lizzie didn't think she could handle any more hand-holding or hugging. She was feeling pretty fragile, ready to break apart at any moment. It was as if Charlie sensed it and after a few seconds of stunned silence she regrouped.

"Your dad's not coming back, Liz."

"I know that. And then I go to visit my mom, and—" She was mortified to realize that tears were slipping down her cheeks and she scrubbed them away with her hands. "She asks where he is. She doesn't remember that he died. Or she'll say he's been to visit her when that's impossible, and it's like ripping open a wound again."

"Sweetie," Charlie said, and her thumb rubbed reassuringly over the top of Lizzie's hand. "I'm so sorry, Liz. I wish I could make things better."

But Charlie couldn't, not really. Though simply being here helped.

"I can't put things off any longer. Everything is such an unholy mess and somehow I have to fix it. I'm so angry!" Liz admitted the dark truth with a burst of frustration, relief sliding through her as she finally said the words. She was angry at a disease she couldn't do anything about, turning her mother into a stranger. She was angry at the suddenness of the stroke that had taken her father, a cruel irony for a man who'd dedicated his life to saving others. And she was angry at herself for slipping up and the devastating consequences that followed.

"Your dad loved you. You know that." Charlie ran a hand over the swell of her belly, the action making Lizzie feel suddenly left out. "Your mom adores you, too. Of course it's going to take some time for you to grieve. You just shouldn't be going through this alone. I wish you had someone . . . the way that I have Dave." A wistful smile touched her lips.

Lizzie couldn't help the small smile. Charlie was head over heels in love with her new husband. "I knew this would come back to my love life eventually."

"What love life?" Charlie raised an eyebrow.

"Exactly." Lizzie focused on picking shortbread crumbs off her jeans, glad she'd gotten some things off her chest and very glad they'd changed the subject somewhat.

"Whatever happened to that doctor you were seeing at Christmas? The cute one with the reddish hair and big laugh?"

Lizzie felt her cheeks heat. "That's over."

"I can tell by your tone who ended it. I thought you were crazy about him?"

Lizzie shook her head. "Ian's last act as my boss was to tell me to take a leave of absence. He's not on my list of favorite people these days."

Charlie shut her mouth. Picked at her shortbread. Took a sip of cold tea.

"Oh for God's sake, say something," Lizzie snapped, unable to take Charlie's silence.

Charlie got up, picked up her chair, and moved it so

she was sitting knee to knee with Lizzie. "He did you a gigantic favor in my opinion," she said firmly. "Look, here's what I know for sure. Russell Howard loved you. You loved him. No, hear me out. He was human, and you're human, too. If you're angry, be angry. My question to you is, what do you want to do now? Because whatever you want to do, I'll help you."

Anxiety seemed to tumble around in Lizzie's stomach.

"Everything feels so out of control, Charlie. I don't know how to deal with it. And I haven't been able to admit that to anyone before now."

Charlie smiled softly. "If you had the answers you wouldn't be finding this so difficult. And honey, you don't need to decide today. I know that's hard for you to accept, but it's true. Stay the weekend and stop worrying. Look around. The offer is still open to take my place for a few months. I'm planning on starting my leave July first, as long as I can find someone to cover."

Lizzie dropped her chin. "My head is so messed up. I can't bring all that into the practice you've built."

"Don't worry about that. The other doctor is great. I'm already working reduced hours. It'd just be . . . backup." She smiled encouragingly.

"Colds and ingrown toenails. Lovely." But Lizzie's lips twitched. Charlie was like a dog with a bone when she got an idea in her head. Nothing was going to make her give it up. "Besides, I'm sure the town is nice, but isn't it a bit . . . dull?" Dull as in dead. There probably wasn't a movie theater, or a martini bar, or decent restaurants.

"I know you're impossible when you're bored. But there is a lot to do here." At Lizzie's skeptical look she insisted, "There is! Including sleep. You look like hell, Liz. Besides, Portland isn't far away if you need something more . . . cultured. There's more to Jewell Cove than you think. It's only for a few months. It's not like it's forever or anything."

Finally, Lizzie laughed. Charlie was better for her than any prescription. "Thank you, Charlie. For inviting me to visit." When Charlie raised a doubtful eyebrow, she capitulated, "For *making* me come. I didn't know who else to turn to."

"I'm always here; you know that."

"But just because I'm on leave doesn't mean I'm saying yes."

"It ups the chances. And I'm not above using a little blackmail."

"More shortbread?"

Charlie put her hands on Lizzie's knees. "If you stayed the summer, it means that my best friend in the whole world would be with me when my baby was born."

Lizzie's nose stung and her bottom lip quivered. It was no secret that Charlie's mom and dad weren't exactly the nurturing type. Lizzie couldn't imagine them being doting grandparents, or Mrs. Yang sitting through the undignified process of childbirth, even though she'd gone through it once herself. "That's playing so dirty," Lizzie whispered.

"It's true," Charlie answered. "You need someone, Lizzie. And I need you. You're the closest thing to a sister I've ever had. I want you to be our baby's godmother."

Lizzie felt herself slipping. But she had to be strong. She hadn't even seen the town yet. Or met the other doctor. And where would she find a place to live this close to tourist season? Surely everything was rented in advance.

"I'll think about it," she replied. It was all she was able to commit to at the moment.

CHAPTER 2

They took Lizzie's convertible, driving with the top down in the late-spring morning. The drive into Jewell Cove was short but pretty. Once leaving Charlie's cottage, the road connected with Route 1, tracing the jagged coast like a curving snake. This morning the fog was melting in the morning sun, giving the light soft edges, like a picture from a magazine that had been photoshopped—but this was the real thing. Lizzie filled her lungs with the sea air and felt her hair blow back in the breeze. She had never been in such a naturally beautiful place in all her life. Maybe she could finally try windsurfing, or go hiking in Acadia National Park. *Whoa*, she reminded herself. She wasn't actually considering taking Charlie up on her offer, was she?

"We'll find a place to park," Charlie ordered. "Somewhere near the café, I think. We can shop and then come back for lunch." Lizzie crawled along Main Street, looking for an open parking spot, following the direction of the finger Charlie pointed.

"Do you ever think of anything besides food?"

"Believe me, after a solid thirteen weeks of throwing up . . ."

Lizzie laughed. "Fair enough. If my turn ever comes . . ."

"Do you want it to?"

Considering Lizzie's current situation, the idea of a family was so far removed that it seemed a lifetime away. "I don't know. I haven't thought about it much. I've been too busy. And there's the tiny issue of a husband. Not a lot of Daves floating around for the taking, you know. I know in this day and age it's not necessary . . . but I'm still a little old-fashioned when it comes to marriage."

"You're far more conventional than you let on, Liz."

"Don't let that get out and ruin my reputation," Lizzie replied. "Like I said. Long way off." But she'd been truthful about her view of marriage and family. Her upbringing hadn't been perfect. Her father had been a bit of a workaholic, which put a strain on the marriage from time to time. But her parents had loved each other and persevered, even through tough times, and they'd always made an effort to make home a fun and welcoming place. Lizzie would rather be alone than settle for anything less.

"Well, take notes just the same. You've already missed the morning sickness bit. Least you can do is hang around for the varicose veins and hemorrhoids."

Lizzie laughed. "Gee, what fun. And here I thought small-town medicine was boring."

They made their way along to the northeast end of Main. Only a few parking spots remained along the curb, and the small lot by the wharf was half-full. In another few weeks Lizzie figured the tourism traffic would hit full force for the Memorial Day weekend, turning the relaxed little town into a hub of activity.

As they halted at the stop sign next to the wharf, Lizzie saw a pleasure boat slowly make its way around the slip. The words on the side were still clear: *Jewell's Constant*. Farther out in the bay, the pristine white sails of a pair of clipper ships glided above the water. What would it be like to escape for a day's sail on the ocean? When had Lizzie last taken time to do something so frivolous?

She turned her attention back to Charlie. "You're really happy here, aren't you?"

"Yes," Charlie replied, "I am. Look, Liz. I know this isn't your speed and I know it's not where you want to be in life, and that's okay."

Lizzie pulled into a spot and killed the engine. "Small-town life isn't for everyone same as city living isn't, either."

Charlie frowned. "All I know is that I'm worried about you. I was worried after Russ died and I'm even more worried now. And yes, I can't think of anyone I'd want taking my place more than you. There's no on call, no night shifts. It's regular hours, which, after your insane schedule, is nearly like a vacation. The people are wonderful. There are beaches and parks. You could do worse." She looked Lizzie right in the eye. "I want the old Lizzie back. The one who smiles easier and isn't so afraid."

They got out of the car and Lizzie could smell the rich fragrance of coffee mingled with bacon coming from the café. The town was built on a hill, so each street climbed up a step and was dotted with postcard-perfect buildings painted an array of colors. The café was cobalt blue with white trim. An inn across the street was brick red, and Lizzie's gaze caught on a large building the next street up painted lavender, of all things. How could she be anything but cheerful when faced with such a rainbow of architecture? But cheerful was not the same as happy. Charlie's idea was an intriguing one, but Lizzie wasn't sold yet. Charlie was right. It wasn't her speed. And yet . . . it wasn't like it was a permanent position or anything. It would be . . . vacation. It had been a long time since she'd taken one. She bit down on her lip. Had she actually forgotten how to let her hair down and have fun? Be spontaneous and daring? In the past she'd jumped at the opportunity to travel, to try something new. But in the last six months . . .

Charlie let the topic rest as they spent the morning browsing shops. First they visited the Three Fishermen gallery featuring pieces by New England artists, including a stunning selection of painting on glass. There was a clothing boutique with hand-painted silk scarves and intricately beaded handbags that Lizzie drooled over. They laughed over lobster-shaped salt-and-pepper shakers in a touristy souvenir shop, and when Charlie wistfully touched a hand-pieced quilt she'd been eyeing for the baby's room Lizzie bought it on the spot.

"Are you crazy?" Charlie turned over the price tag to show Lizzie.

"No, I am not." She carefully took the quilt off the display rack, smiling at the yellow and white bunnies peeking over the squares. "It's gorgeous and you're in lust with it. It's the least I can do."

"But today is *your* birthday."

Right. She'd pretty much forgotten that little detail. "Then buy me a cupcake."

At the bookstore Charlie bought Lizzie an illustrated guide to the Maine Midcoast, another tool, she said, in her ongoing blackmail ploy. But the real clincher was lunch at Breezes Café. Grilled panini sandwiches and sweet potato fries would have done it all on their own, but the warm blueberry buckle with vanilla bean ice cream toppled Lizzie over the edge.

As they left town, Charlie casually directed her past the doctor's office two streets up, a large saltbox-style house with precisely two parking spots. It looked very proper with its deep-green rhododendrons flanking the door and a sign hanging on the front lawn. Lizzie figured the detour had been a strategic move on Charlie's part.

"Dr. Collins used to be an army doctor," Charlie said as they pulled up to the curb. "He retired from the military, and after his wife died, he came back to Jewell Cove to set up practice. He took over for Phil Nye, who was the town doc for decades."

"What's he like?"

"Phil or Joshua?"

Lizzie chuckled. "Joshua."

"Kind. Smart and efficient. People trust him because he's local. Jewell Cove might be small, but he keeps up with the latest. He's been fine to work for. No drama, which from what you've said would be a plus. He's very . . . uh, professional."

Charlie made it sound like that was a negative, but Lizzie figured professionalism and efficiency were fine traits in a doctor. After her disastrous affair with Ian, an ex-army widower sounded positively perfect. No chance of romantic conflicts in the workplace. "I haven't even come close to saying yes," Lizzie replied, putting on her signal light to pull away.

And yet the town had charmed her with its colorful buildings and unique shops. She looked in her rearview mirror at the house. It had a certain appeal. There was a level of friendliness in the town she wasn't quite comfortable with, but she suspected that would change when the tourists started rolling in and the strangers outnumbered the townies.

What else was waiting for her that was any better? If she was perfectly honest with herself, it was wishful thinking that she would be able to convince Ian to let her go back to work. Especially while the threat of a lawsuit still hung over her head.

"I don't know where I'd live," Lizzie said, as if she and Charlie had already been having that conversation. "And don't say with you and Dave. No way. I refuse to impose on you two that way. And then there's my mom. . . ."

"Not that it would be an imposition, but I already thought of that," Charlie replied smugly. "And as far as your mom goes, it's not that long of a drive. With your lighter schedule, it won't be difficult to visit often. No more difficult than finding time when you're working over sixty hours a week."

"You're probably right about that last part." Lizzie sighed. She should have known. Charlie always had a contingency plan, always had her bases covered. Lizzie suspected she'd never stood a chance. Not that she'd truly put up much of a fight. God, she was weaker than she thought. What did that say about her?

"Does this mean you want the job?"

"Are you really going to make me ask?"

Charlie's smile was so big Lizzie thought her cheeks might crack. "You're really thinking about it?"

Charlie looked so excited it was impossible to remain immune to her enthusiasm. The idea of going back to Springfield and begging for reinstatement filled Lizzie with dread. There were memories back there, too, memories she'd rather not face. Why not give herself a break?

She'd been top of her class at Harvard. Every step of the way she'd gotten what she wanted. It had really thrown her to have someone else call the shots in her career. She was more daring in her personal life; maybe it was time to employ a different strategy professionally.

So she laughed and threw caution to the wind. "I can't believe I'm going to say this. I'm not just thinking. I'm offering. Just for the mat leave, though. I don't think I could stand more than six months in a place so small there isn't even a Starbucks." She gave a false shudder. "Where am I going to get my macchiato?"

Charlie let out a squeal. "Hot damn, Dave owes me ten bucks. I told him I could do it!"

They had been sitting at a stop sign for so long the driver of a truck behind them laid on the horn. "Keep your shirt on!" Lizzie called back, and Charlie giggled.

"You sure you want that? The driver seems awfully cute. Definitely shirt-off material."

Lizzie gave a cursory glance in the rearview mirror. She could make out streaked blond hair and broad shoulders. Okay, so he was kind of good-looking. She sent Charlie a stern look as she proceeded through the intersection. "Look, you've already played havoc with my professional life. No matchmaking. I mean it, Charlie." All teasing aside, the last thing Lizzie needed in her mess of a life was a romantic entanglement.

"I promise." Charlie crossed her heart.

"When would I start?" Despite Lizzie's reservations, excitement fizzed through her veins.

"End of June, first of July? It's nearly six weeks away. Lots of time to make arrangements."

"So where are we going?" Lizzie checked the rearview mirror again, and the truck turned off on a different street.

Charlie smiled. "Put on your turn signal and get back on the highway. I'm going to show you the cottage at Fiddler's Rock.""

The afternoon was getting on when the Realtor met them at the cottage, less than two miles away from Charlie and Dave. The property agent smiled as she turned the key in the lock. "The owner got married and moved somewhere bigger," she explained, shoving open the door. "He rents it out now."

"I can't believe it's not rented already," Lizzie replied, stepping onto the wraparound deck.

Charlie grinned. "Dave was renting it when we met."

"Tom, the owner, likes a long-term renter, none of those rent-by-the-week vacation types," the agent replied, sticking her head back out the door. "You coming in?"

Lizzie looked back at Charlie. "Come on. This is your party."

Charlie laughed, her brown eyes twinkling at Lizzie. "You were a lot easier to convince than I expected."

"You caught me at a vulnerable moment."

They stepped inside the cottage and Lizzie caught her breath. It was perfect. Solid wood cupboards in the small kitchen, a drop-leaf dining table in front of sliding deck doors. The kitchen led into a living room with warm oak flooring, and at the back of the cottage were two bedrooms and a beautiful bathroom complete with an old-fashioned claw-foot tub for long evening soaks. Trees around the cottage added privacy; endless windows provided views from every angle. The décor was decidedly masculine, sturdy, with dark-plaid upholstery on the sofa and chair. But it worked, somehow. It felt settled, and comfortable and welcoming. Very different from Lizzie's modern condo in Springfield but cozy like her childhood home had always been.

The agent wisely kept quiet. Lizzie opened the patio doors and stepped out onto the deck. She thought she understood now why the knob of land in the middle of the cove was called "Fiddler's Rock." From this vantage, the shoreline curved in the shape of a violin, until widening out into the bigger bay, then on to the open ocean.

Her life had been spiraling for some time now. Maybe this was a desperate move in the current circumstances, but it was a deliberate one, and one she was making on her own. It was both heady and terrifying.

"I'll take it," she said.

She pretended not to see Charlie's fist pump the air.

CHAPTER 3

Six weeks later

Josh Collins grabbed a still-warm oatmeal muffin from the plate and ate a third of it in his first bite on the way to the coffeepot. His mug was already sitting on the countertop waiting, a sickly grayish ceramic one with "World's Best Skipper" painted on it in bright blue. Another one of his sister Sarah's craft classes gone wrong. Why Jess had gotten all the handicraft genes and Sarah had none was beyond Josh. Sarah was always signing up for Jess's classes at her store, Treasures, claiming they were fun and not all about artistic talent. Personally Josh thought Jess's evenings above her store were more about the gossip and wine than about crafts, but he'd never be stupid enough to say that to either of his sisters. Besides, what Sarah lacked in artistic talent she more than made up for in the kitchen. She was a tremendous cook.

"Fog's in again," Sarah said, wrinkling her brow and gazing out the kitchen window at the harbor. Sarah tended to mother them all. She'd let up on Jess recently since Jess had gotten married. That only left Josh. He let Sarah hover because he understood. She was a nurturer, and she didn't know how else to help him. Poor, poor widower Josh. He was fine. Had been for some time, really. But she did make great coffee and muffins, so the morning ritual was one he enjoyed. Most of the time.

"The fog will burn off well before lunch," he answered easily.

"You're going out today, then?"

"Not today. I'll be at the office."

She seemed relieved to know he wouldn't be out on the water, even though it was just some fog and not a storm. "I thought it was your day off."

Josh had thought so, too, and had looked forward to taking out the boat, doing some fishing, not to mention peace and quiet. "Not anymore. Charlie's replacement is starting work today and I'm going to show her around."

Sarah's brow knit into a frown. "But Susan has a checkup today. Besides, Charlie isn't due for a few months yet."

"Well, Dr. Howard was available and Charlie said she'd like to have some time before the baby arrived. It doesn't matter to me, really, so I agreed. Today you'll be seeing the new doc."

Sarah didn't look appeased. One thing he'd realized about his sister—she liked things a certain way. She didn't like leaving things to chance or change. He rather suspected it had been that way since their father had died at sea. One morning their dad had been eating breakfast at the kitchen table, and hours later he was just gone, leaving Josh as the man of the house.

He was familiar enough with grief to know that it changed people in small but important ways. Sarah's need for control was one. Her urge to nurture was another.

So he poured her a cup of coffee and put it on the table before her. "Look, I trust Charlie. If she says Dr. Howard's a fine doctor, I believe her." He smiled. "I'm pretty sure Susan doesn't want her uncle giving her a checkup. But if there's a problem, we'll set you up with my friend in Portland, okay?"

She nodded. "Yes, okay." She let out a sigh and raised her mug, taking a test sip of coffee. "I'm sorry, Josh. I don't mean to be difficult."

He smiled, jostled her free elbow. "You're not. I know you worry about me. I'm fine, Sarah. I've been home over a year now and I'm happy. Truly. I've got a great practice, I'm around my family, and I've got a brand-new boat and fishing rod. Life's good."

And so what if he was alone? Even during his marriage he'd felt alone. At least this way it was stress-free.

He turned away, focused on pouring his own coffee. It wasn't just his family who was concerned about him. The whole damn town worried, for that matter. He clenched his teeth. He was *fine*. Absolutely fine. He wasn't going to break.

"You want some eggs?" he asked. "I'll cook."

"Oh," she replied, jumping up. "I forgot you haven't eaten."

"Sit down, Sarah. I'll get it. By now I know your kitchen as well as my own." Josh went to the fridge, taking out eggs and butter.

Sometimes his family's concern got claustrophobic. He could have stayed at his own place this morning, he supposed, as he melted butter in the pan and broke eggs into a bowl. But they'd settled into this pattern months ago, ever since he'd returned to Jewell Cove. To ignore the routine now would mean worried phone calls from his sisters, a lecture from his mother, and fancy tap dancing around everyone. The last thing he wanted to do was upset the family applecart, so it was easier just to show up a few times a week, have breakfast, and keep everything on an even keel.

Not that he could blame his sister entirely. He put up with the hovering because she'd been the one to pick him up when he'd damned near had a breakdown after Erin's death. Dealing with the repatriation and the funeral . . . it had stretched him to the limit. Grief and guilt were not a good combination.

Then there'd been Erin's parents to deal with. They'd absolutely hated that their precious Erin had gone into the Army as a medic. Erin had always felt like a disappointment to them. Their expectations had run much higher. He'd often had the thought that they'd only tolerated her "mild rebellion" because their future plans had been for Josh to go into practice with her dad and they'd be one big happy family. Afterwards, trying to work day in and day out with Erin's father . . . it was too much. And it had been time to come home.

He stirred the eggs and put some bread in the toaster. Butter and jam followed, plunked unceremoniously in the middle of the table.

Sarah's face finally cleared of its worry as she grinned. "I still can't believe you're in the medical profession with a bedside manner like that," she groused, teasing. "Thank God you were never a waiter."

He scooped eggs onto a plate, added toast, and put

it before her before filling a plate of his own. For a few minutes they ate in easy silence. He was glad she seemed to be out of her doldrums. The last year had been a rough one, and he didn't want to add to that.

And even though he knew the Collins women tried to mother him, Josh had never been able to shake the protective feeling he had for his sisters. Part of the reason he kept up with the day-to-day charade was because he worried about them as much as they worried about him.

"I'm gonna run," he said, getting up and going to Sarah's side. "I've got to catch Tom before he heads to work, and then hit the office."

"There's a lunch for you in the fridge," she replied as he pressed a kiss to her cheek. "Say hi to Tom. Tell him not to forget the big picnic on the Fourth. We're all supposed to be at Jess's by six."

"Will you make potato salad?"

Sarah laughed and handed him a paper bag. "Oooh, a request. I'll make you a deal. I'll make the salad if you'll bring a date."

Josh sighed, wishing everyone would stop with the matchmaking. "Sarah . . . you and Jess have been plotting again."

"And Mom. Don't forget Mom. We were thinking Elaine, you know? From the inn?"

Lainey Price. Nice enough but so not his type. "No matchmaking."

"Or maybe Summer's free. You do tend to end up together at these things."

He sent her a dark warning look. Summer was a nice girl, too, but that was it. Nice. Not for him. "Back off, Sarah," he warned.

"You're lonely."

"No, I'm not. And I can find my own girl if I want one."

"Then why don't you?"

It was a fair question. Erin had been gone nearly two years. Did he still grieve? Yes. But not necessarily for the reasons his family thought. He wasn't sure he ever wanted to go down that road again. Dating in this town was problematic, too. Everyone would know within the hour and would have them marching down the aisle by the following breakfast. There would be no privacy to fall in love, just pressure. It was easier just to steer clear.

"Not yet," he answered, not wanting to get into his personal life with Sarah this morning. All he wanted was to have his breakfast and get to work and treat this like any other day.

Because that's exactly what it was. A day just like yesterday, and tomorrow would be the same again. Until he damn well felt like changing it.

"I still want potato salad. Now let me get going." He leaned over and kissed her cheek again, knowing he could definitely get around her that way.

The fog was thick as he drove to the edge of town and the small prefab that Tom used as an office for Arseneault Contracting. He dropped off the circular saw he'd borrowed to cut some new deck boards and then drove the six blocks to the clinic. It was oddly quiet after he shut the truck door. On mornings like this, the sounds of the bay held a different, mysterious quality that almost felt otherworldly.

He could see the moisture hang in the air and he tried not to let the dismal weather drag down his mood. This was the life he'd chosen. His own practice, back with his family. At the time it had made the most sense.

But lately there was something missing. Something more that left him unsatisfied. He wished he could put his finger on it.

This damned fog wasn't helping matters any. He opened the back door to the office and flicked on the lights. Their assistant, Robin, was already ten minutes late, and when he booted up the computer the e-mail showed she'd be an hour late because her kid had popped a wire on his braces, requiring an emergency trip to the orthodontist. Josh turned on the radio for background noise and set to work making coffee.

"Dammit," he muttered, running a hand over his hair. "Why do I bother hiring people when they never manage to show up on time?" Now he was on the hook for pulling the first patient files and making sure the exam rooms were prepared.

When the back door opened and shut again, his irritation spilled over. "It's about time!" he called out. "Your appointment go faster than expected?"

"I didn't realize I was late," said a soft voice, and Josh paused, his hand on the trash can that hadn't been emptied the night before.

He looked over his shoulder, knowing it had to be Dr. Howard but unprepared for the sight just the same. Medium height. A bit too skinny for his taste. Good eyes, though, he thought, and he suspected her dark hair would be quite a sight to behold if she ever let it down. Today she had it pulled back in a low, demure ponytail. Professional. He liked that. His own personal reaction? Not so much a fan. It had been a long time since the sound of a woman's low voice made his pulse jump.

"I'm Elizabeth Howard," she said smoothly, raising a perfectly groomed eyebrow at him.

"Josh Collins."

"You're Dr. Collins." Her other eyebrow rose to meet the first, making it more of a question than a statement despite the inflection.

He wasn't sure what it was about her tone that set him on edge, but it did. "Who did you think I was?"

"I don't know. The janitor?"

Josh chuckled tightly and put down the trash can. Dr. Howard, on the one hand, was dressed in neat trousers and a pressed blouse and sensible flats. He, on the other hand, was in faded jeans and a golf shirt in muted orange. It was Jewell Cove, after all, and not Johns Hopkins. "I actually do have an assistant who normally looks after this stuff. She has an orthodontist emergency this morning. I thought you were her."

"Oh." Her lips thinned in disapproval, as if the tardiness was a reflection on the entire setup. "Where can I put my things?"

"Your office. End of the hall on the right. You'll see Charlie's name on the door."

"Thanks." She brushed by him but not before he caught a telltale pinkness coloring her cheeks. "I'm gonna kill Charlie for this," he heard her mutter.

Josh trusted Charlie and she said that Howard was the best doctor she knew, but they hadn't gotten off to the best start. He wasn't quite sure if Dr. Howard was disapproving or embarrassed, but either way it was awkward.

He looked down the hall and saw Dr. Howard slide her arms into a white coat. At least she was on time—unlike his other employee. He liked Robin and she kept the office running like a well-oiled machine, but she did take liberties with the time clock now and again.

Dr. Howard came back down the hall and Josh decided to try a friendly overture to break the ice instead. "There's coffee in the kitchen. I was just going to get a cup before I unlock the front. Want some?"

She followed him to the kitchen—a closet, really—and he pulled down two mugs from the cupboard. "There's milk in the fridge, and sugar here," he said, reaching for the coffeepot. He poured two mugs and handed her one. She stared at it for a moment before taking a cautious sip—black.

Josh grinned. "I like mine black, too. If the military didn't teach me to drink it that way, twenty-four hours on hospital shift would. You take what you can get, huh?"

"I have an espresso machine at home, so I prefer macchiatos."

Of course she did. With that one sentence Josh felt entirely inadequate. Erin had been that way, too, at first—an air of accepting nothing less than the best. Growing up rich and privileged seemed to bring with it a general expectation of standards and this Elizabeth Howard had the same way of looking at him that made him feel just a little bit . . . lacking. Provincial and unsophisticated. Like his little practice was beneath her. Then again, she was probably right. He'd seen her qualifications. Why she'd ever accepted Charlie's proposal was beyond him. Even with Elizabeth's current troubles, another hospital would have snapped her up in a heartbeat.

Josh's family had never looked down their noses at anyone; there hadn't been the money or the time. It wasn't something he apologized for anymore. Maybe blood was thicker than water, but he'd take Sarah's and

Jess's meddling any day of the week over the cold formality of Erin's family.

"Well, no fancy coffee machines here. Just plain family medicine. Blood work is done at the local lab, radiology at a clinic in Portland. You'll find requisitions in each exam room." The back door opened and closed once more. "That'll be Robin, I hope." He looked at his watch. "Make yourself at home and any questions, ask."

He took his coffee and made his way to the front office and waiting room. The true test would be Howard's attitude toward her patients. And luckily for Josh, he had the perfect insider already scheduled for two forty-five. Susan would be brutally honest with her opinion of the new doc.

Lizzie had meant every word. She was going to kill Charlie.

Charlie had known all along that Joshua Collins was drop-dead gorgeous. She had known all along that he was in his early thirties. A military vet and widower indeed. Lizzie had pictured a retired army doc, perhaps with a little gray hair and a crusty demeanor. That's who she'd prepared for and she'd been relieved—she could handle that sort of boss right as rain. But Collins? Faded jeans and a golf shirt passing for professional attire . . . good Lord.

She flushed a little and tried to turn her attention back to her chart. He did wear the faded denim well. Too well. She'd gotten a good look at his backside when he'd bent over that trash can and she'd called him "the janitor." Janitor! She'd been so flustered that the only words she could think of to say were to ask where her office was and to tell him she had an espresso machine at home. What an idiot she was. . . .

Even worse was the knowledge that Charlie had deliberately kept quiet about such an important detail. That day they'd been touring the town, it had been Collins in the truck behind them, Collins who had laid on the horn and made Charlie laugh. Heat rose into Lizzie's cheeks. This was the problem with letting people know you too well. Charlie knew that Lizzie would have said no if she'd admitted her partner was a young, sexy, single doc.

Maybe he wasn't single. Charlie had mentioned he'd moved back after his wife died, but that didn't mean there wasn't a new Mrs. Collins. And Lizzie hadn't checked to see if he was wearing a ring. Or there could be a girlfriend in the picture.

Robin tapped on the door. "Dr. Howard? Your two forty-five is here, in room one."

"Thanks," she said, pushing aside the chart. She was already going crazy. Today she'd seen a total of ten patients. The most exciting one had needed a slight adjustment to his blood pressure medication. God, she missed the emergency room. Missed the activity and the challenge. Maybe this one would actually need some real medical care.

Outside the exam room she plucked the file off the door and skimmed it. So much for challenge. A ten-year-old patient for a checkup. She sighed. *No such luck.*

When she opened the door, a pretty woman in her early thirties was sitting in a chair and the patient was already on the exam table, her hair in a perky ponytail and freckles dotting her nose. "Hi, Susan. I'm

Dr. Howard." She smiled what she hoped was a welcoming smile.

"I'm Sarah, Susan's mother." The woman stood and held out her hand.

"It's nice to meet you. You're here for a checkup?" Lizzie shook Sarah's hand with the odd feeling that the woman was somehow familiar.

"Josh is my uncle!" Susan announced.

It was tough to keep her smile in place. *Oh goody.* Josh's family and on her first day. Was this a test or just a coincidence?

Sarah let go of her hand and sat down again. "I know it must be strange, on your first day and all. We always saw Phil Nye when he was here, and then when Josh came back to town we started seeing Dr. Yang. It's a little weird thinking about Josh being our doctor." She gave a lopsided grin and Lizzie relaxed a little.

"Yeah, more like eeew," Susan answered. "That's definitely TMI."

Lizzie laughed. Maybe today's appointments weren't a total loss. She rather liked Josh's niece. The tone was just a touch snooty, Susan's eyebrow raised in a sarcastic arch. The girl had just the right amount of attitude and spunk.

They went through the usual stuff—height and weight marked on a percentile scale, blood pressure and heart and lungs . . . a formality, as Susan appeared to be a perfectly healthy little girl. Lizzie chatted to her about school and what activities she liked, including piano lessons and soccer and an upcoming sleepover where the girls were going to make their own pizzas and ice-cream sundaes with a zillion toppings.

She was a chatterbox, but a delightful one.

"Well, I think you're all set here, unless you have any questions for me," Lizzie said, closing the chart.

"Do you have a boyfriend?" Susan asked, unfazed by the dire look her mother sent her way.

Lizzie felt a blush heat her cheeks.

"Don't answer that," Sarah said, turning to Susan. "Suze, that was rude."

"You're always saying you want Uncle Josh to date. You can't throw Summer Arnold at him forever."

Now it was Sarah's turn to blush and Lizzie gave an uncomfortable laugh.

"Where on earth did you get that?" Sarah demanded.

"Grandma said it last week after church."

There was a moment of awkward silence. "Sorry," Sarah apologized. "Sometimes I think she's ten going on twenty-five."

Lizzie flapped a hand. She'd seen a lot of things in emergency departments, had been propositioned and proposed to once by a man dressed in drag with alcohol poisoning who was brought in by his friends during a bachelor party gone wrong. One ten-year-old being slightly inappropriate was really no biggie.

Except that it did make her blush, because she actually had noticed Josh that morning and found him quite attractive.

"Your uncle and I work together, that's all," she said with a polite smile. "And you, Susan, are perfectly healthy. It was good to meet you."

Susan hopped down from the examination table. "You won't tell Uncle Josh what I said, will you? About Summer?" She looked a little worried. The bravado of earlier had been curbed by her mother's sharp admonitions.

Lizzie smiled reassuringly. "Of course not." Like

she'd repeat the notion to Josh, or talk about her personal life at all. That was strictly off-limits. She winked at Susan. "Doctor-patient confidentiality. It's our secret."

Susan smiled . . . and so did her mom.

As Susan tied her shoes, Sarah picked up the conversation. "So, how are you enjoying Jewell Cove?"

Lizzie thought of her morning run along Fiddler's Beach and had to admit the fresh air and space were growing on her. "It's very beautiful. And everyone has been so friendly." Too friendly. Even out at Fiddler's Rock, her arrival had prompted a basket of baked goods and a casserole showing up from well-intentioned neighbors. So much for privacy.

"Our Fourth of July celebrations are in a few days. There's always lots happening on the docks, and there are fireworks, too. You won't want to miss it." Sarah angled her head a little. "In fact, our family always throws a picnic on the Fourth. You should come. Charlie and Dave have accepted an invite, and you are Josh's coworker after all. You could meet some people in town."

Way to put her on the spot. She certainly didn't want to horn in on a family event, especially since she and Josh had only shared a few sentences today that weren't about work.

"I'll definitely think about it," she offered, trying to be positive but noncommittal. "Thanks for the invitation."

Sarah nodded. "Our family is always coming up with excuses for get-togethers. If you can't make it, there's always the next time."

After Sarah and Susan were gone, Lizzie took a moment to sit on the rolling stool and let out a breath. How did Charlie manage to keep the patient/doctor relationship professional in such a small, intimate town? Lizzie had already noticed how residents waved and greeted each other on the street. The gossip mill was alive and well, too, if the chatter at the café was anything to go by.

This wasn't her style at all. And yeah, maybe she needed the change of pace to de-stress, but the thought of staying here indefinitely? Not in a million years.

She left the exam room and went to the reception desk to find Robin and instead found a wicker basket covered with a pretty napkin sitting on the middle of the counter. She lifted a corner and saw plump, golden muffins tumbled about the inside. There was a small card attached to the handle and she removed it, sliding the little cardboard note from the envelope.

Welcome to Jewell Cove, Dr. Howard.

It was signed from the Jewell Cove Business Association. *Good heavens, a welcome wagon?*

At that moment Josh came from his office and stopped, lifting his nose to the air. "What's that smell? I'm starving."

"Muffins," she answered.

He sauntered out, curiously examining the basket and lifting the napkin. "Banana chip. Yum. Welcome present?"

She swallowed. "How'd you know?"

He chuckled as he selected a muffin from the assortment. "That's Jewell Cove for you. Always there with a warm welcome and a helping hand."

There was something in his voice that made her think he didn't necessarily consider that a perk. "I think it's a lovely gesture," she answered.

"Hey," he said, taking a bite of the muffin and chewing thoughtfully. He swallowed and frowned a little. "I obviously love this place. I grew up here. I moved back, right? But I'll be the first to admit it can get a little too small and well-intentioned sometimes. "

Hmm. Curiouser and curiouser. "But you're the town golden boy, aren't you? I mean Charlie said—"

And then she stopped talking, rather abruptly, because she'd been about to say "after your wife died" and had realized how callous it would have sounded.

"Charlie said what?" One eyebrow lifted as he took another bite of muffin, catching a few crumbs in his hand.

She scrambled to come up with better words. "She just said that when you moved back, everyone was happy about it. That you belong here."

His gaze sharpened, as if he was trying to puzzle her out. She wasn't quite comfortable with the intensity of it. It made her feel rather transparent. A little bit naked.

"It can be a little claustrophobic at times. Very little privacy."

She smiled at that. "Really? So you didn't plan for your niece to have her checkup on my first day in the office?"

The answering grin he gave her made her catch her breath. It lit up his whole face, transforming it. He looked younger, despite the crinkles at the corners of his eyes. Lighter, less burdened.

"Suze is great, isn't she? A real firecracker."

"She asked if I had a boyfriend." She wasn't sure what prompted her to admit that, but Josh's answering laugh made her glad she had.

"And do you?" he asked, and the smile slipped from

her face. He put the nearly finished muffin on the countertop. "Bad question to ask?"

"It's no biggie. I was seeing someone a few months back. It didn't exactly end well." She hoped Josh would leave it at that. How humiliating to admit that she'd been dating her boss. Particularly when she was talking to her new boss.

"Sorry," he offered kindly. "That sucks."

Truly, she felt way worse about the bigger situation in Springfield. The relationship had just been a casualty of that, really. No permanent damage. Not like that poor family—

"Elizabeth? You okay?"

He was looking at her with concern now, so she shook off the disturbing thoughts and smiled. "I'm fine. And call me 'Lizzie.' Please."

"Lizzie," he repeated, and their gazes caught once more.

CHAPTER 4

Josh loved the feel of the wind in his hair, the smell of the water, the taste of the salt on his lips. He loved pulling away from the dock in the morning, the vibration of the engine beneath his feet, sometimes in a secretive mist, sometimes to a bright-blue sky that somehow sharpened the lines of the rocks, cliffs, even the whitecaps on the waves. There was freedom in the openness that he craved. No orders to follow beyond his own. He could take the route he wanted, up the coast, out to the small islands, wherever the seals bathed in the sun, or out farther into the bay, searching for whales feeding. Being at the wheel, feeling the rise and fall of the swell beneath his feet, was just about as perfect as he could handle.

As he steered the *Jewell's Constant* toward the slip, he wiped a hand over his face and pushed all his stress away. He took a deep breath, filling his lungs with the brisk, salt-scented air. Focus on the positive, that's what he needed to do. Live in the present. The afternoon had been a good one. The trip out of the bay had been smooth, and he'd encountered a pod of humpbacks after the first hour. Intrigued, he'd quietly adjusted his position and waited for the awesome moment when over thirty tons of mammal breached and splashed back into the water with incomparable force. He'd finished the trip by piloting around Aquteg Island, getting close enough to the south beach that he could see the seals, hear them grumbling bad-naturedly at each other. He and his cousins, Tom and Bryce, and best friend, Rick, had spent hours upon hours on the rock locals had dubbed Lovers' Island, looking for the treasure rumored to have been buried there in the 1800s. They'd never found a thing, but Josh had good memories.

He enjoyed his life, and his level of contentment was one more thing he felt guilty about now and again. He was happier here than he'd ever been in Hartford. The life he'd planned with Erin was over. When it was all said and done, he'd wanted to be home. To have a small practice, a little boat where he could get away, get lost in the vastness of the ocean. At least there he could breathe.

Once the *Constant* was secure, he hopped out onto the dock and gave a long, satisfying stretch. If he was honest, he wasn't really grieving anymore. He could look back on the night the news had come and put it in perspective.

He remembered the slow footsteps, the hollow sound of them on the verandah, then the knock on the door. Not the doorbell. A fateful, heartless knock. He'd known what he would find on the other side before he ever put his hand on the doorknob. An officer. And a chaplain.

Josh had his whole life blown apart in the space of

two minutes. There'd been shock, and anger, and more than a little guilt. But there was peace now. Particularly between himself and his cousin Tom.

Josh's truck was parked in the wharf lot and he got inside, starting the engine with a growl. What he needed was some music, something upbeat to drive home to and shake away the doldrums. He flipped open the glove box and shoved his hand in, looking for a CD when a flash of pain shot through his hand.

"Shit!" He pulled out his hand and scowled. It was already bleeding—a lot. He grabbed a roll of paper towels from the back and tore off a strip, wrapping it around his middle finger. Carefully he checked the glove box and found an open utility knife.

"Goddammit." He rolled the blade back into the handle and shut the glove box. Blood was already soaked through the towel and he took it off, staring at the deep gash before tearing off a new strip and wrapping it around his finger.

Waiting for stitches in an emergency room on a Friday night was not how Josh wanted to spend his evening, and suturing his own wound didn't hold much appeal, either. He checked his watch. If he was lucky, Dr. Howard would still have the office open and could stitch him up in a flash. Josh put the truck in gear and headed to the office.

The streets were full of tourists, the annual season of clogging the roads and alternately bolstering the economy in full swing. It was part of Jewell's lifeblood. The vibrancy was part of what drew him back here. Life went on.

A silver convertible was the only vehicle outside the doctor's office—Lizzie's ridiculous excuse for transportation that was a little too flashy for his liking. She was wicked good at her job, though. Perhaps she was seeing a last patient for the day, Josh thought. He wrapped another square of towel around the already-soaked clump on his finger and headed to the door. Unlocked. A few stitches and they could get on with their weekend plans. The waiting room was empty, though, and a quick glance down the hall showed both exam room doors open. Josh frowned.

"Hey, Doc, you here?"

There was a shuffling sound in the back, and the clunk of a drawer closing.

"Sorry, I'm closing up," her voice said, and Josh spun to the left and the reception desk. She took one look at the bloody towel and her lips dropped open.

As soon as he saw her stunned expression, Josh's knees went watery. *Shit.*

She recovered quickly. "You've lost some blood there. Let me have a look."

Josh gazed stupidly at his finger and back at Lizzie. He took a few steadying breaths, feeling ridiculous. It was just a cut finger. Lizzie stepped forward, took his hand firmly in hers, and turned it over, examining the slice, her fingers cool and soft on his. She was close enough that he could smell her light perfume and as she looked down at his hand he looked at her face, marveling at the fine cheekbones and long eyelashes . . . but more than that, her hair was down. It had been pulled back yesterday, but today she'd left it loose. It was glorious, just as he'd imagined.

"You're going to need stitches," she said.

"What?" Josh struggled to come back to the present. He'd been thinking about sinking his hands into the thick mass of her hair, tilting her head back, exposing the pale column of her neck. *Wow.* He had to be light-headed, because those thoughts were really inappropriate, considering she was a new doctor in his practice.

"Oh. Stitches. Yeah, I know. I was hoping you could do it and save me a trip to the ER."

Lizzie circled his wrist with her fingers and led him into the first exam room. "You'd better sit down," she said gently. "You look like you're going to faint."

It was enough to pull him out of his stupor and he shook his head, looking up at her clearly. "I don't faint at the sight of blood," he replied, his tone suggesting the very idea was preposterous. He'd be damned if he'd explain that it was her turning his brain to mush rather than any blood loss.

She raised one eyebrow. "You sure?" She moved to a cupboard and took out a tray. "When was your last tetanus?"

"Tetanus?"

"You hurt your hearing as well as your hand?"

He heard the smile in her voice and tried to relax. "No, ma'am. Last year. I was updated last year."

"Well, I can forego sticking you with a booster, then. Lucky for me I still get to poke you when I freeze your finger." Her smile looked a little bit smug, he noticed, liking the way her lips titled a bit at the corners as she teased him. He found the hint of sassiness crazy sexy.

In no time flat she'd given him a local anesthetic and grabbed a suture pack and was sitting on a rolling stool putting four stitches in his finger.

"Nice stitches."

"And you're done." She pushed back and peeled off her gloves. "Keep it clean and I'll take those out for you next week."

"I can take them out myself, you know." He sent her a sarcastic grin. "Easier than putting them in."

She shrugged. "You're the doc. But you're also a man, and you'll want to take them out before they're ready."

She was right, not that he'd admit it out loud.

She was up and tidying and he was still sitting on the chair. "You need something else, Josh?"

Did he need anything else? He couldn't think of a thing. Not one single plausible reason to keep her with him a moment longer. Except . . .

"You settling in okay?" It was a fair question, right? She'd only been in town a few days.

She put the used needle in the dispenser and dropped the rest of the mess in the garbage can. "What's this, the end-of-the-first-week debrief?"

"Jeez. Just making conversation. Sorry I kept you late. You probably have plans."

She laughed, the sound a little brittle for his liking.

"Plans? In Jewell Cove? Just me and a glass of chardonnay. Real exciting."

She didn't make it sound like a good thing, and he definitely didn't want to pry. He got up and made his way to the front door but turned at the last minute. She was behind the reception desk again, the phone receiver to her ear as he raised his hand in farewell.

She fluttered her fingers and smiled, the sharpness of a moment before gone. His heart did a little lurch again. Being attracted to her would be such a mistake. She was a coworker. And she was temporary. He got the distinct impression that she'd rather be back in the big city than killing time in his hometown. Hell, that smile and fluttering of her fingers was about as warm as she'd been the entire week.

But it had been warm enough to fuel something he hadn't felt in a long time. And that was very, very inconvenient.

July Fourth was as big of a deal in Jewell Cove as it was anywhere else in America. Lizzie'd seen that right away when she'd arrived in town, her suitcases piled into the back of her convertible, at the end of June. Red, white, and blue decorations appeared all week: flags, bunting, flowers, the works. By the time the actual day rolled around, celebrations were in full swing. Lizzie found herself accompanying Charlie and Dave to several events beginning at noon, charmed despite herself at the cheerful, patriotic mood that enveloped the town.

The mayor, a crusty ex-fisherman named Luke Pratt, made a speech in Memorial Square, the statue of Edward Jewell looking on approvingly. There was a tribute to the members of the armed forces and the announcement of the Most Patriotic Display for local businesses, which went to Cover to Cover Bookstore for their window featuring the Declaration of Independence as the centerpiece with a huge stars and stripes collage as a backdrop. All day long there were special events. A hot dog barbecue in the square; face painting sponsored by the local store Treasures. There was to be a ball game at the park between the current high school team and alumni and games for the younger kids down on the wharf where, incidentally, Sally's Dairy Shack was giving out free soft ice cream with special tickets handed out by members of the business association.

Dave was just finishing his cone when he looked over at Charlie and Lizzie. "Okay, you two. I've suffered through speeches and the two of you oohing and aahing over flowers and God knows what else. It's time for some manly pursuits. Can we head over to the ball game? The first inning just started."

Charlie looked pained, but Lizzie nodded. "That sounds like fun." She never made a big deal of it, but she and her dad had often enjoyed watching the Sox play and she liked the game. It was one of the things she'd missed this past spring. Besides, it was sunny and hot and what better way to spend the day than at America's favorite pastime?

Dave, bless him, looked relieved. "Charlie told Josh we'd show up to the postgame barbecue, so we can head over there afterwards."

Lizzie put her tote over her shoulder and hesitated. "Maybe I'll just head back home after the game. I don't need to play third wheel."

"Don't be silly," Charlie argued, nudging her elbow as they walked to the clinic where they'd parked. "Half the town was invited, including Robin from the office. Besides, I know for a fact that Sarah expects you."

Lizzie frowned. "How do you know that?"

Charlie laughed. "Because I ran into her at the grocery store and she said to be sure I brought you with us."

Lizzie didn't argue. She could always make up an excuse later if she didn't want to go. Right now she was actually having fun. The sun was hot on her hair, her nose was sweating just a little bit around the nosepiece of her sunglasses, and she was thirsty for water now that she'd finished her vanilla soft-serve cone.

The ball field was behind the high school, northwest of the waterfront. Cars already filled the school lot, and when they reached the bleachers the game was under way. The scoreboard read 2–0 for the high school team in the second inning, and the alumni were up at bat.

Sarah's daughter, Susan, ran up to greet them. "Mom says to give you these." Susan handed over three ball caps, brown ones that said: *Old Dogs*. "She said you have to cheer for the old guys."

Charlie laughed. "Your uncles aren't exactly old."

Susan shrugged. "They're no spring chickens."

Lizzie burst out laughing as Susan ran off again. "I like that kid," she said, taking the hat and pulling her ponytail through the hole at the back as she placed it on her head. "What are they calling the high school team?"

Charlie pointed at a teenager standing nearby, watching through the fence. His ball cap was red and said: *Young Pups* on it. Lizzie grinned. "Cute," she said, chuckling a little.

They made their way into the stands, Charlie and Lizzie picking seats while Dave bought them sodas from someone with a big cooler. Lizzie had just popped the top on a root beer when one of the "old-timers" struck out, causing lots of good-natured trash talk to erupt on both benches. "That's Josh's cousin Bryce." Charlie nodded toward the burly player making his way back to the dugout. "He's the police chief. Boy, he's going to have a hard time living that one down."

The next batter was Rick Sullivan, who Charlie pointed out was Josh's brother-in-law and had a prosthetic hand. Lizzie watched curiously as Rick gripped the bat, his prosthetic at the bottom, his other hand above it. The first pitch came in slow, and Lizzie saw Rick scowl as he stepped out of the batter's box, refusing to even swing. "Come on, Danny," he groused. "No wimping out just because I'm a cripple. Might as well bring out that fastball like you do for everyone else on the second pitch."

She swore the kid, Danny, blushed on the mound. Rick stepped back inside the box, dug in his front toe, and waited.

Sure enough, the next pitch came zooming in, a perfect fastball. And Rick swung, connecting with a sharp crack as the ball went just over the shortstop's head and dropped in front of the left fielder, giving him a single.

The pitcher kicked his foot in the dirt and hoots and howls came from the other bench. "He had your number, son!" More laughs and high fives, and Rick had a ridiculous grin on his face as he stood next to the first-base bag.

Josh was up next. Lizzie couldn't deny that her pulse gave a little jump as he strode out from the on-deck circle and swung his bat a few times. Hot damn, he looked good in ball pants. The gray material hugged his butt perfectly, making her mouth go dry, and the shirt emphasized his lean waist and broad shoulders. He sent the pitcher a crooked grin, tapped his batting helmet with his knuckles, and put one foot in the box while the other one remained out, taking his time. "Now Danny," he called, "I don't need that fastball. I kind of like the inside curve, if you don't mind!"

Shouts erupted from both benches. "Don't listen to him, Dan!" mingled with laughs, and everyone on the benches had smiles on their faces.

Lizzie remembered that Josh's right hand still had stitches in, but he didn't seem to be favoring it any. His batting gloves would give him some extra padding, she supposed. And she admired his perfect form as he finally put his back foot in the box, raised his left elbow, and got ready for the pitch.

Josh's face had lost all traces of teasing and was perfectly focused as Danny wound up for the pitch. He'd known exactly what he was doing, she realized, as Danny didn't throw the curve but instead hit him with another fastball, straight down the middle. It was just what Josh had wanted, wasn't it? Because he took a mighty swing and she watched as the bat came around, his hips swiveled, and torso and shoulders rotated in perfect form as he followed through. The ball went up, up, and long, heading for the fence. The fielders ran back, but it was too late. The ball sailed over the fence, bringing in two runs and tying up the game.

The team lined up for high fives as Josh rounded home, and the high school team's faces showed a new determination. Dave laughed. "I think those Young Pups thought they'd walk away with it, but they've got some competition. I heard Josh, Rick, and Tom were all on the State champion team back in the day."

Local star, hometown hero, Jewell Cove's favorite son. Lizzie scowled a little. She was sorry about his wife, of course, but gosh, it certainly seemed like Josh Collins had had an all-American dream upbringing. He was damn near Mr. Perfect.

At the seventh-inning stretch, Lizzie made a point of reapplying sunscreen while Dave went down to the bench and Charlie sipped on ice water to keep cool. "Are you okay?" Lizzie asked her. "It's a lot of sun. We don't want you getting sunstroke."

"I'm okay. The breeze has come up a bit and it's helping."

"Say the word and we can go somewhere cooler. With air-conditioning."

Charlie laughed. "And miss this? Not a chance." Charlie lifted her hand and sent a wave to a woman behind the visitors' bench.

"Wow, who's that?"

Charlie looked over at her. "Oh. That's Josh's other sister, Jess Sullivan. She was doing the face painting this morning. You haven't met, have you?"

"She's stunning. Holy cow." Very pregnant, Jess Sullivan was still one of the most gorgeous women Lizzie had ever seen.

"I know, right? She's married to Rick. The guy with the prosthetic. She owns Treasures, the purple store on Lilac Lane. Rick runs it with her and paints, too. On glass."

"The stuff we saw at the gallery that day?"

Charlie nodded. "That's his. Oh good, Jess is coming over. I'll introduce you."

It shouldn't have made her nervous to meet Josh's sister, but it did. It was funny. Everywhere she went, everyone she met . . . she felt like she had to pass some sort of test. It was the weirdest thing. She didn't usually have a confidence issue.

But then again, that was all before she'd lost her dad, lost her edge, and screwed up.

"Jess, hi! This is my best friend in the whole world, Lizzie Howard. Liz, this is Josh's sister Jess."

Jess smiled warmly. "Good to finally meet you. Josh said you stitched up his finger the other night." She rested her hand on the fullness of her belly.

"He took on a utility knife and the knife won, I'm afraid." Lizzie smiled. Jess had a warm, easy way about her that Lizzie liked. "When are you due?"

Jess sighed. "Another month. Second trimester was

a breeze. I'm heading into the 'let's get this show on the road' stage now."

Lizzie laughed. "You haven't dropped yet, so it'll be a while."

Jess winced. "That's what Charlie told me just before she went on her maternity leave. My mom calls every day, too, to ask how I'm feeling."

"Josh is really going to be surrounded by babies in a few months, isn't he?"

"My cousin has a seven-month-old, too. Lots of babies these days."

Jess took a moment to cheer a play and then turned back to Lizzie. "You're coming over later, right? Rick's grilling ribs and Sarah's made enough potato salad to feed both teams and there's all sorts of food."

"I . . . I'm not sure."

Charlie elbowed her. "She's coming," Charlie informed Jess. "Don't mind her. She's being all new and stuff."

Jess laughed. "Like you were, Charlie? You didn't come out of your shell until Dave dragged you out of it." Jess looked at Lizzie. "Charlie was so quiet for her first few months here. But we've gotten to know her a lot better since Christmas. She even took a knitting class I ran in March."

"I figure I'll finish that bunting bag by the time I need it this winter," Charlie joked.

Babies and knitting . . . Lizzie really did feel out of place. But now that she'd had an official invitation, it would be rude to refuse. "No need to drag me anywhere," Lizzie informed them both. "I'll go, for a while, anyway." She offered a smile. "Girl's gotta eat."

The Old Dogs took the field again and Lizzie

watched as Josh took to the pitcher's mound. The score was close, with the Young Pups ahead by a single run. The game was getting serious now, with less trash talk and more honest-to-goodness cheering. Josh had the count at two-and-two when the young man at bat cracked one straight down the third-base line.

The third baseman caught it easily and sent it humming to first. Lizzie recognized her landlord, Tom, playing first and smiled as the big man stepped forward to catch the ball, anticipating that the throw was slightly short. But he stepped right on the baseline just as the runner came barreling toward the bag, his foot extended.

Tom held his spot, his glove hand extended, focused entirely on the ball.

The collision knocked him back a step, but he was a big man, well over six feet and sturdy as an ox. The kid didn't stand a chance, particularly when his knee hit Tom's thigh.

The kid went down like a rock, while the crowd fell silent.

Josh dropped his glove and went straight to first base while teammates on both sides crowded around. Lizzie and Charlie both stood, and then Lizzie raised her eyebrow. "You stay. I'll go."

"You're sure?"

"Yep." Lizzie hopped down off the bleachers and made her way to the field.

"Excuse me," she ordered, pushing her way through players to where Josh knelt next to the runner. She tapped Josh on the shoulder just as he was pushing up the player's pant leg to examine the knee. "What's up, Doc?"

It was easy to see that the boy was in a lot of pain. The moment Josh eased up the fabric past the knee, they both knew what had happened. The kneecap was dislocated, shifted to the outside of the leg. "Ouch," she said lightly, looking down at the player. "Hey, sparky," she said, kneeling down. "Take a deep breath for me and relax."

He did and opened his eyes to look up at her. "You a doc?" he asked. "Nothin' against Josh and all, but it's kind of humiliating to have the enemy fix me up, you know?"

"You guys and your pride," she responded, giving a little laugh. "Hurts like hell, doesn't it?"

"Yes, ma'am."

She looked at Josh and nodded, and he nodded back. "Don't call me 'ma'am,' it makes me feel old, and I just turned thirty last month. And don't say thirty is old."

"No, ma'am. I hurt it bad, didn't I?"

"It could be worse. You dislocated your patella, but that's easily fixed. Let's see if we can get your leg straight, first."

He shouted as they manipulated his leg, and Lizzie tried not to wince. "Hey, guys? Can someone go get an ice pack or two?" There were too many people around, hovering. Still, this wasn't the first time she'd seen one of these. When she was working in the emergency room, all sorts of sports injuries came through the door. This was pretty straightforward.

She looked back at Josh, and once again he nodded. Now was the time to trust him. "You wanna switch spots?" she asked quietly.

"I got this," he answered. For a moment her ego flared to life, but she reminded herself that Josh had been a doctor in a war zone. He could handle an itty-bitty kneecap.

"So, what's your name?" she asked. "Might as well make some small talk while we wait for that ice."

"Shawn."

"Okay, Shawn. It kinda hurts running into a big bruiser, doesn't it?"

"Tom's like a friggin' tree."

She laughed. "Did you run right into his leg or what?"

"I could see him there. At the last minute, I tried to pivot out of the way—"

Ah, that was it. He'd planted and twisted and pop! She put her fingers behind her back and started counting down from three.

"So you planted your foot?"

"Yeah, but I just couldn't get around him and—" He yelled as Josh deftly put the kneecap back in place. "Holy shit!"

Lizzie laughed and patted Shawn's hand. His face had gone white for a few seconds, but the color was coming back now. "You're still going to have to have it checked out, and no weight on it. We're going to wrap some ice around it and carry you off the field. But everything's back where it's supposed it be. Say 'thank you, Dr. Collins.'"

"Yuh, thanks," he mumbled, but then turned his gaze back on her. "You're a nice distraction—"

"Dr. Howard. And thank you. Now stop flirting. I'm old, remember?"

He blushed and she laughed, then stood up. She'd worn cutoff denim shorts and a blue T-shirt today and the rusty-brown dirt of the field stuck to her knees. She brushed it off as Josh wrapped the ice pack around the leg and he and a couple of the guys carried Shawn off the field as the players and spectators clapped.

She didn't get a chance to speak to Josh again until after the game was over. The Pups won, but only by a run, and the Old Dogs were looking a little less spry than the kids, who were already talking about heading back to a teammate's house for a barbecue and then picking up girls for the fireworks later in the evening. The older guys were ready for cold beers and some downtime.

Charlie was starting to really feel the heat and Dave had taken her back to the car in the middle of the ninth so she could sit in some air-conditioning. Lizzie was making sure everything was in her tote bag when Josh, his gray pants streaked with brown from a slide into second, made his way over to her.

God, he looked good. His tanned skin contrasted with his dirty-blond hair, which curled out from beneath his cap just a little bit. Then there were his eyes. It seemed like all the Collins kids had inherited the same clear, blue eyes.

"Hey, good teamwork out there, huh?" he asked.

"It was okay. You still lost." She kept her tone nonchalant, deliberately misunderstanding his meaning.

He laughed. "I meant you and me."

"I know you did." She couldn't help but smile now. "That probably really hurt. Hitting Tom had to feel like hitting a brick wall."

"He's a big lad."

She chuckled. "When I signed the lease on the cottage, I was like, holy cow, who is this lumberjack dude?"

Josh really laughed now. "Hold up. Dr. Howard, did you just say 'dude'?"

"So?"

"So, I didn't know such vernacular was in your vocabulary. It's not . . . um . . ."

She shouldered her tote. "Not, um, what?"

"Never mind."

She had a feeling she knew what he was going to say. "Are you saying I have a stick up my ass, Collins?"

He looked shocked that she'd suggested it. "Of course not! Just that you're very . . . uh . . ."

She knew she'd been short with him at times. Stupid truth was that when she felt awkward she reverted to her professional self. Ian had told her once that she sometimes seemed cold. She wasn't, not really. She was just . . . unsure. Of course she'd never admit that to Josh. She didn't like people knowing about her weaknesses. Especially capable, hunky people she had to see every day.

"Good thing you're a doctor," she teased. "Your vocab sucks."

"I was going to say 'professional,'" he finished.

"'Uptight.'"

"Maybe." She was playing with him a bit, and what was more, she was enjoying it. She let him off the hook. "Hey, I'm new, still figuring out the dynamic and stuff. Cut me some slack."

He grinned at her. "You surprised me today. You seemed more easygoing than usual."

"I take my work seriously. But after hours I like to be more chill. It's how I balance things out. My day is organized and efficient. My outside-of-work life is more spontaneous. The game was fun. I do know how to have fun once in a while. I can tell you stories that'll curl your hair."

His eyebrows went up. "Really? Like what?"

She tilted her head to the side. "Well, I think one of my favorites was cliff diving in Hawaii."

He blinked. "You did that?"

"Sure I did. And walked volcanoes and learned to surf. I didn't do so well with the surfing. Hurt my pride a fair bit."

"Excuse me, but that does not seem like the Dr. Howard who shows up at my clinic pressed and dressed for a day of diagnoses."

She hesitated for a minute. "You know, I think you aren't all that you seem, either."

He looked over at her. "Me?"

"I think the amiable guy who goes casual in faded jeans and T-shirts might be a bit of a front. You, Dr. Collins, are not as laid-back as you appear. Am I on the right track?"

That he didn't look at her this time said a lot; at least she thought it did.

"I'm no workaholic."

"Okay." She wasn't about to press the issue. And he had taken a day off and left her at the clinic on her own earlier in the week. The day he'd cut himself on the utility knife. Maybe he wasn't a workaholic, but there was an intensity about him, a restlessness. Maybe small-town medicine wasn't enough for him, either. It was pretty slow compared to a city emergency room.

Damn, she was all curious now. And it really wasn't any of her business.

"I'd better check on Charlie. The heat really seems to get to her these days."

"You're coming to Jess and Rick's?"

"Apparently." They paused at the edge of the parking lot. She realized Josh's old truck was only a few vehicles away, dusty and with rust patches along the bottoms of the doors. "Josh, I have to ask. Why the old truck? You're a doctor. You could afford something so much nicer."

His face hardened and he met her gaze. She wished she could tell what he was thinking, but she realized he knew how to do this thing where he could look right into the person he was talking to but not reveal anything of himself, like a two-way mirror. She wondered if he'd learned to shutter away personal feelings as a doctor or if he'd mastered the art of it when he'd been in the Army. Either way, it was very effective.

"Why do I need anything nicer? It does what I need it to do and gets me where I need to go. I've never seen the point in status symbols. Just because I'm a doctor doesn't make me anything special."

He spun on his heel and walked away, and she was rooted to the spot, nonplussed. There'd been a hostility in his voice that was unexpected. Like she'd touched a nerve.

She came to the conclusion that sure, they'd worked together just fine this afternoon, but on a personal level he didn't like her very much. Not that she needed him to, but she was a little offended. All she'd done was ask a simple question. And his response had felt personal. Like it was obvious she thought she was something special and drove a fancy car.

She shook her head, coughing a little as his truck spun up a bit of dust as he pulled away. If he only knew how unspecial she was, he'd maybe keep his opinions to himself.

CHAPTER 5

Josh knew he hadn't been fair.

He twisted the top off a bottle of beer and took a long swig, standing in Rick and Jess's big backyard. Their new retriever, Riley, romped around, going from person to person with a ball in his mouth, looking for someone to play with him. Most of the alumni team-mates were already present with their spouses and kids, laughing and munching on the snacks Jess had put out to tide people over until dinner. Music played from outdoor speakers placed on either side of the steps that led from the back porch, which used to be Rick's studio. Now the long and narrow room was decorated with wicker furniture and a profusion of plants. Jess came out through the screen door, carrying a platter of something for the buffet table, looking blissfully happy.

What was it about Collins family meals that put him on edge? It was only a little more than a year ago when he faced his cousin Tom for the first time since Erin died, at a similar backyard party. A lot had changed since then. Josh had faced a lot of truths about his marriage, and he and Tom had patched things up. Progress. Back then Rick had been drinking too much and dealing with his own demons. Now Rick and Jess were blissfully happy and expecting a baby. Tom and Abby had been married since last October and were happily settled at the Foster mansion on Blackberry Hill. Heck, even Josh's sister Sarah and her husband, Mark, seemed to be doing better after her miscarriage a year ago.

And Josh was back home where he belonged and going through the motions of being happy. Fake it until you make it was his policy, but that went out the window last week when Lizzie Howard came to work with her uptight hair and flashy convertible and capable ways. Confidence was so not a problem with her, was it? He'd done some checking up, and his suspicions had been verified. She was the daughter of Russ Howard, who'd been one of the top trauma specialists on the East Coast. Talk about money and privilege. Sounded like another family he knew. Erin's. Overachievers and so concerned with status and appearances.

And so he'd snapped at Lizzie today when she'd done nothing to deserve it. All because she'd made a simple comment about his truck and he'd gotten all up in arms about her elitism.

He was in the middle of a ladder golf game with his nephew, Matt, when she walked in with Dave and Charlie. Charlie looked refreshed—they'd likely gone home after the game to change—and Lizzie had dressed up as well, in a flowery sundress with a light sweater draped over her arm. She'd let her hair down, and soft curls touched her shoulders. Josh watched as Jess went over and said something to Lizzie and she smiled, popping a dimple he hadn't realized she possessed.

Because she hadn't had much cause to smile at him, had she?

"Hey, Uncle Josh. It's your turn. Quit staring at the girls."

He looked down at his nephew, who was grinning up at him cheekily. "What do you know about it, short stuff?" Josh looked at the ladder and noticed two of Matt's throws had scored three points each. "Damn. No fair. I was distracted."

"Too bad, so sad," Matt answered.

When the game finished, Matt went off to meet up with a couple of his friends to play fetch with Rick's dog and Josh wandered over to the snack table. His contribution to the day was chips and salsa, but he'd made an attempt to be festive and bought red, white, and blue corn tortilla chips. Apparently Sarah's need to have every food group represented was quashed today, since the other offerings included chips and dip and pretzel twists.

From the corner of his eye he saw Lizzie, holding a glass full of something that was a greenish yellow and looked very citrusy and refreshing. She put the straw to her lips and took a sip of her drink, not a hair or thread out of place.

He'd had time to think about her on his way home from the game this afternoon, think about why she set him on edge so often. It was the two Cs: Competence and Class. Lizzie had them in abundance. Erin had them as well. And he'd spent a good part of his marriage feeling like he wasn't good enough. Part of it was because of where Erin came from. The other part came from knowing that deep down his wife had really been in love with another man. Lizzie made him feel the same way. Like she was way out of his league. It was hard on a man's ego.

As if she felt him staring at her, she looked over and met his gaze. She smiled and gave a little wave before turning back to her conversation. To his surprise, she put her hand on Sarah's arm and seemingly excused herself. His pulse sped up as he realized she was coming his way, his palms started to sweat, and he wondered why on earth it should matter at all. She was his coworker, for Pete's sake. He was technically her boss. He shouldn't feel this way . . . like the unpopular kid on the sidelines of the gym, wondering if the girl walking toward him was going to ask him to dance.

"Hey," she said softly as she caught up with him.

"Hey yourself." Why the hell was he so nervous? "You look nice."

She looked down for a moment. "Um, thanks. I wasn't sure what the dress code was for this sort of thing."

He realized she was the only one wearing a dress. "Things tend to be casual around here. My mom hasn't worn a dress since Jess's wedding, I don't think, and the girls . . ." He looked sideways, then back up at Lizzie. "Jess tells me that she hates dresses right now."

Lizzie took a sip of her drink. "Your sister is beautiful, Josh. Almost eight months pregnant and rockin' the boyfriend jeans look. I don't know another pregnant woman who could pull that off."

Boyfriend jeans? Before he could ask what that meant, he heard Lizzie apologizing.

"Josh, I'm sorry about this afternoon. I didn't mean to criticize."

He met her gaze evenly. "No, I should apologize. I was touchy and I shouldn't have been."

"It's just that we have to work together and I'd rather there wasn't any friction." She took another sip and he wondered if she was doing it just to mask her discomfort. She didn't seem like the kind who would enjoy this sort of conversation. Put her in the middle of a medical emergency and she was in her element. This, though? Awkward.

"I agree." He did, and then some. She looked far more approachable today, without her white coat and neat bun. "Look, what you said . . . it's my issue, not yours. Basing things on appearances is a bit of a hot button for me, that's all."

"Like me asking why you drive a death trap?"

A laugh burst out before he could help it. "Hey. The Beast is not a death trap." When she smiled around her straw, he added, "No more than driving around with the top down."

"Touché." She laughed lightly. "Honestly? The car was my dad's. He treated himself to it two years ago, when he was looking for something fun. I was driving a plain old boring Toyota until a few months ago. And I mean plain. Like *beige*." She emphasized the color with an eye roll.

He laughed despite himself.

"I do know how to have fun, you know. Ask Charlie. She was the stick-in-the-mud when we were in college."

"So what changed?"

"What do you mean?" She picked up a blue tortilla chip and bit off a corner.

"I just . . . You seem, I don't know, guarded. So serious all the time."

Her cheeks flushed a little. "Oh. Well, my dad died last winter." She shrugged casually, but her eyes were dark and sad as she said the words quietly, the somber tone a contrast to the happy summer music and laughter filling the yard.

Josh felt like a jerk. "I'm sorry to hear that. Was he ill?"

She shook her head. "No. He was semiretired. A trauma specialist. He wasn't even seventy, so we didn't see the stroke coming. He's the reason I became a doctor, and we were really close. It seems weird, not having him with me anymore."

"It can be hard to live up to your family's expectations."

She frowned. "Oh, Dad didn't put that kind of pressure on me. When I was little, he used to tell me, 'Lizzie, no one ever got anywhere by dreaming small. Dream big. Have adventures.' And then when I got older he was the one who advised me to leave work once in a while and cut loose." She smiled wistfully. "He wasn't always like that. When I was little, he worked a lot. But one time I heard my mom put her foot down and say that he had a marriage to look after and not just a job. He really made an effort to balance life after that. We used to take these ski trips every year. My mother nearly had a fit when he decided the two of us were going heli-skiing." Her face softened, and then she blinked quickly four or five times.

No mention of where her mother was now, but Josh didn't want to pry too much when Lizzie was already upset. Clearly she had adored her father. Josh also found it very telling that she mentioned his death but not a word about the situation at her last job. For some reason he liked her more for it, and what it said about her that she'd chosen losing her father as the defining moment of the past six months.

"I lost my dad when I was young," he offered. "It was also really sudden. I know it can throw you for a loop, especially when the presence has been a strong one. It'll get better, though." He smiled at her encouragingly, and when she looked at him, her lashes slightly damp, something changed inside him. She wasn't the uptight city girl who drove into town in her flashy car and made judgments. In that moment of honesty, Lizzie Howard went from being temporary coworker to friend. And Josh always made sure to look out for his friends.

"Uncle Josh, Mom says to stop hogging the chip bowl." Matt popped up beside them and let out the string of words all at once, without a pause. "Oh, and to ask you if I can get you a refill, Dr. Howard."

The interruption broke the strange spell between her and Josh, and he took a step back. Lizzie let out a breath and smiled. "Oh, that would be lovely, Matthew." She handed over her glass and Matt dashed away. "He's a cute one," she murmured.

"A good kid, but all boy, too," Josh said affectionately, somewhat relieved they'd left the heavy conversation behind them. "It's too bad he doesn't have any brothers or cousins. When we were little, the four of us—me, Rick, Tom, and Bryce—did everything together." He grinned. "Good and bad. Do you have any siblings?"

"Nope. Only child. Charlie's the closest thing to a sister I've ever had."

"She says that about you, too. She's really mellowed out since she and Dave got together. It's kind of cute."

They both looked over at Charlie and Dave, who

were holding hands as they chatted to Todd Ricker and a young woman Josh didn't recognize. "They're adorable," Lizzie said. "It's almost sickening, except I'm so glad to see her happy that, well, you know."

"Wedded bliss isn't for you, Dr. Howard?"

She tilted her head and gave him a sideways look. "I wouldn't know. I haven't been close enough to it to give it a serious thought."

He laughed. He couldn't help it. She was so dry, so delightfully cynical, that he felt an instant bond. "God, and here I thought I was the only one not enthralled with the idea of marital bliss."

Matt came back with Lizzie's drink and she thanked him briefly before he went running off again. "But . . . you were married before. You don't intend to do it again?"

He'd walked right into that question, and he should have known better. This was what happened when you got comfortable with someone. You tended to forget the walls and boundaries you'd built to protect that soft underbelly. And for Josh, that weak spot was Erin.

"I loved my wife," he said, knowing that was the truth. "But it wasn't enough. And now she's gone."

With that cryptic response, he offered a quiet "excuse me" and went to help Rick at the grill.

As the guests kept coming, the noise in the backyard rose. Lizzie met a ton of new people, all of whom were friendly and welcoming. The lime coolers were deliciously crisp and tart and by seven she was grateful for food. She found herself sitting at a picnic table with Josh's mom, Meggie, and Tom and Abby Arseneault, and an older woman who introduced herself as the town busybody and member of the historical society. Lizzie hadn't talked to Tom since the day she'd moved into his cottage, and they got caught up chatting about the house and the nearby beach. Abby, she learned, was relatively new to Jewell Cove, having arrived just over a year earlier, and it was nice to talk to someone else who had a newcomer's eyes.

Rick's ribs were fall-off-the-bone delicious, and Jess had cooked corn in a massive canner that Lizzie figured was also used for lobster and other backyard "boils." Sarah's potato salad disappeared quickly, and there were fluffy white rolls and coleslaw, too. Just when Lizzie was sure she couldn't eat another bite, Jess came out carrying a cake to rival any July Fourth dessert she'd ever seen.

It was a huge rectangular sheet cake with white icing. Blueberries were in the top left corner making the "stars" part of the flag, with rows of ripe raspberries forming the "stripes." Right in the middle was a sparkler ready to be lit, and all the kids in attendance bounced around, wanting to see the sparkler and get the first pieces. Before long the younger crew was temporarily quiet as they gobbled up cake and vanilla ice cream.

It was a very fun evening, but the whole time Lizzie was aware of Josh. The serious expression from earlier was gone, and he smiled and chatted and laughed and looked all-around happy. She wondered how much of it was an act. There'd been something strange about what he'd said. Not that he'd loved his wife or that she was gone—that was expected. But the part about not loving her enough. What did he mean? Had their marriage not been as happy as everyone let on?

She held off on the coolers now; she'd started feeling fuzzy around the edges and had no desire to drink too much and possibly say something inappropriate. She wondered if that actually did make her a stick-in-the-mud as Josh had intimated earlier.

"Sue me for being responsible then," she muttered to herself. Maybe she should check with Charlie. See if she and Dave were anywhere near ready to leave.

But Charlie was determined to stay until the fireworks at ten, which would take place on a barge out in the cove and could be seen right here from Rick's backyard. Lizzie helped clean up the mess from dinner and when it was over found herself perched on the edge of a picnic table with a cup of coffee.

Alone.

Despite what Sarah and Charlie had insisted, there weren't singles here. The crowd was a mix of late twenties and thirties, with the odd older couple in attendance. There were babies and toddlers and elementary school children, and while hearing their happy laughter was nice, it did serve to make Lizzie feel more out of place. Sure, Josh's mom was attending alone, but she was sitting with her sister, Barb, and brother-in-law, Pete, and that didn't count. As far as Lizzie could tell, she and Josh were the only two singletons in the bunch. And she wondered if her invitation had been more than just a friendly one or if she'd been maneuvered in his direction.

How mortifying.

To make matters worse, Josh came over and hopped up on the table next to her. "So," he said conversationally, as if the earlier tension hadn't existed, "are you counting by twos as well?"

She laughed. If he wasn't going to bring up their last talk, she wouldn't, either. "You noticed."

"I think we were manipulated. Or at least you were.

I would have been obligated to come as both team member and family."

"Well, maybe I should be flattered." At Josh's questioning look, she smirked a little. "Hey, according to a reliable source, they can't throw Summer Arnold at you forever."

The scowl on his face made Lizzie's evening, and she caught herself chuckling.

"Have you met Summer?" he asked. "She's nice enough, but I can't get past the constant hair color changes or the nose ring. I suppose that makes me the uptight one, huh?"

"If the shoe fits," she replied. "So . . . was she the one painting faces today? She stood out."

"That's her." He took a sip of his coffee. "How was your dinner?" he asked, resting his elbows on his knees. "I saw you ate with my mom, and Tom and Abby." He looked over at Lizzie. "Almost like you were avoiding me."

"I don't avoid people. Besides, you were the one who walked away from me."

"About that . . ."

She noticed he 'd put his hands together and was rubbing his right thumb over his left knuckle. Nerves?

"I don't know what people have told you about me. But it'll get back to you eventually. I should probably just give you the lowdown now to avoid any future awkwardness."

"Jeez, Josh. We're coworkers. If this is about your personal life . . ."

"In a town this size, personal life gets talked about. It just goes with the territory."

"Right."

"The thing is—"

He started but then stopped, and Lizzie simply waited. Jess turned on strings of patio lights that lit the yard in a soft, colorful glow, and someone brought out glow bracelets for the kids who were running furtively between lots, looking for "ghosts" as the evening deepened and the sky slowly melted into darkness.

He cleared his throat. "The thing is, my cousin Tom was sweet on Erin first, and I stepped in and stole her away. I was in med school and her dad is a doctor. They approved of me whereas Tom . . . not so much. I had prospects and he had a tool belt. And it wasn't that I didn't love her. I did. But I knew she didn't love me the way she loved Tom. And I married her anyway."

Lizzie let out a big breath. "Holy crap. And you and Tom still get along?"

Josh made a choked sound that she figured was half laugh, half "are you kidding?"

"Last year I moved back home. At my homecoming party, I coldcocked him. I was a pretty big jerk. We've made peace since then. Tom fell in love with Abby, and I stopped blaming him." Josh paused and stared out over the bay. "It wasn't like he ever made any trouble for us. He didn't have to. Erin's feelings for Tom were more than enough to stand in the way of our being happy. Anyway . . ." He put his hands on his knees and pushed so he was sitting up straight. "What I said before was me letting a little bitterness back in. I try not to. Sometimes I just get caught up in looking back and wish I could have changed things."

"She broke your heart."

"She did. And did a good number on my ego, too. Everyone seems to think I should get back out there again. Get married and have kids and act like my life before didn't happen. I just wish they'd let me do it on my own time."

"I get that."

"You do?"

"Yep." Her insides were trembling a bit. Josh had been really open with her. A lot of disclosure, and she felt a little obligated to share in return. But there was more than obligation, too. She was starting to like him. Sure, she'd been surprised by his casual dress and manner at the office, but she'd also come to see that he set exactly the right tone for the clinic. He built relationships and trust with his patients, patients he would see year after year, unlike doctors who worked behind the revolving door of an emergency room.

She didn't have to worry about ongoing cases or seeing people more than once. Emergency medicine was like that. You triaged and assessed and moved them on . . . and then you moved on.

At least that was how it was supposed to work. But the Miller case was not something she was going to talk to Josh about.

"Liz?"

She looked over to find his eyes watching her closely. Goodness, he looked like he cared. Like he was really listening. She swallowed. No wonder he was a good doctor. If this was his bedside manner . . .

"In my case, the people pushing me to move on is actually, uh, me," she admitted. "Hanging with Charlie again has been good for me. She made me see that I was pushing myself too hard to avoid dealing with my own pain."

"From your dad's death."

Her stomach twisted. "Yes." It was partially the

truth, anyway. Everything that had happened since then was a result of her not dealing with her grief. A result of her own denial.

"And what about your mom? Is she still in Springfield, too?"

Lizzie nodded, the sense of sadness and futility seeping into her again. "Yes, but she's in full-time care. She has Alzheimer's. My dad was having a hard time caring for her at home. He cut back his hours, but there came a point where she required more than he could provide, even if I tried to fill in the gaps."

"So you've lost two parents, not one."

"Essentially, yeah."

The first firework of the night popped and then exploded with a bang. Everyone stopped what they were doing and turned their faces to the sky, waiting for the next sparkly shower.

"I'm really sorry, Liz. That's a lot to deal with."

"I haven't done that great of a job. I kind of burned myself out."

Another *pop, pop* and "ooohs" from the partygoers.

"Know what? Take it from one who's been there. This place can be really great for finding your feet again. I'm glad you're here."

"I can't believe I'm going to say this, but me, too."

The fireworks really hit their stride and Josh and Lizzie fell quiet, simply enjoying the colorful display. When it was over, the music started up again, the smaller children started to snuggle in mothers' arms, and the older ones went on the hunt for leftover cake.

"You want a lift home?"

Josh's voice was close to her ear, the warmth of his breath sending delicious shivers down her spine. "I came with Charlie and Dave. . . ."

"And Charlie just went inside to look at the nursery. They're going to be talking babies for a while."

She looked at him, wondering what he was asking, whether it was simply a courtesy and friendly gesture or if . . .

But no. They'd both been clear that romance was not even on their radars these days. "That'd be nice. It's been a long day."

"You want to tell Dave? I'll go fire up the Beast."

"Okay."

A minute later and she was at the gate to Rick's yard, looking out at Josh sitting in the cab of his truck.

Why did she feel like a teenager sneaking out to meet the town bad boy?

CHAPTER 6

The interior of Josh's truck was clean, but the vinyl trim was worn and there was a rip in one of the seats. Lizzie smiled to herself at the imperfection. From everything she'd seen at the office, Josh was a very conscientious doctor. He didn't brush people off but instead listened carefully to what they said—and didn't say. He had a penchant for cleanliness, which was a definite plus in her book, and also for punctuality.

But she could see a laid-back side to him, too, like the casual dress, the hair that was a smidge too long, the easy way he talked to people. She liked both sides, really. He was easier to be with than she expected, with none of the awkwardness she'd anticipated feeling away from the office. And now he was driving her home. He smiled at her from the driver's seat as he put the truck in gear, and a warning slid through her head. It would be okay for them to be coworkers, even friendly. But anything more would be a mistake. After the disaster of her relationship with Ian, she wasn't about to travel that road again. Might as well cut that idea right off at the knees.

"Thanks for the drive home," she said, trying to set the proper tone. "I didn't want to cut Charlie and Dave's time short. She's really enjoying becoming part of the community."

He pulled away from the curb and turned left at the stop sign. "And that's not you?"

She shrugged. "Not like I'm going to be here long enough anyway."

"Oh, you never know." There was a smile in his voice. "Abby said that, and she ended up staying. So did Dave."

"Well, I'm pretty sure that there's not room for three doctors in Jewell Cove," Lizzie rationalized. "Besides, I'm an ER doctor. And those departments are generally found in the city."

"Hey, there are departments in Rockport and Brunswick and lots of other places."

She looked over at him and gave him a look that said, *Real emergency departments.*

He chuckled. "You like the fast pace."

"I do. And the unpredictability. I'm afraid small town just doesn't do it for me. I mean, Springfield is about as small as I go. I'm more of a big-city girl."

Josh tapped the wheel with his fingers, along with the beat to the song on the radio.

They turned off the main road, heading up a hill that was not part of the route home. "Hey," she said, suddenly feeling awkward and a bit uncomfortable. "Where are we going?"

If he was going to attempt to take her parking, this was going to be really, really humiliating. Off to her left she saw a stately house, complete with white pillars that stood out in the moonlight, giving it a grand yet ghostly air. "What's that place?"

"That's Tom and Abby's. Her great-aunt left it to her and Tom renovated it. You should see it inside." But he drove past the lane, farther up the hill, until they encountered a gate. Josh put the truck in park, got out, and opened the gate, then hopped back in and kept going.

"Uh, Josh, I'm not sure if I gave you the wrong impression or what, but . . . I think I'd rather just go straight home."

He laughed. "Lizzie, we're adults. If I wanted to proposition you, don't you think I'd just offer a 'my place or yours'?"

She hoped her hot cheeks weren't noticeable in the darkness of the truck cab.

He crested the last steep curve of the hill, turned to the right, and then backed up so that the back end of the truck was facing the view below. "Come on," he urged, opening his door. "There's something I want to show you."

Reluctant but undeniably curious, Lizzie got out of the truck and went around to the back, where Josh was letting down the tailgate. Without offering, he simply put his hands on her waist and boosted her up while her lips dropped open in surprise. She couldn't deny it was a little exciting.

Josh hopped up beside her and let out a long, satisfied breath. "Welcome to Blackberry Hill," he said softly. "You can see Tom and Abby's house from here, see?" He pointed down the hill, where the shape of the house was visible, surrounded by the darker, well-defined perimeter of their lawns and gardens, illuminated by moonlight. "And beyond that is the cove. The town is that way"—he pointed a bit to the left—"and your cottage is over that way, just past Fiddler's Beach." He pointed a little to the right this time. "And straight out, you see that dark lump way out in the water?"

"Is it an island?" she asked, intrigued despite herself.

"Yes. You can see it from up here, but not from the harbor. The natives call it 'Aquteg,' meaning 'hidden.' Which is pretty fitting considering rumor has it that during the Civil War a privateer buried treasure on that island. A privateer with the last name of Arseneault."

"As in Tom's family?"

He nodded. "The very same. Arseneault was good friends with two other names you might recognize. Jedediah Foster and Edward Jewell."

Lizzie crossed her legs and rested her elbows on her knees. "Okay, is this just some nautical fairy tale that you guys tell all the newcomers to add mystery to your town?" She laughed lightly, though the story had caught her interest more than she cared to admit.

"Not at all," he assured her. "Arseneault was a Southern privateer who fell in love with a local woman—an abolitionist. The story goes that he buried some sort of treasure out there before reforming his wicked ways and joining her as part of the Underground Railroad." He grinned. "Which is why the locals now call it 'Lovers' Island.'"

"That *is* a romantic story," she admitted, staring out at the faraway lump of rock in the middle of the shifting sea. Stupid thing was, she could see it all in her head. The risk of sailing on the seas in wartime, the sails billowing in the wind, women waiting on the shore in dresses with enormous skirts, a rake tamed by an honest woman—

Damn. It was like something out of one of those historical romance novels that she devoured, a secret little pleasure that felt indulgent and frivolous. She just bet everyone expected that she read dry medical journals in her spare time. Pirates and damsels and treasure? That was right up her alley, though she doubted Josh knew it.

"There must be some truth to the tale," he continued. "A few jewels have shown up over the years. Abby's engagement ring is an Arseneault family heirloom. And Rick ended up with a necklace that was traced back to Jed Foster." He paused, looked over at her, and grinned. "A bunch of us used to go out there and search for buried chests and the like."

"Did you ever find anything?"

"We thought we did." He laughed, a soft, alluring sound in the dark. "We made up all kinds of things that we imagined were clues and trails. Mostly, though, we packed peanut butter sandwiches and cookies and explored."

"Sounds like a fun childhood," she remarked, trying to picture him as a boy.

"It was. Once we rigged up some sort of metal detector and headed out for the day and put a hole in Tom's dad's dory and sank it. He was not happy about that at all. I don't know what bothered us most, the way he yelled at us or losing that metal detector."

She smiled, picturing it. "I never had any brothers or sisters, so I never got up to stuff like that. The way you tell it, I kind of wish I had, though."

"I guess what I'm saying is Jewell Cove isn't a bad

place to be. Especially when you're trying to sort yourself out."

She'd been super relaxed up to that point, but his slight insinuation raised her guard. "And you think I have something to sort out?"

"Don't you?" he asked. The evening was so quiet that the only thing they could hear up here at the top of the hill was the breeze in the leaves of the trees. "I was kind of waiting for you to bring it up. I know about what happened in Springfield, Lizzie. It's on record. I didn't just take Charlie's word for it about you, you know. I did my due diligence. This is my medical practice."

She wasn't sure if she was angry, embarrassed, or hurt at the reminder of why she'd been asked to take a leave of absence.

"I screwed up. But I'm not supposed to say that to the lawyers."

He sighed. "Because they'll settle, right?"

"That's right. Too bad the settlement doesn't make me feel any better about my mistake." Just talking about it made her sick to her stomach.

"What happened?"

She swallowed, a bitter taste in her mouth as she recalled that day for what seemed the millionth time. "Group B strep. During a normal pregnancy, the screening would have already been done. But they'd been in an accident and the baby was coming early and fast. I never even thought about a test—mom was bleeding a lot from her injuries and the baby was crowning." That one day seemed to change everything Lizzie believed about herself as a doctor.

She'd been up all night on shift, and she'd been dog tired. She'd been solely focused on triaging and treating and packing mom and baby off to the proper departments.

She'd peeled off her gloves and scrubs and called it a day. But the mom had insisted something wasn't right and Lizzie had blown her off as distressed by her injuries and the chaotic events leading to the delivery. She and the baby had been moved to the neonatal ward and Lizzie had gone home, never giving them a second thought.

"The baby got sick." It was a statement, rather than a question. He knew all this already, didn't he? But he was asking for her side . . . and she found herself sharing it even though talking about it was the one thing she *hadn't* done in weeks.

"And I missed it. Two days later the baby contracted pneumonia and it was too late. All because I was in a rush and I was tired and I wasn't thorough."

Her throat tightened. It hadn't been her job to tell the father and mother that their baby was dead. She was just the ER physician who happened to be on duty that first morning. But she'd seen the couple leaving the hospital. She'd never forget it. The mother, her belly still soft from pregnancy, weeping quietly, and the father with red-rimmed eyes, holding his wife as they walked to the exit without their newborn son.

"I'm sorry."

"Not as sorry as I am." She knew her voice had hardened, but she couldn't help it. It had been months now and she still couldn't escape the guilt. "I get that we all make mistakes. I've made mistakes, but none this disastrous, and I've always known in my heart that I did all I could. Every other time, I've been there in the room making all the calls. But this time I was tired, distracted, and careless. That's what I can't seem to move past."

"Your boss said you are the finest ER doctor he's ever seen and that he hates that this has happened to you."

Ian had said that? For a flash she was pleased and flattered at the praise. But it was quickly erased as she recalled seeing his too-handsome face the day he'd called her into his office. There'd been pity, but there'd been distance, too. Ian had to cover his butt. Besides, civil suits happened all the time. Her leave of absence was far more a reflection of his opinion of her abilities rather than on the case itself.

"He only said that because we were in a relationship until the end of April."

That must have surprised him, because Josh didn't say anything for a few minutes. Instead he lay back on the bed of the truck and stared up at the stars. "Well," he drawled, "that does complicate things a little, doesn't it?"

"It's definitely a mistake I won't repeat," she said acidly. "I should've known better than to get involved with the boss."

Josh chuckled. "I guess that tells me where I stand, doesn't it?"

Once more her cheeks heated. She looked down at him and couldn't help but admire his flat stomach, the curve of his muscles in his T-shirt as he put his arms behind his head. "You're joking, right?" She sincerely hoped so. It would really suck if things got awkward on the job a mere week after she started.

"Yes, I'm joking. I'm not looking, Lizzie. Though my family thinks I should be."

"Hence the Summer what's-her-name comments."

"Exactly." He sighed. "When the time is right, I'll know. Maybe it'll never be right. For now I like running the practice, hanging with my family, going out on the water in my new boat. Keeping it simple."

Keeping it simple sounded wonderful, actually. And there was no reason why she shouldn't treat this summer like a lovely seaside vacation in a rented cottage. So what if she had to work a few days each week? It kept her from being bored. And how many people could say they were spending the summer only footsteps from the beach, anyway?

Encouraged, she flopped down beside him and looked up at the stars. "Gosh, does this mean we're becoming friends?"

She wasn't looking at him, but she got the sense he smiled. "Maybe. Maybe I just wanted you to be a little more comfortable around here, so things aren't so tense at the office, you know?"

She stared at the stars. "Have I been uptight?"

"A little. Listen, I have no complaints about your work, other than you can relax a little. Time moves a bit slower around here. Stop and smell the roses." He paused. "Or look at the stars."

She did, for the space of ten long breaths. The weird thing was that neither of them said anything and she didn't find the silence awkward, either.

A falling star streaked across the sky, leaving a whispery trail behind it. "Whoa, did you see that?" Josh asked.

"Yeah, I did." She searched the sky for more. "Where my condo is, there's too much light pollution to really see the stars much. This is cool."

"When I was deployed, I used to love looking at the

stars. It kind of linked me to back home, you know? Because I'd look up into the darkness and know that back here, the people I loved could see the stars, too. It doesn't make much sense, with time and hemisphere differences, but there you go."

She imagined him doing that and once more realized that there was far more to Josh than met the eye. "Josh?"

"Hmmm?"

"When I'm nervous or unsure I tend to get . . . officious. That morning when I first arrived, and I thought you were the janitor? I was embarrassed. I know sometimes people think I'm stuck-up. I'm really not."

Josh turned his head and looked at her. "A few weeks here has started to thaw you out," he replied, and it was hard to tell in the darkness, but she thought he winked at her. "I'm glad you're here, Lizzie. Now, are you ready to go home?"

"I think so." She sat up, pulled her knees into her chest. "This was really nice, though. Maybe I *have* been wound a little too tight."

"Ya think?" he joked, hopping down from the tailgate. He extended his hand to help her, but she sent him a grin instead and jumped down herself.

They were soon back in the truck, slowly descending the hill. Lizzie looked closer at Abby's house and shook her head. "Wow, that really is a showpiece, isn't it?"

"Yup. Years ago, her great-aunt Marian ran a home for unwed mothers there. She left it to Abby when she died, but it needed a lot of work. Last year, we had our Fourth of July celebrations there, a real garden party with servants in period dress and everything."

"She seems nice."

"She is."

Lizzie looked over, and a shadow had come over Josh's face. "Hmm. Bit of a story there?"

He perked up. "A long story, and a fairly convoluted one. The most important thing is that she and Tom are really happy. "

And Josh wasn't. He didn't have to say the words for her to know. This whole side trip tonight hadn't just been for her, she realized. He'd needed the space, too. Josh was more complicated than she had originally thought. Maybe it was the death of his wife. That had to be a terrible thing to try to get over, but she wasn't going to ask him. That would be prying into something incredibly personal. Even if they were becoming friends, they'd bared enough of their souls for one night.

She could still barely believe that she'd told him about the baby . . . but then, he'd already known, hadn't he?

He turned back onto the main road, and it was only a few minutes and they were at her cottage. It was dark inside and out, as she'd never thought to turn on the outside light before she left this morning. For a quick moment she considered asking him in for a drink, but she didn't want to give him the wrong idea and they'd already spent a fair bit of time together tonight. "Thanks for the lift," she said, injecting her voice with false enthusiasm.

"Anytime," he replied, leaving the truck running. "I'll see you at work."

"Yes, boss," she joked, but the silence turned uncomfortable. For a while tonight they'd both forgotten that he was her boss. The whole situation seemed so strange, so foreign. So very far away from what her life had become.

He waited until she got inside before backing out of her driveway and heading back to town.

CHAPTER 7

The hallway was cool and clean and Lizzie knew she should feel comfortable in this, a medical setting. But she didn't. The facility her mom now called home wasn't like a regular hospital. Sure, there were doctors and nursing staff, and Lizzie would meet with them after and discuss dosages and progress and all the other factual elements of her mother's illness.

But the truth was, Lizzie's mom lived here. She lived in a room and had her meals provided and her needs catered to. As a doctor, Lizzie knew this had been the right decision for her mom's day-to-day care.

As a daughter, she felt guilty as hell.

Lizzie paused outside the doorway, then poked her head around the corner. She never really knew if she'd find her mother at home in her room or a stranger who didn't recognize her. Today Rosemary was sitting in a chair by the window, staring outside while a skein of yarn and a crochet needle sat abandoned on her lap.

"Hello!" Lizzie called lightly, stepping to the door-way.

Rosemary Howard turned her head and a smile lit her face. "Elizabeth. Hello, dear."

Relief rushed through Lizzie. Her mom's eyes seemed clear and sharp, her smile genuine and not confused. "Hi, Mom." Lizzie held up a little vase. "I brought you some lilacs."

"Oh, they're beautiful. Let me smell." Rosemary was only sixty-five, but when she got up Lizzie could tell her hips and knees were stiff. Lizzie held out the vase and watched with bittersweet pleasure as her mom took the flowers and buried her nose in the fragrant blossoms. "I love lilacs. Where did you get them?"

Rosemary put them on her windowsill and Lizzie put down her purse. "Actually, I snipped them from the bush at the cottage where I'm staying. It's the last of them, I'm afraid. Next time I'll bring some roses from the bushes there."

"Lizzie, are you gardening?" Her mom's eyebrows lifted in surprise, and they both moved to the seating area provided in the room, a little cozy spot with a television, a small bookshelf, and a side table that currently held a few puzzle books Lizzie kept bringing to help keep her mom's mind sharp. Sudoku was her favorite.

"Only a little," Lizzie replied. "I'm working in Maine for a while." She repeated the information, unsure if her mom remembered her mentioning it last time. "I'm renting a cute little cottage on the coast. You'd like it."

Her heart gave a little lurch. Her mom really would like it up there. She'd always liked the ocean and she'd always kept beautiful flower beds at their house. Perhaps that was what bothered Lizzie the most about her mom being here. So many of the things she'd enjoyed all her life were stripped away, one by one. It didn't seem fair.

"A cottage?" Rosemary frowned. "But you've always liked the city. You don't want to be bothered by a yard and upkeep. Do you remember that plant I got you for an apartment-warming present?"

Lizzie nodded, tears stinging her eyes. Oh, it was a good day. At least so far. "It was an African violet and I killed it within a month."

Rosemary nodded back and laughed a little, and Lizzie was so lonely for her mom that an ache spread through her chest.

"So," she said, trying to keep things light. "I thought we could have a picnic for lunch. What do you think? I have a cooler in the car, and the nurses said we can eat in the garden at that little table overlooking the pond."

"You cooked?"

"Of course not." Lizzie laughed. "I'm not quite that domesticated. There's this café in Jewell Cove. The cook's name is Gus, and his fried chicken will make you weep and thank your maker. Not to mention potato salad. And I brought dessert."

"It's so good to see you," Rosemary said, reaching over and patting Lizzie's hand. "Let me freshen up first, okay?"

Lizzie waited while her mom went to the bathroom. So far, the disease hadn't progressed to the point where she needed help all the time and today she was remarkably clearheaded, so Lizzie let her have her independence and simply waited. When Rosemary emerged, Lizzie tried to hide her dismay and put on a bright face. Not bright enough to match Rosemary's, though. She had put on cherry-red lipstick and brushed on some blush that was far too heavy for her delicate cheeks.

"Okay, Mom, let's just tell someone we're heading to the garden and we'll have a nice lunch."

Rosemary followed close to Lizzie as they stopped at the reception desk and then went to the car for the soft-side cooler she'd brought. It was only a few minutes and they were settled at a small iron table and chairs set in the middle of the English gardens, an oasis of tranquility remarkably free of the telltale scents of medical facilities.

She unpacked a container of fried chicken, a dish of potato salad, and another of cool sliced cucumbers, plus two soft buns from the Main Street Bakery, sandwiched together with a thick layer of real butter. Then came the plates, real ones, as Lizzie knew how her mother despised paper, and proper knives, forks, and napkins. Lizzie's one plastic concession was glasses, but the ones she'd picked up were cute, with little flowers painted on them, and she took out a thermos of cool, fresh lemonade.

When she'd served both plates, her mom looked up with worried eyes. "Won't your dad be joining us? Where is he? Is he working late again?"

Lizzie's heart plummeted to her feet and she swallowed against the lump of futility in her throat. "It's just you and me today, Mom," she said, forcing a smile and handing over a napkin. "Try the chicken."

"Your father works too hard. He never comes to see me," Rosemary complained, her voice taking on a plaintive quality that grated on Lizzie's nerves, making her feel even more guilty.

"Then let's just make this a girly day," she suggested lightly. She got up and spread the napkin on her mother's lap. She would not cry or let her frustrations show. She would be patient, kind . . .

Sad.

No, she had to lock that away for later. So she poured lemonade into her mother's glass and handed it to her. "I know I'm not much of a cook, but I made the lemonade myself, just this morning. What do you think?"

She saw Rosemary's hand tremble a bit as she lifted the drink to her lips and sipped. "It's tart," she replied, puckering her lips. "Just the way your father likes it. Will he be joining us today?"

More swallowing of tears. "Not today," Lizzie replied. She forced herself to take a bite of chicken, trying to lead by example, but it didn't taste good anymore. She was desperate to change the subject. "What are you crocheting, Mom? The yarn looked so pretty, a really nice shade of pink."

Finally Rosemary picked up her fork and started to eat. "Hats. For the neonatal unit." She tasted her potato salad, then daintily cut a cucumber slice in fourths. "A few of the other ladies and I work on them and the nurses take them to the hospital." She met Lizzie's gaze. "It makes me feel like I'm doing something important."

"It *is* important," Lizzie agreed. "I'm glad. Can I do something to help? Buy you some yarn? There's a craft shop in town that I think probably carries it."

"Some yellow or light green would be nice."

"I'll bring it next time I visit, how about that?"

"Thank you, dear."

Lizzie noted with some pleasure that her mom had eaten a good portion of her meal, rather than picking at stuff as she often did. Encouraged, Lizzie reached down into the cooler for one final dish. "Mom, I brought dessert. Your favorite, coconut cream pie." She put the container on the table and removed the lid.

Rosemary made a face and looked at the pie with disgust. "But I hate coconut. That's never been my favorite. Whatever made you think that?"

Oh, maybe just the fact that every special occasion since Lizzie could remember Rosemary had offered to make coconut cream pies. If they went out to eat it was her favorite thing to order for dessert, and years ago, before her memory had started to slip, she'd had a list of the best places to get it and the ones to avoid. Who made the best pastry and where the filling was the creamiest.

Lizzie felt like weeping for the umpteenth time. The only parent she had left, and her mother was slipping away by degrees. And today had been a good day. Now even the good days wore on Lizzie and she found it harder and harder to rejoice in the lucid moments.

"I'm sorry, Mom. My mistake." She packed away the pie before Rosemary could get upset and smiled. "Maybe we can sneak some ice cream from the kitchen. What's your favorite flavor?"

"Vanilla," Rosemary answered clearly. "But shouldn't we wait for your father? He'll be so sorry he missed lunch."

Lizzie felt like banging her head on the table. It hurt to think of her dad at the best of times, but to be reminded this way by her mom was nearly unbearable. How many times could a person's heart break anyway?

"Let's sneak into the kitchen, then. See what's in the freezer."

She packed the dirty dishes into the cooler and zipped the top, then walked with her mom back over the lawns, through the gardens and flower beds to the low building that housed the patients. It looked like a lovely, restful place . . . until you got to the front doors and recognized the security features in place to keep patients from wandering away.

Lizzie guided her mom to the kitchen, where they managed to sneak a scoop each of vanilla ice cream before Rosemary started to show signs of fatigue and Lizzie helped her back to her room. "Thanks for having lunch with me today, Mom." She put her arms around her mother, closed her eyes, and realized once more that the woman before her was her mother and yet bore little resemblance to the woman she'd known all her life. Rosemary had lost weight over the last few years, and she didn't smell the same, like her preferred laundry soap mixed with Chanel perfume, a scent she'd always called "classic."

What surprised Lizzie the most was that she wasn't only grieving for one parent. She was mourning two.

Gently, she helped her mom to her bed. "You're tired. Why don't you rest your eyes for a bit? It's time for me to go anyway, but I'll be back soon. Is there anything I can bring you?"

Rosemary sat on the edge of the bed, acquiescing to Lizzie's attentions, her body totally submissive. "I wish you could bring Russ back. I miss him so, Lizzie."

Christ, what a moment for lucidity to return. Lizzie continued removing her mom's shoes, but the view of them was blurred by tears. "I miss him, too, Mom."

"He was so proud of you. So am I."

Lizzie sniffed, gathered herself together, and lifted

her head with a smile. "Thanks. He was a really great inspiration, you know?"

Rosemary nodded sadly. "Yes. Better than I ever was."

Lizzie sat beside her mom and took her hand. "You are the best mother I could ask for," she whispered. "And don't you forget it."

But Rosemary would. As she usually did. It never seemed to make sense, what she pulled from her memories. But Lizzie was highly doubtful her mother would remember today. Certainly not the things they'd said.

As if she could read Lizzie's thoughts, Rosemary squeezed her hand and looked at her with a tired but concerned expression. "Lizzie, did you remember to pay the bill for lunch?"

"It's taken care of, Mom. You rest." She eased her mother down on the bed and covered her with a light blanket. Lizzie, who wasn't generally prone to emotional displays of affection, leaned over and kissed her mom's forehead in a way similar to how Rosemary had kissed hers when she was a little girl, being tucked in for a nap or bedtime. "Love you."

"Mmm-hmm." Rosemary sighed, a contented sound. "Maybe Russ will be by later. He promised."

"Maybe," Lizzie replied, feeling like she'd been through an emotional wringer, wondering exactly when she and her mother had made such a complete reversal of roles.

She left as Rosemary was drifting off to sleep, stopped to chat briefly with staff, and then hit the road, heading back to Jewell Cove. And wondered what it meant that she was relieved to be returning to the little cottage instead of her condo in Springfield. Somehow the little spot overlooking the inlet was exactly where she needed to be.

Not in the bustle of the city or the chaos of an emergency room. *Good God.* She might actually be losing her edge.

Honest to God, if Sarah tried to set him up one more time he was going to lose his cool and be very blunt in telling her to back off.

This time it was an impromptu family trip to Sally's Dairy Shack for banana splits. Josh shook his head as he stood in line, wondering why he hadn't seen it coming. Summer Arnold was behind the counter taking orders, her pink-striped hair pulled back into a weird twist and covered with a hairnet. Her diamond-stud nose ring was visible, and with her hair pulled back so was the row of earrings in each ear, including one ear cuff hooked by a chain to a dangling daisy earring.

She was so not his type. Not that she wasn't a nice girl. She was. He'd known her for years. Sarah and Jess thought a lot of her, which was why he'd tolerated a certain amount of interference. But really, they had to stop doing this. He wasn't interested. Full stop. And it was getting damned awkward.

Matthew and Suzie placed their orders, and then Mark and Sarah ordered splits for six—the two of them, plus Rick and Jess and Meggie and Josh. When Josh went to collect his, Summer gave him a sympathetic smile. "Extra pineapple on yours. I know you like it that way."

He hoped he didn't blush. "Thanks, Summer."

He started to take the plastic boat from her hands, but she held on just a second until he looked up at her.

It surprised him to see she had understanding written all over her face. "Don't worry about it, Josh. Eventually they'll stop pushing."

He didn't know what to say. Everyone was milling around and he really wanted to respond, but now wasn't the time or place. He should have realized that Summer had to feel the pressure to pair them up, too. It was fairly obvious. Before he could change his mind, he found himself asking her out.

"Listen, do you want to grab a bite or go for a walk or something . . . sometime?" Boy, he sounded like an idiot. "It'd probably be better to talk without an audience."

She leaned a little bit forward. "That'd be nice," she agreed. "And definitely better than dancing around the topic. I work at the café until seven tomorrow, but I'm free after that."

"Sounds good. I'll pick you up there." He stood back and raised his voice slightly. "Thanks, Summer."

"Anytime." She smiled and moved on to the next customer while Josh took his banana split and plastic spoon and headed toward the picnic table where the rest of the family was waiting. Had he seriously just asked her on a date? This could be the perfect way to get people to leave him alone. Or it could just backfire in a big way. God, women were complicated—and that included his sisters and mother.

The kids finished their sundaes in record time and decided to go look for jellyfish beside the wharf. The adults sat around the picnic table, chatting in the soft summer evening. The conversation all centered around Jess's progressing pregnancy, what Sarah's kids were doing over the summer, and Mark's "vacation" now that school was out for the year and he and Sarah could take the kids on day trips. Josh felt spectacularly left out, though he knew it was unintentional. These were their lives. He had his. If things had been different, he and Erin might have been here now, with a kid or two, talking about the same things. It certainly wasn't Jess's or Sarah's fault and Josh certainly didn't begrudge them a bit of their happiness.

The simple truth was that Erin hadn't wanted his babies and their marriage hadn't been a strong one to begin with. Everyone in Jewell Cove thought it was his grief over her death that kept him from exploring a new relationship, and he didn't bother to disabuse them of that notion.

He simply refused to enter into a relationship that didn't have a strong foundation. Things had to click from the get-go. They had to want the same things, have the same values and . . . well, whatever it was that made perfect couples mesh. That magical, special something that said someone was The One.

Erin hadn't been his One. He'd known it and ignored it and he would never, ever do that again. He wouldn't—couldn't—settle.

He wanted a partner. Someone as committed to him as he would be to her. There had to be love and desire and trust and a best friend. The kind of partners his sisters had found, he realized. His cousin, too. They'd been incredibly lucky, he realized. It was a lot to ask of one person.

"Josh, how's Dr. Howard making out?" Sarah was the first to pose the question, and he pushed his thoughts aside.

"Fine. More than fine, actually. She's very professional, efficient, and sharp." He shrugged a little. "Truth be told, her talents are probably a little wasted here in Jewell Cove. But Charlie was right on. She's a great doctor."

"Pretty, too," Rick said, earning him an elbow from Jess. "What? I still have eyes, you know." He sent his wife a soft smile. "Besides, no one is as pretty as my wife."

Sarah made gagging noises that made everyone laugh.

"So what's she doing here, then? If she's such a hotshot?"

Josh considered what to say. Lizzie had confided in him a bit, but it wasn't his story to tell, not at all. Her reasons were private, so he merely responded, "Charlie's her best friend. And hell, it'd be silly to pass up the opportunity for a paid summer in Jewell Cove, wouldn't it?"

That seemed to appease them for the moment, but not for long. Sarah leaned against Mark's shoulder when her banana split was gone and studied Josh with an affectionate expression softening her face. "Josh honey, really, isn't it time you started dating again? You're a real catch, you know. Not that many handsome doctors around. And you can't be alone forever."

Would the woman never let up? He chuckled, though it felt forced. "Seriously, Sarah, can't you focus on something more important than my love life?"

"Come on, Josh," Jess teased. "When was the last time you got laid?"

"Jessica!" Meggie interrupted, but when Josh looked at his mother her lips were twisted as if she was trying not to laugh.

"I haven't forgotten how, if that's what you're worried about."

"I'm not listening, na na na na. . . ." Meggie covered her ears, but her eyes twinkled.

"Leave the guy alone," Rick stood up for Josh. "He'll get around to it. Sometime before he's eighty."

"Et tu, Brute?" Josh remarked, sending Rick a sideways glare. *What the hell,* he thought. Maybe letting the cat out of the bag would get them off his case. "For your limited information, I'm meeting Summer after she's done work tomorrow night. So get off my back, all right?"

The teasing continued until even Josh had to laugh. Was he prepared or did he need to go to the drugstore, be home by midnight . . . it went on and on. He took it because he knew it all came from a place of love. They just wanted to see him happy.

"Okay, you hooligans," he joked, getting up from the table. "I still have to work tomorrow. Time to head home."

"Wow, you're going to be a fun date tomorrow. Home by nine! Grampie needs his beauty sleep!"

Jess was on a roll tonight. It was good to see her come out of her shell more and more, a definite by-product of her happiness with Rick after her previous ordeal. "What can I say?" Josh replied, patting his hair and sucking in his cheeks. "I'm not just another pretty face."

Everyone was laughing when he walked away, and when he glanced at the Dairy Shack Summer met his gaze and gave a little wave.

He really didn't feel like heading home, though. The air was fresh and the waves were calling, so he drove down to Fiddler's Beach, parked the truck, and decided to take a walk on the sand. This time of night there were only a few stragglers left, sitting around little bonfires on the beach, steaming clams and having a few drinks. A dog from one of the houses above the stretch of sand came galloping over and Josh paused to pat him, grinning at the tongue lolling out and the excited wiggle of the dog's butt as he wagged his tail.

"Hey, buster," Josh crooned, giving the dog a good rub over his back. "Aren't you a friendly one?"

"Roofus! Come on, boy!" A teenage boy came charging down to the sand. "Sorry. He was supposed to be in the backyard."

"It's fine. He's real friendly."

"Too friendly." The teen pulled a face. "The next-door neighbor said if he came near her labradoodle again she'd call Animal Control."

Josh laughed. Clearly this dog was a mutt and not a purebred. He winked at the kid. "Trust me, dog, you want to stay away from the classy broads."

The kid laughed. "Tell me about it. C'mon, Roofus." He grabbed the dog's collar. "Thanks, man."

"No problem. Nice dog."

They took off up the beach to the cottage above and Josh took off his sandals, letting his toes soak into the sand still warm from the afternoon's heat. Next to being out on the ocean in his boat, this was his favorite thing. He wasn't sure he could take not living by the ocean again. There was something about the air, the sound of it, that soothed him like nothing else. It took away the stresses of his day, leached away the memories of his tours overseas and what he'd seen there.

He swallowed tightly. He didn't regret coming home. But some things couldn't be fixed or forgotten with a home-cooked meal and familiar settings.

The beach tapered to a thin line of sand, edged by tall grass and then trees. The first star appeared, and then another, and the sliver of a moon began to rise into the indigo sky. The ocean darkened to a secretive black, the rhythmic waves lulling him to a calmer place. Before he realized it, he was almost all the way up to Fiddler's Rock, where the shoreline curved like half of a figure eight and the little knob of land sat squarely in the center of the tiny cove.

And then he realized he wasn't alone.

A runner made their way through the sand, coming in his direction, but he didn't think they'd seen him yet, as their pace was strong and sure. Looking closer, he could tell by the build that it was a woman, in loose shorts and a T-shirt, strong legs and arms churning through the sand. She picked up her pace for about fifty yards, and Josh stopped, simply admiring the strength and form. It didn't occur to him to identify the runner until she suddenly stopped, put her hands on her hips, turned her face to the sky. He saw the dark ponytail silhouetted in the moonlight and he knew.

Lizzie. And just like that, his stomach did that weird weightless drop thing. A feeling that had been distinctly missing when he'd asked Summer out earlier this evening.

Shit.

CHAPTER 8

Lizzie fought for breath. The run was supposed to help, and it did, for a while. The feel of the sand beneath her toes, the tang of the sea air, the openness of the sky.

Anything to wash away the feeling of helplessness and self-blame.

But in the end it was futile. She pushed her muscles to the breaking point, sprinting back along the beach to the cottage, running until they quivered and threatened to give out. Her calves burned with the added exertion of running in the sand and her breath came in harsh pants and still the hole of nothingness was open, right in the middle of her chest.

Her head told her the home was the right decision. Her mother needed round-the-clock care that Lizzie simply couldn't provide. But her heart ached with the knowledge that she was completely alone. Her father was dead and her mother was a polite stranger most of the time and Lizzie had no brothers or sisters to share those early memories with. She fought to catch her breath, but her quadriceps gave out and she sank into the sand, pulled her knees to her chest, and let out the grief that had been threatening to overwhelm her for weeks.

She wanted her family back. She wanted everything the way it used to be, with the three of them together for holidays and talking about old times and plans for the future. She wanted to talk to her father about the mistakes she'd made and wanted to taste her mother's apple pie and feel the warmth of her smile again.

She needed that. Someone, something, to keep her grounded. She'd pretended for a while, lost herself in her work, but it wasn't the same. So she sat on the sand, still warm from the heat of the sun, and let the tears come. Hot, heartbreaking tears that she'd held inside for months.

The touch of a hand on her shoulder made her jump, and she lifted her head, scrambling to wipe her face. "Shhh," she heard, and a quick glance told her it was Josh behind her, his face creased with concern.

"God, I'm so sorry. I'm such an idiot," she began, moving to get up. But his hand remained firm on her shoulder.

"Hush," he murmured, the sound so soft it was almost part of the waves. He sat down on the sand, a little behind her, and pulled on her shoulder until she gave in and leaned back against him. He felt so good and she ignored the voice that said she was making a huge mistake. She needed to feel connected to someone rather than floating alone on an endless sea. His arm came around her and he tucked her head beneath his chin. "If you need to cry, cry," he commanded. "Just let it out. You'll feel better."

Her eyes stung again, not just at the emotions she

hadn't yet released but because of his kindness. "You're my boss," she said, giving her head a little shake. "I can't cry all over you."

"I'm not your boss tonight," he said quietly yet definitively. "I know that sort of crying, Lizzie. I've been there, and holding it in isn't doing you any favors."

She hiccupped. "I was okay until I . . . I went to see my mother."

That was all she needed to say for the waterworks to start again, and to her surprise Josh said nothing. Just looped his arms around her and gave her a safe place to fall. She was just weak enough to take advantage of it—this once.

His chin rested on top of her head and his hand rubbed along her arm, a rhythmic, soothing motion. After several minutes she was spent, emotionally and physically. What the run hadn't accomplished the crying had. She didn't even have the energy to pull away from his embrace like she knew she should. She was tired, so very tired. And he felt just a little like a port in a storm.

"Better?" he whispered.

She nodded. "A little embarrassed. I didn't expect an audience."

"I had to get away for a while. Looks like we both turned to the beach. I like the wind and the sound of the waves."

"Me, too." She nodded against his T-shirt. "I should get back. . . ." Losing it was one thing. Willingly staying in his embrace was another. He was so strong, so solid. And as much as he said right now he wasn't her boss, it wasn't something they could turn on and off. It was *his* practice. She worked for him. There was no getting around it.

"Sit still, and chill," he said. "And tell me what set you off. You said you went to see your mom?"

She nodded. "She's just outside Springfield, in a home there."

"She can't be that old, if you're only thirty."

"My mom is only in her sixties."

"I see." And the seriousness in his tone told her that he did, indeed, understand.

And then she let out a deep sigh. A sigh of relief from having purged the emotion, a sigh of resignation that there was nothing she could do. And perhaps that was what bothered her the most. There was absolutely nothing she could do to fix the situation. What good was being a doctor if she couldn't help the ones she loved?

"How advanced is it?" Josh asked quietly.

"It's been getting worse since my dad died. He really struggled with putting her into care, but he was almost seventy. It was getting harder and harder for him to look after her alone. Particularly when she would forget who he was and be afraid."

Josh shifted his weight and moved his right leg so that she was sitting more in the lee of his legs, still leaning on his chest. It felt so good, so right. His hand brushed her arm, and his unique scent of man and clean laundry and fresh air imprinted on her memory. "Josh, I'm pretty vulnerable right now, so if this is, well, you know . . ." She was too embarrassed to finish the sentence.

"It's not. I'm just here if you want to talk, Lizzie. I know how grief feels. I know how guilt feels. I know what a hurting person looks like. "

"That's all this is?"

His breath was warm on her hair, strangely intimate even though he hadn't made any advances whatsoever.

"That's all this is. So why don't you tell me about your mom. Did something happen today that was especially difficult?"

Somewhere up the beach a group of vacationers started setting off fireworks. The cheers and laughs filtered through the air and mingled with the *lap lap* of the little breakers on the sand. Lizzie took a big breath, let it out slowly, imagined the tension leaving her body through her feet, letting go of the stress and pain.

"I took us a picnic to have in the garden. She was actually pretty good when I got there, but during lunch she kept asking if my dad would be joining us. Sometimes she remembers he's gone, but other times she expects him to walk through the door. And I feel terrible because she's the one with the disease, not me, and yet I'm the one who gets upset and . . . and . . . afraid."

His arms tightened around her. Another rocket burst in the air, a huge bang followed by a cascade of pink and blue sparks.

"It's silly, but the worst part of the day was when I took out dessert. I'd bought her favorite, coconut cream pie, from the bakery right here in town. And it wasn't just a guess. It really was her favorite, for years. It was a running joke in our family. And she looked at me like she was angry that I even insinuated she liked coconut when she hates it. It's a damned pie, so why should I be so upset? But it made me so sad and angry. Nothing I say or do makes a damned bit of difference. I got her some ice cream in the kitchen and took her back to her room and all of a sudden she's back to making sense and when I asked her if I could get her anything she asked for my father back."

"Oh, Lizzie. I'm so sorry."

"Me, too. She's slipping away more each time, and with my dad gone . . . dammit, Josh, she's the one who's sick, not me. So why do I feel so horrible?"

He kissed her hair. "Because you feel helpless. Because you're a doctor and helping people . . . fixing people . . . is what you do. And this time you can't."

She closed her eyes. He understood. Someone understood. And the really odd part of it was that Josh was really a stranger when it came down to it. They'd only worked together a few weeks. How was it he could see things so clearly?

"I miss them," she whispered. "How do you get past the grief, Josh? Does it ever go away?"

He sighed. "It gets better." Josh was quiet for a moment, and she got the sense he was wondering what to say next. She gave him time to decide, keeping her eyes closed and listening to the waves.

"When my dad died, it was really terrible. It was such a shock, you see."

"What happened?"

"I forgot you don't know, you're not from here. He was a fisherman. He went out like he always did, and never came back."

Lizzie turned in Josh's arms, looked up into his face. "Do you mean they never found him?"

He shook his head, his blue eyes darker in the dimness of the starlit sky. "Not him, not his boat."

"God, Josh. That's horrific. How awful for all of you, and your mom . . . it's got to be a special sort of hell, dealing with a death without a body."

A flash of pain transformed his face for a moment,

and then she watched as he shuttered it away. But not fast enough.

"And then for you to lose your wife . . ."

He nodded. "That was different, though. At least . . . well, we got to bring Erin home and give her a proper burial. We know what happened. The not knowing . . . that's the book that never gets closed, you know?"

Lizzie touched his arm with her fingertips. "We had a burial for my dad, but that doesn't mean it was easy or I've managed to let go. How do I do that, Josh? How do I move on as if it doesn't matter? Please, tell me what to do to let me see my mother as a medical patient and not my mom, because it's killing me and I don't know what to do about it."

"You get through it," he said calmly. "One day at a time. That's all any of us do, Lizzie. And you look for joy. Moments of it at first, and eventually there's more than you expected."

She turned, half in his arms and half out, meeting his gaze evenly. "Is that how it is for you, Josh? A life of joy?"

He shrugged. "I'm still in the moments part, but the moments are getting longer and more frequent." He smiled, a little sheepishly.

"I'm the last person to judge," she admitted.

He chuckled down low, a sound that made something secret and delicious run through her. "People in glass houses?"

"Exactly." She let out a deep sigh. She'd been doing that a lot tonight, trying to regain her equilibrium. Lizzie shifted out of Josh's arms now, feeling like she was on a bit more solid ground, worried she was crossing a line between accepting comfort and longing for more. Still, the emotional purge had been good for her.

Josh leaned back on his hands, his fingers disappearing in the soft sand.

"After losing your parents, being told to take some time off must have really freaked you out."

Lizzie let out a big breath. "I felt like I'd lost everything. You're a doctor. You know what the hours are like. What you need to do to work your way up . . ."

"Hmmm. I guess I've never really cared about that sort of thing. Being in the sandbox changed a lot of that for me. I couldn't have cared less about prestige or reputation when I was putting men and women back together."

Right. She'd nearly forgotten he'd been a doctor in the Army before now. Of course he'd seen things that were vastly different from a city emergency room.

"Well, when you're Russ Howard's daughter, there are expectations."

Josh was quiet for a few moments. The silence made her uncomfortable, like she'd somehow said something wrong.

"I bet there are," Josh said.

"You don't understand. It's like . . . I'm held to some higher standard than anyone else. Because he was such a hotshot, I have to be, too, or I'm letting people down."

"Letting who down? Them? Or yourself?" He frowned. "We're not talking about the expectations or the normal pressures of the job. Tell me the truth. Do you think your leave was justified?"

"That's an odd question." She looked away. The question had hit its mark.

"Just think about it. I don't know your old boss, but I'm guessing he knew you and knew you needed to take a break and get yourself together. To make that call, knowing that you were going to hate him for it? That took some 'nads."

She looked over at Josh, her discomfort and annoyance growing to irritation. "It wasn't his call to make. He took advantage of the fact that we were sleeping together."

Josh held her gaze. "Did he? Or did he make the professional call despite the fact that you were sleeping together?"

She scrambled to her feet, angry at his assertion, even more uncomfortable that they were talking about her sex life when only minutes ago she'd been cradled in his arms and she'd been thinking about how strong he felt and how good he smelled.

"You don't know anything about it," she snapped, brushing the sand off her butt.

"I know more than you think." He stood up, too. "I worked for my father-in-law, Lizzie. Do you know how weird that was after Erin died? The thing that linked us together no longer existed. You don't have the corner on awkward situations. And you certainly aren't the first to come to Jewell Cove to find their feet again."

"That's not why I'm here."

"The hell it isn't."

"I came for Charlie—"

"And I call bullshit. And you'll make peace with stuff a whole lot faster if you start telling yourself the truth. Truth is, you're messed up."

Josh stepped up to her and put his hand on the side of her face. She was too surprised to move away, and her gaze shot up to his automatically, as if drawn there by magnetic force.

She half-hated that he was right and half-admired the fact that he'd known that about her.

He leaned forward and dropped a tender kiss on her forehead. "Go home, Lizzie. Have a glass of wine. Give yourself a break. Get some sleep. You seriously need to learn to relax."

She gave an emotional laugh. "That's not exactly in my vocabulary. My kind of relaxation comes from adrenaline. Now, if you suggested bungee jumping at dawn, I might be your girl."

He shook his head. "Crazy," he muttered.

Josh turned and started walking back toward her cottage, and she fell into step beside him. "Spend some time with Charlie, then," he suggested. "Sit on her deck and listen to the waves and the seagulls. Go out on the ocean. Go shopping. Eat ice cream. Whatever it takes."

"What works for you, Josh?" Lizzie wasn't convinced any of those things would distract her from the issue at hand. Her toes squidged in the sand as they ambled back along the beach where she'd been running, following the curve of the "fiddle" for which it was named.

"My boat. I go out in the bay and take my fishing rod and let the wind and the waves and the quiet work their magic. Nothing can touch me out there."

"It sounds nice."

"You could come with me sometime."

She laughed. "Fishing? Really? Do I look like someone who goes fishing?"

"Why?" he asked. "Because you did your degree at Harvard? You might break a nail? Or is that pastime a little too pedestrian for you?"

"Ouch. Great. Now I'm elitist and you have a chip on your shoulder." But she was teasing him.

"Then maybe you'd like a trip out to Lovers' Island. To search for treasure."

She rolled her eyes.

"Before you say no, there are some neat caves there that you can explore at low tide. And a fabulous beach. Think about it. The clinic is closed on Sunday. We could go then."

"Is this one of those you're not going to take no for an answer things?"

"Consider it for your own good."

"Try again."

"Because your boss is telling you to?"

"And this is why I want to be the boss."

He laughed. "Indulge me. If you hate it, we'll come back. It's not like it's that far, and you can leave your car right at the marina. I'll be taking the *Constant* out for a rip regardless. If you're interested, meet me at the dock at eight. That's a little late for me to be going out, but any earlier and you'll have an excuse not to come."

They'd reached the crooked wooden steps leading from the cottage down to the beach. She faced him, tempted to accept the invitation and wanting to say no just so he got the message that boss or not, he wasn't in charge, particularly of her days off.

"Good night, Josh. Thanks for . . ." She thought of how she'd huddled in his arms and cried, how she'd snapped at him, how they'd gone from that to this calm, quiet conversation. It was the strangest thing. "Thanks for the chat."

Wow. That was a rather underwhelming description of the last hour.

"You're welcome. I won't even charge."

She punched his arm and he laughed.

"See you at the office!" he called as she started up the steps. "Think about Sunday."

"Good night, Josh," she repeated, but a warm feeling

was spreading from her core outward. She turned when she reached the top and looked down over the waving grass to the sand, but he was gone, walking up the beach with his hands in his pockets.

CHAPTER 9

Josh met Summer at the parking lot for Breezes Café at the end of her shift. The sunny weather of the day before had shifted and the evening was misty with a fog creeping in. A walk was out of the question. Plus Summer had been on her feet most of the day. As she approached his truck he smiled at her and said, "Have you eaten? We can go out. Someone can serve you for a change."

She laughed. "Just not here. Can we get out of Jewell Cove for a few hours?"

He'd had the same idea, wanting to avoid gossip and speculation. "I was thinking Rockland. We could get out of town for a bit. Have some . . . privacy."

"Afraid to be seen with me, Josh?"

Actually, he was. Not at all because he was ashamed but just because he didn't want assumptions to be made. "Going out in Jewell Cove is like being on a reality TV show."

"It is a bit of a microscope." She put her hand on the handle of the passenger door. "There's a nice coffee shop I know. The food's all organic and they roast their own beans."

"That sounds perfect." Actually, it sounded a little earthy and not his usual style. He'd had more of a pub in mind, a more laid-back and blend-in atmosphere. But it didn't really matter where they went, did it? Besides, she'd been around food and customers all day. Maybe this coffee shop was a bit quieter for her to wind down after her crazy shift.

The drive didn't take long. By some unspoken agreement, they both chatted simply about their day, their jobs, inane little things about Jewell Cove. Josh relaxed a little, but it still felt strange. Just last night he'd been holding a weeping Lizzie in his arms and he'd felt something shift inside him. It had been incredibly intimate, yet they hadn't even kissed beyond the peck he'd given her on her forehead. So why had he thought about her all day today? Even at the office it had been odd, like they had gone out of their way to avoid each other. Like it had suddenly gotten weird.

Was he embarrassed about last night? Or just taking a step back, as she clearly wanted?

"Josh? Did you hear what I just said?"

"What? Sorry." He was pulling into the parking lot and Summer laughed.

"I lost you there for a minute. I was talking about the baby shower for Jess. Abby's holding it at her place." She leaned closer. "Are you okay? You seem distracted."

He was, and it wasn't fair to Summer. He wasn't even sure how he was going to bring up the subject of the two of them . . . or rather the lack of the two of them. They'd been paired together a lot, but they'd never discussed whether or not they wanted to be. If

Summer was under any illusions, it would be better, kinder, to set the record straight now.

God, he hated this sort of thing. He felt like a complete ass.

He promised himself to stay present in the moment and focus on her. "It was just a long day. I could use a cup of coffee."

The mist had turned to steady rain as they parked, and they jogged to the door of the shop, anxious to be in out of the wet. Josh's first impression was that this was a hipster sort of place, with the rich scent of coffee beans and a chalkboard that introduced the specials of the day including a free-range chicken sandwich and a salad made from local vegetables with an organic raspberry dressing, as well as an avocado chocolate cake, which to his mind sounded both intriguing and disgusting.

They ordered at the counter. Josh eyed the cake suspiciously and ordered a slice out of sheer curiosity, as well as a bowl of black bean soup that looked somewhat more appetizing than the ground-round chili. Summer, who hadn't eaten yet, either, went with the roasted vegetable panini sandwich and some sort of raw vegan macaroon for dessert.

Thank God for plain old regular coffee. Rich, strong, and black.

Summer got a chai tea.

New Agey stuff played on the speaker overhead, reminding Josh of the prenatal yoga class he'd picked Jess up from one day earlier this spring. There was a reason why he was more comfortable at the Rusty Fern, with the dartboards and cold beer and yeah, even the terribly unhealthy loaded nachos or half-pound burgers with fries. This wasn't exactly a *guy's guy* kind of place. He and Summer settled at a table by the window, and he cautiously dipped his spoon into his soup and had a taste.

Okay, so it wasn't half-bad. He was relieved about that, at least.

When he looked up, Summer was grinning at him with a foolish look on her face. "What?" he asked.

"You're not too sure about this place."

"It's not my usual speed." He smiled back, gave a small chuckle. "It suits you, though." Which was kind of his point, if he'd actually manage to get to it.

"It does, yes." She picked up her panini, took a bite, chewed thoughtfully. "I like the atmosphere. It's very calm, very . . . centering. I like how it focuses on whole ingredients, not a lot of processing, locally sourced."

He must have blushed, because she laughed again. "It's okay, Josh. It's not for everyone, but it works for me. It took me a long time to be okay with myself, and part of that was learning to accept who I was. I did that through a lot of natural principles. Getting back to basics. Simple. Clean. Uncluttered."

Accept who she was? He had no idea that had been a struggle for her. "But you always seem so confident. Like with the, uh, hair. And the nose ring."

She touched the tiny stud in her nose and laughed a little. "For a long time that was a disguise because I didn't like the real me. Now I just do it because I like it." She took a sip of her tea, cradling her hands around the thick mug. "Growing up is kind of nice like that. You stop caring so much what other people think."

They each ate a little more dinner and then Summer spoke again. "Josh, why did you invite me out tonight?"

He met her gaze. She was watching him with a forthright expression and he figured he might as well be honest. "Because my family has this notion that we ought to be together and we both know it. I wanted to clear the air."

"Because you're not interested in me that way."

Guilt spiraled through him, as well as a longing to not hurt her feelings. But it was only fair to tell her now. "No, Summer, I'm not."

She laughed out loud and picked up her sandwich. "Thank God for that," she said, taking a huge bite.

He put down the spoon that he'd forgotten he was holding. "Oh," he said, unsure of what to say now.

"You thought I was? Hey, I could see people pairing us up. Similar age, single, you know how it goes. And you're a nice guy, Josh. A real nice guy. But I never quite got that whole woo woo feeling in my stomach when you walked into a room. And I knew you didn't, either."

"You knew that?"

"You are always very nice, but there's a pained look around your lips when you're in an awkward situation. I see that quite often."

Damn. He truly hadn't realized he was that transparent.

Summer's gaze softened. "Besides, I remember how you used to look at your wife. You don't look at me that way. At all."

"Jeez, Summer. Ouch."

"That's why you asked me out, though, right? To make sure we're on the same page?"

He nodded.

"We are. Eat your soup. We can have a nice hour or so as friends, and that's that."

Josh looked down at his bowl and laughed a little. "Why do I feel like you've just let me down easy?"

She reached across the table and put her fingers on his wrist. "Because I don't play games. I decided a long time ago that I would say what I think and be honest with people and not pretend to be someone I'm not. I'm much happier that way."

He squeezed her fingers and then pulled away. "You're some woman, Summer. Some guy's going to be pretty lucky to get you. And you'll keep him on his toes, no question."

She raised an eyebrow. "I doubt it. For some reason I seem to naturally repel men. I'll probably have to get a few cats in a year or two."

"What, no hunky hotties at your yoga class?" he teased.

She laughed, and they both seemed to relax a lot more. "Way to stereotype. As a matter of fact, at my last Vinyasa class there was a firefighter there. At least that's what the bum of his shorts said. I made sure I put my mat behind him." She fanned herself and winked at Josh. "And I probably stand a better chance of hooking up at yoga than you do in your office."

Which immediately switched his brain back to Lizzie. She'd been her regular efficient self this morning, dressed in sand-colored trousers and a pink blouse under her white coat. Her hair had been up, as it usually was at work, and it was like the night before at the beach had never happened.

But he remembered. Remembered the wistful sound of her sigh, the heartbreak in her tears as she asked why it had to hurt so badly. He remembered the smell of her hair and the feel of her firm, toned body under his hands as he held her close, wishing there was some way he could take away her pain.

Whoa. What the heck? He'd just tried to help . . . not get personally involved or care too much—

"You okay?" Summer asked, a wrinkle forming between her perfect eyebrows. "Where'd you disappear to?"

"Nowhere," he replied, forcing a smile. "Now that we've set the record straight, we should finish eating before it all gets cold. Besides, I'm dying to try that avocado cake."

They made it through the rest of the date just fine, but something stuck in Josh's mind. Or rather someone. Because Josh was sitting with a perfectly nice, perfectly attractive woman and all he could think about was Lizzie.

It was unexpected. And more than a little bit unwelcome. Particularly since she was so adamant that their association be 100 percent platonic and he'd already made plans with her to go out on the boat Sunday morning. It had seemed an innocent invitation, but Josh knew it wasn't as innocent as it should be. Because it hadn't been just a friend helping out another friend. There'd been a moment, more than one moment, last night when he'd considered tipping up her face and kissing away the tears that streaked down her cheeks, her soft lips puffy and swollen.

For the first time since returning to Jewell Cove, he wished he were attracted to Summer. He got the feeling it would have saved him a lot of headaches.

Lizzie was shocked at the amount of activity on the docks at seven forty-five on a Sunday morning. It appeared that the pleasure craft demographic was alive and well, with groups preparing to hit the water for the day, carrying fishing rods, coolers, or both. A lineup of tourists was ready for the first whale-watching tour of the day, while another company was preparing for a later-morning lighthouse cruise up the coast. The morning was crystal clear with a piercing-blue sky; the sun was already warm on her face with the promise of a scorcher ahead. On the water was the perfect place to be.

She put her hand up to shade her eyes as a smallish white boat approached the dock. It was easy to make out Josh at the wheel, his dirty-blond hair shining in the sun, aviators shading his eyes. He wore a white T-shirt with the sleeves ripped out that wasn't quite tight—but tight enough that it emphasized his muscled torso and arms. As he pulled into the dock, she saw he had on swim trunks. Orange ones, with tropical flowers all over them. She walked over to meet him, watching as he leaned over and kept the boat from bumping against the gray wood.

"My, my. If you aren't the very picture of summer."

He smiled. His teeth looked extraordinarily white. Good heavens, he could be a poster boy for a Coppertone ad at this rate.

"And you look ready for a day on the water."

She felt like a schoolgirl going out on a first date, and how ridiculous was that? First of all, she was a grown woman and getting all fluttery was silly. And this wasn't a date. It was spending the day with a coworker, a friend. There was nothing between her and Josh.

Which didn't explain why she'd painted her toenails last night, agonized over what swimsuit to wear under her clothes and what to pack in her oversized tote. Sunscreen, hairbrush, lip balm, water, beach towel . . .

He held out his hand to help her aboard, and she took it, knowing it would be far more conspicuous to refuse. She hopped into the boat, holding her balance as it wobbled from side to side just a little.

"Oopsie, there you go," he said, steadying her with his hands and then stepping back. "Is there anything you need out of your bag? It'll stay drier if we tuck it in under the seat."

"Oopsie?" she asked, giggling.

"Don't judge. It just came out." He shook her bag, raising his eyebrows in a manner of repeating the question.

"Sunscreen?" she asked, shrugging.

"I've got some up here. Let's head out first, and when we stop for a bit you can apply."

"Sounds good."

She stowed her bag and took the other front seat, the interior surprisingly comfortable, as he pushed away from the dock and eased his way out into the harbor. She pushed her sunglasses up, shook her hair over her shoulders, and let out a big breath. She couldn't remember the last time she'd taken a day like this, one that was entirely for pleasure and escape. The closest she'd come was shopping with Charlie, but even that had a purpose. Today's only purpose was relaxation, and as Josh slowly made his way into the wider cove her muscles began to unwind.

"Ready?" he asked as they advanced through the cove. From out here she got a good glimpse of the small lighthouse at Refuge Point, the white shingle siding bright against the backdrop of the gray rock and scrabbly green bushes.

"Ready," she replied, raising her voice to be heard over the motor.

Josh moved the throttle and the boat shot forward, gaining speed as he headed for the corridor that marked the departure from Jewell Cove into the wider, deeper waters of Penobscot Bay.

Lizzie gave a little whoop of surprise as he made a smooth turn to take them past a marker, and the wind blew her hair back from her face. Oh, the freedom of it! Josh looked over at her and grinned and then gave it a little more gas so that they were flying out over the waves, bobbing over the crests, bottoming out on the slight waves just enough that it was a little bit rough and wild.

"Okay?" he shouted over, and she nodded. It was more than okay. It was exhilarating, even the jarring thump as they moved into open water and larger waves.

For several minutes they headed away from shore until the light at Refuge Point was just a speck and the coastline was a blur of gray and green. Spray flew up over the side of the boat and misted her skin, the salt water soft and refreshing. "Where are we going?" she called over, and Josh pointed a finger ahead of them.

An island, a hazy dark form, met the horizon. This, then, was the great "hidden" island he'd told her about, the one with the Indian name she couldn't remember but the nickname she could—Lovers' Island. The boat bobbed over the waves as they moved closer and closer, and features of the formation became clearer. It wasn't big; unless it stretched out long and narrow behind what she could see, it couldn't be more than half a mile in diameter. A wide, sandy beach gave way to rugged white and gray rocks, with straggly evergreens and bushes weathering the rough sea winds. Josh pulled to the right, circling it slightly.

It looked untamed and lonely and isolated, and Lizzie was suddenly aware that there wasn't another person for miles. It wasn't really an uncomfortable feeling, but more . . . intimate. Private. She swallowed and felt a familiar tension low in her belly. She didn't want to be attracted to Josh, but the very idea of being alone with him, like this, without a living soul around . . .

Just the possibility was enough to tempt her.

She was searching the shoreline for interesting birds when Josh steered closer, pointing at a stretch of the shore that appeared to be a pile of gray rock. "Look!" he called, edging them in, and suddenly she saw what he was pointing at. Seals, well over a dozen of them, sunning themselves on the rocks. Delighted, Lizzie went to the side of the boat and watched them flop across the hard surface, adorable black eyes staring back at her.

She laughed as two popped up near the boat, just their heads above the water, as if investigating who might be disturbing their Sunday morning.

"They're so cute!" She looked at Josh and grinned widely. "And there are so many of them!"

"More now than there used to be. A lot of people say that the increase in the seal population is what's bringing the great whites this far north."

She moved away from the edge of the boat a little and he laughed. "Relax," he said. "I've been in these waters a long time and I've yet to see one."

They watched for a few more minutes, and then Josh increased his speed and pulled away, moving them away from the island.

"Where are you going?" she asked, raising her voice slightly as he sped up, cruising past the south side of the island and into more open water.

"I'm going to take you fishing, just like I promised," he said, grinning. "The depth out here is perfect."

She raised an eyebrow, slightly disappointed they weren't going to visit the mysterious island. She was sure there was more to enjoy than just seal watching. "You were serious about that?"

He laughed. "Of course I was."

She sat, curious, as he picked his spot, cut the engine, and let them drift on the waves. "Now'd be a good time to put on that sunscreen," he suggested. "I know it's midmorning, but it can get pretty intense on the water."

While she applied the cream to her legs, arms, and face, he retrieved rods and tackle. The sun was beaming down and warming the top of her head, so she took a ball cap from her bag and pulled her ponytail through the back. He handed her a fishing rod, which she gripped rather awkwardly. She'd done a lot of crazy things, but she'd never done something as simple as going fishing in her life.

"This is a jig line," he explained. "More than one hook, see?" He showed her briefly, then demonstrated how to work the reel. "You're going to cast, like this." He cast out from the boat, the line whirring until it hit the water with barely a plop. "Let your line drop until you feel it hit bottom. Then you lift, and reel a little bit. Lift, reel. Like this." He lifted the end of the rod, reeling in some line, lowering it again. He'd only done so twice when he grinned. "And I've got something on the line. Ten bucks says it's a pollock."

"You've been here lots before."

"After a while you learn the best spots and depths for certain kind of fish. Pollock is one of our favorites. Nice and mild, beautiful when it's fresh."

She watched as he patiently brought up the line, saw the tip of the rod bend under the weight of the fish. When it was nearly up, he held the line with his hand and brought it over the side of the boat. Two silvery fish, each just over a foot long, wiggled on the line.

"You got two!" She watched, fascinated, as he took them off the line and threw them back.

"You're not keeping them?"

"We'll get bigger ones and put them in the live well. I'll take the extra back home and give some to Mom and the girls. Sometimes on the weekends the guys come out with me and we have a big fish fry in the evening."

"That sounds fun," she said, watching as he reset the line.

"It is. Mom makes these great potatoes with garlic and parsley butter, and in another few weeks there'll be vegetables from Sarah's and Mom's gardens. You should join us for one of those."

It sounded lovely . . . and a little too familyish for her liking. She was supposed to be keeping her distance and not getting overly involved, wasn't she?

He smiled at her. "Pan-fried it's great. But my favorite is when Sarah makes her beer batter and we have homemade fish-and-chips."

What a perfect life he seemed to lead. And it was all well and good for now, she supposed. But eventually she knew she'd start missing her condo and restaurants with real cloth napkins and a wine list. Heck, even a movie theater or a club would be a huge step up.

"Now you try," he said, putting the rod in her hands. "Use this to release the line as you cast, then get a feel for it as it drops."

Her first cast only went about thirty feet, but Josh said that was okay and to carry on. She didn't catch anything but got familiar with the rhythm of lifting the rod and reeling in the slack.

"Try again," he suggested. "Fishing isn't something done in a rush. It's like you have all the time in the world."

This time her cast went out a little farther and before long she felt a pull and jerk.

"I think I've got something!"

Josh's grin was wide. "Awesome. Don't rush. Just be smooth, lift, and reel."

She reeled in the line, the weight of something on the other end terribly exciting and foreign. When she lifted for the last time, she saw the fish on the hook. "I got one! He's still there! What do I do now?"

Josh chuckled. "Just bring it over the side. I'll do the dirty work."

Thank God. She liked fish, but generally it came from the market, all nice and clean and, well, dead. She held the line and waited for Josh, but she had to wait a little longer as he pulled his phone out of his pocket and snapped a picture first. "Come on, you need a picture of you with your first fish," he said, then took the line and gently removed the hook from the fish's mouth.

"Are we keeping him?"

Josh laughed. "He's only about eight inches. I promise, we'll get more. This time we can both cast."

They carried on that way for a half hour, and Lizzie managed to bring up three good-sized pollock as well as a darker, thinner mackerel, which Josh threw back. On her last catch, she insisted on handling the slippery fish herself, removing the hook from its mouth and slipping it into the water of the live well.

Josh's line brought up an ugly, spinier fish, which he identified as an ocean perch and also threw back. Lizzie cast in once more but got a strange feeling in the pit of her stomach. God, she wasn't getting seasick, was she? She swallowed, but her mouth seemed full of saliva. "Uh, Josh?"

"Yeah?" He turned around, took one look at her, and reeled in his line.

"Look at the horizon," he suggested. "Bring in your line, and I'll get us moving. The problem with drifting is that you ride the swells."

He took the lines and secured them and then started the engine again. Lizzie swallowed repeatedly, not wanting to be sick. How humiliating! And Josh looking as fresh as ever. Of course he'd grown up on the water and probably never got sick. She took desperate gulps of fresh air as he sped up, skimming the swells rather than rocking on them. "Better?" he called over to her.

She didn't answer. The sick feeling also made her head feel funny and she wasn't at all sure she was going to be able to hold out.

He slowed as they approached an inlet of the island, and Lizzie knew. She stood up and put her hand on his arm. "Stop," she said, gulping. And before she could say anything more, she rushed to the side of the boat and heaved.

What a great date she was turning out to be.

CHAPTER 10

She gagged until there was nothing left to come up, then let out a breath and turned around, feeling more than a little wobbly on her feet.

Josh had stopped the boat and was waiting, holding out a bottle of water.

"Swish that around and spit it out," he said gently. "And then take a drink. I'll have you on dry land soon."

She obeyed, cleaning out her mouth and spitting the water over the side. Josh started up and guided the boat into the inlet and to a small, ancient dock that leaned to one side but must be sturdy, since he pulled up next to it and tied the line to a graying post.

"It's safe," he assured her. He took the cooler and put it on the dock and then tossed up a rucksack beside it. He hopped out and held out his hand to Lizzie. She'd taken her tote from under the seat and was ready to step onto something firm that didn't rock back and forth.

She put her fingers in his and let him pull her up. He grinned then and nudged her shoulder. "Don't feel bad. It happens all the time."

"Right," she grumbled, adjusting her tote. "You don't have to say that just to make me feel better."

She watched as he put the ruck on his back and then hefted the cooler, the muscles in his arms flexing under the weight. Her vomit didn't seem to bother him in the least, though perhaps that came from being a doctor, because it didn't really gross her out anymore. It was the embarrassment more than anything. And feeling weak. She hated that.

"All right, let's go. You need to get some food into you."

"Food?" *Gah.*

"Did you eat breakfast?" Josh started off down the dock and she followed him, her sandals making flopping sounds on the old wood.

"I had yogurt and fruit, same as I do every morning."

He nodded wisely. "Which probably ran out over an hour ago. It's always worse on an empty stomach. And I should have thought to tell you to take an antinauseant."

"Yeah, thanks for that."

He laughed and kept leading the way, off the dock and down a narrow dirt path leading to a sandy beach.

"You were doing so well," he continued, adjusting the weight of the cooler in his arms. "But you were really focusing on the water, which makes it worse. Your brain messages get all screwed up."

"I know what motion sickness is," she answered tartly, but he only laughed more.

"Lighten up, Lizzie. You're not the first person to get seasick. You actually held out quite well."

She wasn't sure if that was a backhanded compliment or what, but she forgot when they reached the beach and the sparkling sand was spread out before them, drastically different from the rough, rocky shoreline the seals called home.

"Oh, this is beautiful!" Breakers lapped on the shore and gulls circled overhead, wheeling and crying. "Like if you got stranded on a desert island and there was no one for miles and miles."

Josh put down the cooler and took off his ruck. "I always like to think of it as it might have been a hundred and fifty years ago. Whether or not there is treasure buried here, I imagine the ships and cannons and battles. Charles Arseneault was rumored to use the island to smuggle his goods. And people."

Josh reached inside his pack for a blanket. He spread it on the sand and sat down, then patted a spot beside him. "Charles was a Southerner, and he hated what the war did to the place he loved. At the same time, he wasn't all that comfortable with slavery. So he smuggled supplies past the blockade into the Confederacy and snuck slaves out and into the North."

"Talk about playing both sides," Lizzie commented, pulling her knees up to her chest. When Josh had begun to tell her this story on July Fourth, she'd been intrigued. Now that she was actually on the island? She was dying to know more.

"Oh, there's no question he was in it for profit," Josh said, grinning. "He made a killing. Until he met his wife. She was something, I guess. They met when she was here on the island, helping send slaves onward up to Canada. They say the love of a good woman . . . It certainly seemed to turn him around." Josh grinned suggestively. "Maybe they came out here for lovers' trysts, too. It would definitely explain the island's nickname."

"And so he buried treasure here? Why? What would he have to hide if he just, well, quit?"

"Who knows? Evidence? Contraband? Secrets? That's what's kept the legend going all this time. No one really knows what was supposed to be in that treasure. Money that he'd come back for later? He settled in Jewell Cove and never seemed to be hurting for coin. Charles and his wife were both risk takers, passionate about their beliefs. It makes for some interesting reading. You can always check out the historical society for more if you're interested."

Her, dig around at the historical society? It was kind of funny, really. Certainly not her speed. And yet . . . the story intrigued her somehow. It was adventurous and romantic. And it gave the sleepy little town of Jewell Cove a smidgen of glamour when all was said and done.

Her stomach and head were starting to come around, so she nodded at the cooler. "So, you brought us a picnic."

"Of course. Food always tastes better outdoors and it's not like you can find a drive-thru around here."

He opened the cooler and handed her a small bag of buns and a rectangular plastic dish, cold from the ice inside. She peeked inside the lid and gaped. "You brought the stuff to make lobster rolls?" Another container held an assortment of vegetables: carrots, celery, cucumbers, cherry tomatoes. "Josh, this is amazing. Who on earth was open early enough for you to pick this up before we left?"

"Open? Wow, give me a lot of credit, why don't you. I made the salad at six thirty this morning. Bought the stuff last night so it was as fresh as possible."

She looked over at him. "You made this?"

He grinned, and she imagined his eyes twinkling behind his glasses. "Of course I made it. I can cook, you know. What did you think, I lived on mac and cheese and hot dogs?"

Lizzie made a face at the thought of that as a regular diet. "Sorry. I just thought with the take-out containers . . ." The salad was packed in a dish with a black bottom and clear top.

"Chinese food. That I don't make from scratch, but the dishes come in handy."

She put the lid beneath the bottom of the dish and picked up the roll, using a spoon to stuff it full of the tender lobster meat and sauce. At the first bite she knew he wasn't lying. The man could cook. Perfectly seasoned, the lobster salad was scrumptious. The bread she could only assume came from the Main Street Bakery. No baked goods she'd ever had anywhere could compare to theirs, and top of the list was their bread.

"So, is it okay?" Josh opened his roll and filled it with the salad.

"It's perfect. I'm feeling a lot better, too. I think you were right. Having something to eat will help."

"You won't find the trip back bad, I promise. It really is the rocking motion when you're stopped that does it."

She didn't want to think about that right now, so she focused on the roll, wiping her fingers on a napkin Josh handed over along with another bottle of water. She'd figured that was it for their lunch, but then he took out another dish and two forks. "So I didn't make this," he said, grinning. "I totally bought this at the diner last night. Gus's blueberry cream cheesecake is too good to resist."

SUMMER ON LOVERS' ISLAND   135

The cake had a cinnamon crumb topping, and the first bite was pure heaven. "Oh my God," she murmured, dipping her fork into the dish once more. "That's fantastic."

"You know, that's something I've noticed about you, Lizzie." He rested on his hands and squinted over at her. "You really let yourself enjoy things."

She chewed, swallowed, and pondered that for a moment. "I'm not sure if that's a criticism or a compliment."

He chuckled. "Compliment. I'm not real good at that myself. I kind of had the fun beaten out of me for a while. I like to think I'm slowly getting it back."

Lizzie looked down at the cake, torn between finishing the slice and focusing on Josh. With more than a little regret she put the lid on the dish and leaned forward to put it in the basket. "You can't say something like that without me wanting to ask the follow-up," she said quietly. She spun on the blanket so she was facing him and sat Indian-style with her elbows on her knees.

"I told you that I found peace by taking out my boat, that sort of thing. Truth is, bit by bit I hid myself away, and I haven't really opened myself up again."

Except to her. Lizzie let out a breath. "But I'm safe, right?"

He nodded. "Yes, I suppose you are. You're not family. You don't have history in Jewell Cove, and you're not staying. You're just passing through."

It was all truth, so it was perplexing why hearing him say the words bothered her so much.

"Some would say I haven't been as much fun the last few years."

"Life has a way of kicking us in the teeth, doesn't it?"

She inhaled deeply, tasting the sea air. "Not right now, it doesn't. Thank you for bringing me here, Josh. A picnic on the beach was just what I needed."

"Me, too."

His voice was low, with something beneath it that made her sit up a little straighter. The barest hint of suggestion, but it was there just the same. She was acutely aware that they were isolated here on the island. "Hidden" . . . wasn't that the translation for the native word? And then there was the name given it by the locals . . . Lovers' Island.

Lovers.

Once more she felt a pang of regret as she said the words she knew she must. "Josh, we can't mix business and pleasure," she warned.

"How much is really business?" There was a coaxing note in his voice and she was just vulnerable enough to be flattered that he was suggesting what he seemed to be suggesting.

"You're my boss," she said.

"Barely. We work together. And you're only here for a few months. It's not like you're going to be part of the practice forever." He leaned forward. "Lizzie," he said in a soft voice. "I would never use something like this against you. You have to believe that."

She wanted to believe him. Wanted to so badly that specific parts of her body ached in anticipation. The breath seemed to shake in her chest. "I believed that once before," she reminded him. "And you know how that ended."

"We've both believed a lot of things. I'm not looking for forever, and neither are you. But damn, I'd like to start living again. I want to feel alive. I want to take risks and chances and the hell with the rest."

Lizzie was so tempted. A gull gave a sharp cry overhead, plaintive and demanding. And still she and Josh leaned closer, closer, and butterflies winged their way through her stomach, fluttering with anticipation.

What he was asking for was a fling. With no consequences. Once upon a time that was how she'd lived her life. Fearlessly. How had she changed so much?

Maybe this was just what she needed to move past the mess that was her relationship with Ian. She liked Josh a lot. And she was insanely attracted to him. Come January she'd be back in Springfield. If they kept their eyes open . . . agreed to no strings—

She jumped up off the blanket. "You want to feel alive, Josh?"

His eyes looked confused and she couldn't help but smile, feeling suddenly strong, and with a feminine power she'd somehow lost over the past months. Yes, this was what she needed. "Come with me."

"Where are we going?"

She let her grin grow. "Swimming." She reached for the hem of her shirt and pulled it over her head, revealing her bathing-suit top, then laughed at the startled . . . and hungry . . . look in Josh's eyes. "Come on."

Josh got up and pulled his shirt over his head while Lizzie unfastened her shorts and dropped them onto the blanket. Her bathing suit was modest, a halter-back top and bikini-cut panties, but they were light blue and she knew in about twenty seconds they would be translucent. If he wanted to take a risk, she was up to the challenge, and damned if it didn't feel good to cut loose again.

She let her laughter fly on the wind as she ran to the breakers. This was what she'd been missing. The part of her she'd buried beneath her grief and sadness.

"Shit!" She let out a squeal as she plunged thigh deep into the cold waves. To her delight, Josh came dashing past, barreling into the surf in a careless dive, giving her only a fleeting glimpse of his bare chest and shoulders and the swim trunks he'd worn all day.

Taking a deep breath, she took three more steps and then dove under.

She surfaced and scrubbed her hair away from her eyes and saw Josh treading water about ten feet away, droplets sparkling on his lashes and dark-blond hair. His eyes seemed bluer than ever, and the goofy smile on his face made her feel like laughing. "Graceful!" she called out, bobbing on the waves, pushing toward him in a breaststroke. She licked her lips and tasted the salt of the ocean.

"I prefer strength over grace," he commented, and she blinked. *Yes,* she realized, *he would go for quiet power over finesse,* and the idea was incredibly exciting.

"Me, too," she replied. And then, with an impishness she'd forgotten she possessed, she flashed him a quick smile and dove under, pushing away and kicking her feet on the top of the water, giving a saucy splash.

When she surfaced, he was calmly floating on his back several feet away, utterly unconcerned.

She burst out laughing. God, it felt good. Even better when she saw a smile curve his lips, even though he stayed floating and his eyes remained closed.

As quietly as she could, she made her way over to him, studying the still beauty of his face. And he was beautiful. The barest hint of pale stubble roughed his jaws, and his eyelashes just kissed the crests of his tanned cheeks. Whatever he did to keep himself in shape clearly worked, as strong shoulders curved into muscled arms and a broad chest. She hesitated a long moment, wondering if she dare ease her way closer, wondering whether she was being spontaneous and fun or foolish. But then . . . the last impulsive decision she'd made—coming to Jewell Cove—had worked out quite well. Maybe she was on a roll.

She slipped through the water, her progress silenced by the rhythmic slap of the waves on sand.

When he was close enough to touch, she held her breath, then reached out and ran a single finger down the center of his chest.

He broke the back float immediately, surprised by the contact, coming face-to-face with her in the water. The waves had pushed them closer to shore, and when Lizzie dropped her feet her tiptoes touched bottom. So did Josh's, and they stood there briefly, swaying back and forth with the force of the swells.

She closed the few feet between them, gaining better stability, and together they moved slightly toward the shore until they were only waist deep in the water. Josh's eyes drifted down, and the muscles in Lizzie's pelvis tightened automatically as she realized that he could see the shadows of her nipples through her wet bikini top. And that the breeze blowing across the water was making that view somewhat . . . pronounced.

And she saw his throat bob as he swallowed.

Lizzie reached for his hand, lifted it, and placed it on her breast, letting his surprise last only a moment before she moved closer and lifted her chin, placing her lips on his.

His lips were cold from the water, but his mouth was hot on the inside as his tongue swept against hers. His hand molded her breast only for a moment before his arms came around her and pulled her flush against his body.

Hot and cold, soft and hard, all at the same time. Hungry for him, starved for the connection, Lizzie looped her arms around his broad shoulders and let the water buoy her up until she linked her legs around his waist. Her pelvis rocked against the hardness of his groin, and he moaned into her mouth.

Urgency claimed them both. Lizzie was profoundly glad for his strength, not grace, as he cupped her ass in his hands, holding her against him as he walked his way out of the water. The kiss broke off, his mouth sliding away from hers, presumably so he could see where he was going. Lizzie took the opportunity to lick the salty wetness of his neck, giving a little nip when he let out a delicious curse.

He staggered his way through the loose sand to their blanket and dropped to his knees, then let her down slowly on the warm cotton.

"Liz," he said softly.

"Risks," she breathed, capturing his gaze with her own. "Chances."

"I never . . . I mean, I wasn't prepared for . . . Dammit. I'm trying to say I didn't think to bring protection."

There was risk and then there was stupidity. And yet the need he'd fed pounded through her ruthlessly. "Ways and means," she suggested. "Nothing says we have to go all the way." So much for not messing around with the boss . . . and yet his reasoning only minutes ago was conveniently sound.

She sat up, reached behind her neck, and untied her

top. She shimmied it down her arms, let it drop limply on the blanket beside her, reached for his shoulders.

"God, you're beautiful." Josh kissed her once more, then trailed his mouth down her neck, across her collarbone, and finally onto the soft flesh of her breast. She arched, pushing her nipple toward his mouth, gratified when he laved it with his tongue. Everything tightened within her and she gasped, her eyes closed, the light from the midday sun orangey red behind her lids.

"You taste good," he said, cupping her breast in his hand, paying equal attention to each one until she felt like a spring ready to release. "So good, Lizzie. Sweet and salty."

"Don't stop," she ground out, tossing her head against the fabric-covered sand. When he shoved his hand beneath the damp band of her bottoms, she cried out and wished she could find a way to push closer to both his hand and his mouth. She reached down with her hand and rubbed her fingers along the length of his erection, curling her fingers around him through the trunks. Groaning, Josh pushed against her, the same rhythm he employed with his fingers as he pleasured her. Want pounded through her body, and need, and desire stole her breath. Had she ever felt this urgency before? It was beautiful and terrifying in its power.

He sat up, knelt before her, and grabbed her bottoms in both hands, slid them down her legs, and dropped them on top of her top.

She must be losing her mind. She was stark naked on a blanket in the middle of a beach and she couldn't care less.

His gaze burned into hers, and then he slid down

the blanket, never looking away, silently telegraphing his intentions with his eyes.

Vulnerable. That was how she felt at this moment, as Josh indulged in the most intimate of acts. Vulnerable, and yet powerful, and incredibly feminine and sexual. All the tension and stresses of the past weeks melted away as she gave herself over to the sensations.

The orgasm hit fast and hard and she pushed against his mouth, her cries flying on the wind with the call of the birds.

The pulses were still ebbing when Josh kissed her navel, then the hollow between her breasts, ultrasensitive now, and then his swollen lips kissed hers.

"I . . . uh . . ." The circuits of her brain were clearly fried, as she couldn't put a coherent thought together.

He laughed, a low, sexy sound. And then he stood up, stripped off his trunks until he was naked as the day he was born, and ran into the sea.

It was a view she wouldn't soon forget.

He swam out a long way, then turned around and came back, riding the waves and the tide. Lizzie reached for her T-shirt and pulled it on, without the wet bikini top, and did the same with her shorts. Then she laughed at herself for feeling so naughty for going commando.

When Josh stepped out of the ocean, she could see that the cold water and physical activity had done their job in defusing the situation.

Wordlessly she got up, picked his trunks up from the blanket, and handed them over.

"Thanks," he said, pulling them on awkwardly. They were still damp from the first swim.

"Josh, I—"

"Don't say a word," he cautioned. "I want to remember that exactly the way it was."

At the time she'd been caught in the moment, wrapped up in her own desire. Now she felt rather . . . silly.

"We're adults," he stated. "With needs. And I find you really, really hot."

She felt her cheeks flush, and it wasn't just because she hadn't reapplied sunscreen. "Right. And it's not like either of us is looking for a marriage proposal."

"God no." Josh laughed, then reached for her hand and pulled her close. "Look, no one even has to know. I heard what you said, about us working together. I respect that. We'll be one hundred percent professional at work, I promise."

Great. The words were right, so why did they feel wrong? Maybe because he was suggesting sneaking around? They weren't fourteen or anything.

And yet she knew she didn't want her private life to be public knowledge, whether she was fooling around with Josh Collins or not.

"Hey," he said quietly, and he lifted her chin with a finger. "If you're not up to this, it can end here. We can go back to Jewell Cove and be like this never happened. I mean . . . it's not that I want that, but I understand if you do."

More confused than ever, she pulled away and moved to tidy up their things. "Can I take some time to think about it?" she asked.

"Of course you can."

He sat down on the blanket once more and patted the spot in front of him. "Come here."

Hesitantly, Lizzie dropped to the blanket. Josh adjusted his position so that he was sitting behind her, and then put a hand on her shoulder, pulling her back against him. "Relax," he whispered in her ear.

She let out a breath. "I'll try."

"You were pretty relaxed a few minutes ago." He looped his arms around her, cuddling her close. The afternoon was waning and the heat had mellowed, along with the breeze. Lizzie wondered what it would be like to spend the whole day here, build a fire, have a clambake or something. When Josh held her like this, the world of suspensions and illness and messed-up relationships ceased to exist.

She rested her head against the hollow of his shoulder and eased the tension out of her muscles.

"Thank you, Josh. For bringing me out here today."

"You're welcome." He chuckled softly. "You needed it."

She turned her head a bit. "Um, you probably did, too. And I didn't help you out much there."

She could see his eyes and they shone at her with laughter. "You keep an open mind and you'll get the opportunity to make things even."

"Wow. Cocky."

"One can hope."

She giggled, settling in even more. Damn, he was so easy to be with. She'd have to be careful to not get too close.

But for right now, his arms were strong and warm, the sun was beating down on them benevolently, and all seemed right with the world.

Chapter 11

After a while Josh took Lizzie's hand. He didn't want to leave. The afternoon had been too perfect. "We should probably go before we miss the tide." He was reluctant to say the words.

"Mmm," she replied. Despite their earlier swim, he could still smell the floral scent of her shampoo as she shifted her head.

He hadn't brought her here with any expectation. If he had, he would have made sure to have brought a condom. But Lizzie was full of surprises. She was all business in the office, all professionalism and efficiency. He was starting to see that away from work she had an adventurous side . . . a side he couldn't help but respond to. Like he had this afternoon. All it took was one kiss, one touch of her wet, warm body next to his. . . .

She'd been, quite simply, incredible. He still couldn't believe he'd suggested a secret affair. That was so not his style. He'd never had a casual-sex kind of relationship in his life.

He tugged her to her feet, wishing the afternoon didn't have to end. Together they packed up the picnic basket, and he shook off the sand stuck to the blanket before folding it and putting it in the pack. It was almost like the afternoon had never happened.

Except he could still taste her.

They made their way back to the dock, and he marveled at how easy it was to be with her. He didn't feel the need to make pointless conversation, and the silence wasn't awkward, either. They could just be. He didn't feel the need to pretend or be upbeat. He stopped short, though, when he saw how far the tide had gone out. He'd tied up close to the top of the dock, which meant that right now his boat was sitting in about two inches of water and resting on wet sand.

"Oops," Lizzie said, and he saw her raise an eyebrow.

"Looks like we're going to have to wait," he said, feeling completely stupid. He'd misjudged either the tide or the time or perhaps a bit of both. "I'm sorry, Lizzie. It was a dumb mistake on my part. I feel like an idiot."

When she turned around, he was surprised to see a twinkle in her eye. "You know what this means, right?"

He lifted a shoulder. He had no idea what she was getting at.

"It means we can search for treasure."

He grinned. "You didn't actually believe all that claptrap, did you?"

"Why not?" She let her tote slide to her feet. "Did you make it up?"

"Of course not. But it's all legend. The boys and I used to come out here all the time and we never found anything. It was just kids being kids."

"So? That doesn't mean it's not true."

"You know, I'm starting to realize you're very different away from the office."

Her smile widened. "That's the nicest thing you could have said to me. I think I forgot how to have fun over the last few months. Today kind of reminded me."

If what had happened on the beach was her idea of fun . . . he was happy to help. Anytime. Because the truth was he hadn't been that close to a woman since Erin had died. In fact, the months leading up to her death hadn't been great for their marriage, either. He'd wanted a baby. Erin had seemed . . . distant. Before her last deployment, he'd learned why.

He'd found the birth control pills.

But he didn't want to think of that today. Not now, when it felt like he and Lizzie were the only two people in the world. He went to the boat and put the cooler and pack inside. "Come on, then. We can leave our stuff here. Let's walk. Who knows, maybe we'll find something."

"Great!"

She looked almost girlish as she put her tote in the boat and turned around to face him. She'd put her damp, tangled hair in a messy sort of topknot with only an elastic—how did women get so talented at things like that anyway? Her eyes were bright and impish, her smile easy.

She was absolutely stunning.

"Come on. Let's head to the other side of the island. If someone was going to hide something, I'm guessing it would be there. Way more nooks and crannies rather than sandy beaches."

He held out his hand.

She took it.

It felt strange and pleasant and a little adolescent to climb the dirt path hand in hand. He led the way, away from the sand and marsh grass up over a hill, where scrubby brush dotted the landscape along with knobby, uneven rocks. Farther along they encountered evergreens and lusher grass, but that was short-lived. The island was small, a rocky dot in an otherwise endless sea. They stopped at the crest of a hill and looked out. "What do you think?" he asked.

She let go of his hand, took a deep breath, and turned in a circle. "You can't see land anywhere. How can that be, when we could see it from the top of Blackberry Hill?"

"It's not as far as it seems." He pointed. "Look. Right there, see that darker line? That's the coastline. The haze today is hiding it a little, but on a perfectly clear day you can see it better."

"But it *does* seem far. Like we're in the middle of nowhere. It's wild and a little frightening and exciting all at once."

He knew exactly how she felt.

"You really rowed your way out here in your uncle's dory?"

He grinned. "Yeah, we did. Thank God we told them where we were going. Once it sprung a leak, we were stranded. We were lucky we were so close to the island and didn't drown."

"That's a very different existence from my upbringing." She laughed. "My parents didn't even like me walking to the neighborhood convenience store."

"I hear having boys is different from having girls," he said.

She winked at him. "I said they didn't like it. Not that I didn't do it."

"You rebel."

She laughed, the sound floating on the air. "Come on. The path keeps going and I see rocks down there. Maybe there are caves."

"There are."

This time he let her lead the way down the path, picking her way over the rocks. He knew very well that the path led down some natural rock stairs—he and his buddies had traveled this path often enough over the years—down to the rocky shore and the jagged cliffs and caves.

"If Charles hid treasure here, he would have had to anchor offshore and row it in," she mused. "Or dock on the other side and carry it overland. Which is unlikely."

"We thought so, too. But we never found anything. On either shore."

"Nothing?"

"No. Except . . . well, I'll show you. It's supercool."

They cautiously climbed their way down, picking over the rocks carefully, as they were slippery with water and seaweed from the tide. She and Josh had walked only fifty or sixty feet when he stopped, tugged on her hand, and nodded toward the cliffs.

"Look. At low tide you can really see them."

Nooks, crannies, and deeper caves were eroded into the cliffs by years of tides and winds. Lizzie walked ahead, her expression open and inquisitive as she approached the rocks. A smear of dirt ran up the side of her shorts and her feet were muddy inside her sandals, but she didn't seem to care. It was such a switch from the neat and tidy, not a hair out of place woman he knew from work or even outside of work in Jewell Cove. This woman reminded him of the one who'd flirted with a teenager to take his mind off of a dislocated knee, who brushed the dirt from a ball field off her knees and smiled easily, openly. He'd liked her that day. Liked her even more as they watched the stars from the bed of his pickup. But today . . .

Maybe touching her had been a mistake. She was only here for a short time and he was under no illusions about that. When Charlie's maternity leave was over, Lizzie Howard would go back to where she really belonged. He wasn't sure his "idea" of enjoying each other during her stay was a sound one. He could get caught up in her quite easily. And the last thing he felt like doing was getting his heart trampled on again.

The biggest surprise was realizing that this woman might actually be able to put him in that position.

"Come on!" she called. She was walking ahead of him, heading toward the biggest gap in the rock, the wind whipping some of her hair out of her knot. He picked up the pace and worked on catching up with her.

"Josh, look!" Lizzie's voice echoed off the dark rock. "I can actually stand up in here!"

The rock was still shiny and wet from the last tide, and dripping sounds echoed eerily off the walls. "It's creepy in here."

"Don't be such a wuss," she tossed back at him. "Didn't you come in here as kids?"

He had, but he hadn't actually liked this part. Something about being closed in and in the dark. "Well, yeah. Of course we did. I'm just not a big fan of small, dark spaces." He hesitated. "Or being underground."

There was a reason why he preferred being on the open water. Freedom and lots and lots of air to breathe. Any time he'd spent in bunkers in the military had just about driven him bananas.

"I did a tour of the Hoover Dam once when I was a kid," she said, hunching over and stepping farther inside the cave. "You probably would have hated that. Though when I was going through the rocky part of the tour fresh air was piped in."

He shuddered. Anytime he thought of underground mining or anything of that sort, he got a weird, crawly sensation in the pit of his stomach.

"So, any treasure in here, Dr. Howard?"

"Naw," she answered, her voice bouncing off the rock. "How high does the tide come in here anyway? Any treasure's probably buried topside, right? Where it wouldn't get drowned in salt water?"

"Right," he agreed, wishing she'd back out of the cave. He squinted in the darkness, waiting for his eyes to finish adjusting. "Though the story does say that slaves hid in these caves, waiting for their ship to come and take them north. Part of that whole Underground Railroad thing."

"What if the tide came in?"

"I don't know. It's a good question. Which is probably why it's just a story." He took a few short breaths, trying to steady his heartbeat.

A few seconds later and Lizzie was there, right in front of him, a goofy smile on her face. "You really don't like closed-in spaces, do you?"

"Not really." He swallowed, feeling silly.

"Maybe you just need to have a distraction. Something to take your mind off it."

There was a silky quality to her voice that made his nerve endings stand to attention. "Lizzie," he said quietly.

"Shhh." She put her finger against his lips and slid the last few inches, until her body whispered against his. He couldn't help but look down at her lips, slightly parted, shadowed in the dimness of the cave, only a shaft of daylight providing any visibility. Her eyes glowed up at him and that little half smile flickered at the side of her mouth, a playful invitation.

"You want to keep this private. What's more private than kissing in a cave in the middle of nowhere?" Her voice was husky-soft.

"Private . . . look, Lizzie. It's just . . . it's a small town. If we . . ." He hesitated. "If we see each other in plain sight, there are loads of people who will think it's their place to interfere."

"So it's not because you're ashamed of being seen with me?"

He lifted his head sharply, hitting it on the hard rock behind them. "Ouch!" He felt the spot with his fingers as he stared at her. "What? Of course not! Lizzie, I—"

"Relax," she said, laughing. "I haven't been in town long, Josh, but I'm smart enough to figure things out. Your family's pretty focused on pairing you up. If they knew about this afternoon . . ."

"Right," he agreed, relieved. The last thing he wanted was for Lizzie to feel slighted in any way. "Lizzie, I like you. A lot. But we both know what this is, and what it isn't."

"And there's nothing wrong with keeping that to ourselves."

"Exactly."

"And at some point you're going to be quiet long enough for me to kiss you again."

He nearly swallowed his tongue at the sultry tone in her voice. And he let her have the last word, since the next sound from her lips was a soft moan as she curled her hand around his head and pulled it down so that their mouths meshed together, hot and hungry.

The boat ride back to town was definitely better, though Lizzie had been dreading it a bit, worried she'd get sick again. Instead the fresh air was invigorating and she took out her hair elastic and let the wind blow her hair off her face. A check of her phone told her it was early evening, and the sky had softened into shades of coral, pink, and lilac. The breeze was cool, and Josh handed her a sweatshirt to pull on. It was two sizes too big and smelled like him.

Jewell Cove appeared on the horizon and, with it, reality. Lizzie sat back against the padded seat and thought about today. Rationally, she and Josh had both needed to get away, to blow off some steam. And they were safe for each other, she realized. Because she was only here temporarily. Josh didn't want anything major. And neither did she. And yet . . . being together today had been good.

And it was over. They certainly couldn't be that free here in town, with a hundred pairs of eyes watching their every move.

"You're quiet all of a sudden," Josh observed, the engine noise a slight purr now as he pulled into the dock.

She hadn't really said much the whole trip back, but she knew the last few minutes she'd been quiet in a different way that was entirely related to mood and he'd sensed that.

"Reality check," she said, straightening.

"Yeah," he agreed, and he sounded as excited about it as she did. That was something, at least.

Could they ignore everything that had happened today? Rewind to a few days ago and keep things entirely professional? Maybe it was time she tried that. It was what she should have done with Ian—

Her cheeks heated. She'd done exactly what she'd sworn she'd never do again. Get involved with a co-worker. With a boss. No matter how she and Josh justified it or said it was different, it really wasn't. Monday morning they'd be in the same office seeing patients and pretending that she hadn't been . . . oh God. That she hadn't been sprawled naked beneath him on a sandy beach in the middle of the afternoon.

"Regrets?" he asked, easing his way along the dock to keep the boat from bumping.

"Honestly?" She reached out and kept the side from hitting the dock. "Yes and no. Josh, this afternoon was—"

"Awesome."

"Well, yes." She smiled a little. "But now that we're back—"

"Awkward."

"Potentially."

He tied up the boat, got out, and offered her a hand up. She took it, liking the feeling of his fingers around hers a little too much. She hopped up on the wharf and noticed how it felt very different beneath her feet. Solid, but like she was still moving.

"Know what was great about today?" Josh asked, going back into the boat for her bag. He looked up at her and grinned. "You stopped thinking so much."

"Occupational hazard."

He laughed, and her insides got all warm. "Don't I know it," he responded. "The thing is . . . I don't think we have to decide everything right at this moment. We can just figure it out as we go along."

She took the bag from his hand. "See, I'm not as good at that with my professional life. Winging it, that is."

Josh's gaze touched hers. "You really are a study in contradictions, you know that? The first day I saw you at the office, you struck me as so uptight and . . . well . . . snobby. But I think now that's your business face. Am I right?"

She shrugged. "You might be."

"And which version of Lizzie do you like most?"

It was an impossible question to answer. There was a level of expectation associated with her job. Maybe more so because she was Russ Howard's daughter. Plus she was a bit of a perfectionist. Scratch that. A lot of a perfectionist. It was hard to let go of the idea that she didn't actually have to be top-of-the-heap.

And yet today, wandering Lovers' Island with Josh . . . It had been simple. Lovely. Liberating.

He stood close, close enough that he could have taken her hand if he'd wanted to, but he didn't. Probably because they'd both agreed that they wouldn't. "I know what it's like to have to be two different people." His voice was rough, honest. "I've done that every single day since I came back home. Today I got to be myself. Even if nothing else happens, Lizzie, I want to thank you for that."

Her throat tightened at the plain honesty in his voice. "For me, too, Josh," she whispered. "I've been so wound up with my family situation and my leave of absence, I forgot what it was like to just let loose for a few hours. I'm glad you invited me. Glad we . . ."

She couldn't look up at him. "Just glad. I had a good time."

"Next time we'll make sure you don't get sick," he said, stepping back. And she finally lifted her eyes.

There was humor in his, and acceptance, and affection. And God, he had no idea how much she liked seeing it there. He probably didn't realize that other than Charlie, he was the first and only person to see the real Lizzie in the last few years. And that included Ian.

"Next time?"

And a different light blazed in Josh's eyes. "Oh, I think so. Don't you?"

She wanted to say no, almost as badly as she wanted to say yes. The truth was somewhere in the middle, and she knew he was right. They were going to have to feel their way through this. Carefully.

"We'll see, won't we?" she answered.

"You're catching on." He winked. "You're good to get home now? I've got to get these fish out of the live well and get them cleaned up."

"Oh, right." This really was the end of the day, then. "Josh?"

"Yeah?"

"Thank you. I needed a day away more than you know."

"Oh," he replied, giving a half nod. "I know. Believe me."

He hopped back aboard and untied the rope. "See you around, Dr. Howard."

"Likewise, Dr. Collins."

She stood on the dock and watched as he pushed away, then slowly inched out of the harbor, going left toward what she assumed was his house and private mooring. Not that she would know what either of those looked like.

Because Josh liked keeping his private life private, too.

CHAPTER 12

Sliding back into a work groove wasn't as difficult as Lizzie anticipated, and she had mixed feelings about it. Her female vanity kind of wished it were a little harder for Josh to keep things platonic, but it did make things easier on a professional level. It was Josh who set the tone on the first morning, pouring her a coffee and throwing her a smile but then disappearing into his office before seeing the first patients of the day. At work, he treated her with the same deference and intimacy as he did Robin. And Robin, Lizzie reminded herself with a bit of irritation, was married with a kid or two. It had been over a week since Josh and Lizzie's trip to the island, and it was like nothing had ever happened. She wasn't sure if he'd changed his mind about the "next time" thing or if he was waiting for her to make the next move.

She left the exam room, put the chart on Robin's desk, and went to the kitchen for an apple or yogurt or something else to keep her going until quitting time. The problem with this whole platonic/professional thing was that Lizzie was having a difficult time forgetting. Maybe it had been the dry spell since breaking things off with Ian in April. But really, she'd had much longer dry spells than that before and had felt none of the preoccupation she was feeling now.

Which meant, she supposed, that her ego was the problem. Josh was so good at putting that Sunday behind them that her pride was stinging a little bit. Particularly since she was unable to forget a single second. And she spent far too much time, alone in the cottage at night, imagining what it might have been like if they'd had protection and had made love the way their bodies had demanded.

Far too much time. Maybe she should just go for broke and proposition him to a night of hot sex at the cottage.

She was thoughtlessly shoving Greek yogurt into her mouth when her office phone rang. When she picked it up, it was Robin's voice on the other end. "Lizzie, Sarah's on the line for you. Do you have time to talk to her?"

Josh's sister. Why that made Lizzie nervous she didn't know. It wasn't like Sarah knew what had transpired between Lizzie and Josh. "Put her through, thanks, Robin."

There was a click. "Hi, Sarah?"

"Lizzie." Sarah's voice was warm on the other end. "Hope I didn't catch you at a bad time. Listen, Mark and Matt went out this morning and brought back a mess of fish. I'm having a big fry here tonight and wondered if you'd like to join us."

Lizzie hesitated. She wasn't sure who "us" meant. "Tonight?"

"It's better fresh. We pool the deep fryers. One for

fish, one for fresh-cut fries, and Jess makes the cole-slaw. I've got far more than our little family can eat. We do this several times a summer anyway. If you don't have plans . . ."

She should say no, but the alternatives were going home to make yet another salad with chicken on the top and begging for a seat at Charlie's table, where Lizzie always felt like she was intruding on Charlie and Dave's love nest.

"I don't know, Sarah. . . ."

"Well, there's lots if you decide to come. No pressure."

Now she felt bad, because she sensed the ever-hospitable Sarah was a little bit offended. "If I did come," Lizzie asked, "what should I bring?"

Sarah's voice perked up considerably. "I haven't had time to make dessert today. A pan of brownies wouldn't be amiss."

Lizzie felt marginally better. Like she was asked to be included as the provider of a part of the meal, not just a guest. "I can do that."

"Great! Come over around six."

Lizzie sat back in the chair. "Excuse me for asking the obvious, but is Josh going to be there?"

Sarah laughed. "Wow, you guys don't talk at work at all, do you? Of course he's going to be there. I asked him to ask you a few days ago, when Matt and Mark made the fishing plans. But typical Josh. So focused he forgot."

Now Lizzie was regretting agreeing. Josh didn't forget things like that. He'd deliberately not asked her, like he didn't want her included in their family meal. And now she couldn't back out, not without looking like an idiot or, even worse, like she was not going because of Josh.

Damn him to hell.

"I'll see you at six," she replied. "Gotta run. I have an appointment in a few minutes."

"Bye, Lizzie."

She hung up, took one look at her yogurt, and threw the rest of the container in the trash. It would be fine. She'd show up at six, dessert in hand, stay long enough to eat, and then blast off. She could certainly come up with some excuse. A headache, or an early morning, or needing to stop off at Charlie's on the way home.

At four o'clock Lizzie stopped at the kitchen for a glass of water when Josh came out of his office, looking delectable in his customary jeans and golf shirt. Lizzie had noticed the differences in their appearance this week. Josh was right. She leaned toward conservative dress at work, from her hairstyle down to her low heels. Just because it was a small community practice didn't mean she should sacrifice her professional image.

And maybe that was the problem with a town this size. In the city, she was able to compartmentalize work and play. The two didn't encroach on each other, because away from the hospital she could enjoy a sort of anonymity that wasn't possible here. In Jewell Cove it was all tied up together. No privacy.

"Hey," she offered, topping up her glass. "Busy day?"

"Not bad. You?"

"A fun case of poison ivy." She grinned. "In a most unfortunate spot." She hesitated, then felt they needed to clear the air. "Josh, about the atmosphere around here . . ."

She couldn't read his expression. Apparently she wasn't the only one who could put on a work face.

"I just . . . I don't know. I appreciate the emphasis on keeping it professional, but it's almost like . . ."

"Like it never happened?"

They kept their voices low. There were patients in the waiting room; Robin wasn't far away, either.

"Well, yeah."

Josh ran his fingers over his hair. "I thought you'd prefer it this way. To be honest, it's been hellish. I really haven't known what to say to you."

She let out a relieved breath. "It got weird."

"Yeah."

"Okay." Lizzie looked toward the door again and then back to Josh. "Listen, your sister called and invited me to dinner tonight. If it'll be too awkward for you, I can cancel. I'll think of something."

"Damn." Josh closed his eyes for a minute. "That's tonight. And Sarah told me to ask you and I forgot."

"You forgot?" She raised an eyebrow at him.

He shrugged. "I did, to be honest. I was on my way to Mom's to take a look at her kitchen drain when she called, and then it went right out of my head."

Lizzie wasn't sure she believed him, but she could hardly accuse him of lying. "I'll tell her I had a last-minute call or something. Don't worry about it."

"Don't be silly. I should have cleared the air days ago. Of course you should come. Sarah will be offended if you don't."

Lizzie was just deliberating when Robin came rushing down the hall. "Josh? Lizzie? Luke Pratt just came in complaining of chest pain. He's in the first exam room."

The topic of dinner was quickly forgotten. Lizzie

and Josh darted out of the kitchen, making a beeline for the first room on the left. Luke was sitting on the bed. His normally florid face was gray and clammy, and his lips looked pinched as he breathed, a bit too shallowly for Lizzie's liking.

"Mr. Mayor," Josh greeted him, his voice firm and reassuring. "Not feeling so great today?"

"I felt off all morning, but about fifteen minutes ago the pain started." His breath shook. "Thought it was heartburn at first until it started going down my arm."

"Robin, call an ambulance, please. I think we'd best get Luke to the hospital." Josh turned to Luke and gave his shoulder a reassuring pat. "I'm going to get you an aspirin, Luke. Dr. Howard's going to have a listen and see what's going on in there."

She looked up at Josh, wondering why he was stepping back when Luke was clearly his patient. He shrugged. "You probably see more of this than I do these days."

In seconds she'd unbuttoned Luke's plaid shirt and was listening to his heart. The beat had slowed and she was worried he might pass out. Josh came back with the aspirin and told Luke to chew it, rather than swallow. The older man did as he was told while Lizzie rolled up his sleeve and took his blood pressure. It, too, was lower than she would have liked. "Mr. Pratt, I'm going to get you to lie down. The ambulance will be here soon." She made him comfortable on the bed and put a pillow under his feet and then went for the portable oxygen they had on-site. "This will help you breathe a little easier." She checked her watch. With a heart attack, time meant muscle, and she wanted to ensure that Luke was looked after as soon as possible to decrease the permanent damage.

When Luke was resting quietly, Lizzie looked over at Josh. "How long does an ambulance take?"

"Not long. It's only been five minutes, Lizzie."

It was the first emergency situation she'd dealt with since May. Her adrenaline was pumping and she was frustrated that she couldn't simply order the tests she wanted right now. If they were in Springfield . . .

But they weren't. They were here, in Jewell Cove, where an ambulance had to come from the nearest emergency services station and patients had to be transported to another town for treatment. In Jewell Cove she could treat colds and asthma, give vaccines, and do routine physicals, but very little lifesaving was done.

She missed it. Acutely.

The ambulance arrived, and two EMTs came in with a stretcher for transporting Luke, who continued to be weak and clammy. As they moved him to the stretcher, Lizzie gave them the rundown on his condition.

Josh put his hand on her shoulder. "If you want to ride along, I can hold down the fort."

"Are you sure?" She did want to go.

"Yep. Other than the aspirin, you've run this one. Go ahead. Besides, I'll feel better if one of us is with him. He doesn't really have anyone else."

"Thanks, Josh." As Luke was wheeled out to the waiting ambulance, she rushed to her office for her purse. "I'll try to be back for supper, but if not give Sarah my apologies, will you?"

"Of course."

They'd already inserted a cannula for fluids as Lizzie jumped in the back of the ambulance with one of the attendants. The other hopped up front to drive.

As they pulled out of the lot and the sirens blared, Lizzie smiled grimly. Other than the brief time she'd spent on the island with Josh, this was the most alive she'd felt in months.

She knew where she belonged. At some point she was going to have to work on getting back there again.

Lizzie briefly considered not going to Sarah's, but it was too late now. Jeff and Scott, the EMTs, had considerately dropped her outside Sarah's house when they returned to Jewell Cove. She could always walk back to the clinic for her car, but she could hear laughter from inside the house and she was drawn to the happy sound.

It had been a hell of a ride to the hospital.

She shouldered her handbag and walked down the narrow drive to the house, following the chatter of voices through a fence gate and into the backyard. Rick was playing soccer with Josh's nephew, Matt, while his niece, Susan, challenged Josh to a game of bocce ball. Josh smacked his head and let out a cry of disgust as Susan's green ball came closest to the little white one, and Lizzie smiled. This was what family was supposed to be like. It's what things had been like in her childhood, though it was usually friends playing in the backyard and not extended family.

Remembering made her lonely and homesick. For the second time today.

"Lizzie, you made it!"

Sarah called out her name, Josh turned around and saw her, and everything seemed to pause for a long, long second.

She diverted her attention from Josh, who was now dressed in khaki shorts and a T-shirt, and faced his sister Sarah with a smile. "Sorry I'm late. And I didn't have a chance to pick up dessert. The guys from the ambulance dropped me off."

Sarah waved a hand at her, dismissing her apology. "No worries at all. Meggie brought cookies and we always have ice cream in the freezer anyway. You must be hungry. We'll get you something fresh and you can tell us how our favorite mayor is doing."

Lizzie let out a sigh and followed Sarah to the deck.

"Mark? Plug in the fryer again. I'm going to make a fresh batch for Lizzie."

"Yes, dear!" Mark called down, and Lizzie caught him winking at his wife. He disappeared and Lizzie heard some clanging about up top.

"Sarah, don't go to any bother. I know you've already eaten. I just wanted to stop by."

"Nonsense. I'm going to let you in on a secret that no one in the family knows." She led the way up the stairs to the deck, gave her husband a quick kiss, and went on to the kitchen through sliding doors. Once the doors were closed behind them, Sarah went to the pantry and took out a storage container. "Before I tell you, you have to swear you won't breathe a word. My beer batter is a thing of legend in this family."

Lizzie couldn't help but smile and she crossed her heart. "Promise."

Sarah grabbed a bottle of beer, popped the top, and snagged a small mixing bowl. "It's pancakes."

"Excuse me?"

Sarah giggled. "My secret batter recipe! It's pancake mix and beer. Everyone thinks I have this secret recipe, but I leave it up to Aunt Jemima."

Lizzie laughed. "I promise I won't breathe a word."

Sarah whisked together the dry mix with the beer

until it was the proper consistency and then went to the fridge for another container that held fish fillets. "Come on out. We'll dip and fry. There should be some potatoes left, too, we can do up, if you don't mind them cooked in the same grease."

"I can feel my arteries hardening already." She grinned.

Out on the deck again, they were joined by Jess and Abby and Meggie, who'd been out in Sarah's flower garden when Lizzie had arrived. Meggie snagged the rest of the bottle of beer and took a long swig while Jess settled her very pregnant bulk into an Adirondack chair. "God. Now I'm in this thing and I don't think I'll be able to get out."

Lizzie laughed. There was a sizzle as Sarah dropped fish into the hot grease and followed it with a handful of raw potato strips. Tom came up and grabbed a beer for himself and a can of ginger ale for Abby, who sent him a sweet smile. The bocce game ended, and by the time the fish was golden brown and turned out onto a paper towel to drain a bit the whole family was on the deck, a string of patio lights turned on and the mood definitely mellow.

"I love summer," Rick said, snagging a stool and sitting beside Jess. "I especially love being part of this family. Good times," he finished, and lifted his soda.

Jess curled up close to him. "And this family loves you, too," she reminded him.

"You all seem really close," Lizzie observed. "That's nice."

There were some chuckles among the nodding. "Well, we have our moments. But the latest is that Rick and Abby are actually cousins. Their grandmothers were sisters."

"And you didn't know about each other?"

Abby and Rick shared a significant look. "It surprised us both," Abby said, laughing. "Long story. Come over for lunch in the garden and I'll share it sometime."

Garden lunches. Normally that would be a little slow for Lizzie's speed, but it sounded strangely enjoyable. "We'll make a date."

Josh leaned against the deck railing, waiting for the conversation to wear itself out. "So, Lizzie, what's the update on Luke?"

Lizzie sighed as Sarah placed a plate heaped with fish, fries, and coleslaw before her. "Well, he'll be in the hospital for a while. I had hoped that the damage to the heart was minimal, but he deteriorated on the trip." She met Josh's eyes. "He coded once, but we brought him back. When I left he was in the Cardiac ICU, stabilized."

The mood of the family grew somber. "It's that bad, then," Meggie said quietly, her brow furrowed in worry.

"I'm going to check in with his cardiologist tomorrow afternoon, look at his test results." Lizzie smiled at everyone. "Listen, he came in right away, and got prompt treatment. And Luke strikes me as a strong, vital man. I wouldn't count him out yet."

"Thanks for going with him," Josh said. "I'm glad he wasn't alone."

"He's my patient," she responded simply, and picked up her fork.

But as the conversation started up again, she thought about her last words. As an emergency doctor, she triaged, treated, and sent patients on to where they needed to be in order to make room for the next. Sure, now and again she followed up on an interesting case or a patient would stop by the emergency room with a thanks, but for the most part she didn't follow patients through to their recovery. She didn't get *involved*. Luke shouldn't be any different, but for some reason he was.

"How's the fish?" Josh asked, pulling up a chair beside her.

"Delicious." She dipped a piece in homemade tartar sauce and popped it in her mouth. "Best beer batter I've ever had." She winked at Sarah, who winked back.

"Mark puts seasoning salt on his fries. Jess made the coleslaw. It's our grandmother's dressing recipe."

"I was hungrier than I thought," Lizzie admitted, biting off half a French fry. "Have you ever noticed how fish-and-chips taste better outdoors?"

He smiled. "Almost as good as picnics."

Her face heated.

"You're sure Luke is okay?" He asked it in an undertone.

Lizzie wiped her fingers on a paper napkin. "Honestly? No. I don't like that he coded at all. But the tests will give a better picture. I still don't understand why you asked me to go with him and not you. He knows you better."

"Because you're an emergency doctor and I'm a family physician. And you're hanging around Jewell Cove when you're used to a faster pace. I haven't forgotten that."

She hadn't, either. Though she wasn't remembering as often as she usually did. And that was worrisome.

"You're a good doctor, Lizzie. I knew he was in good hands."

Her heart warmed. "Josh, your belief in me is probably misplaced." It pained her to say it, but it was true. "I've made mistakes—"

"Haven't we all," he said firmly. "And I'd like to think that your time here has helped you past the burnout you were experiencing last spring."

It had. More than he realized. It wasn't not working that was the answer but taking time to enjoy life. Sunsets and walks on the beach and yes, work, but not burning the candle at both ends to escape her problems. "I have to admit, I'm feeling much better these days."

"I know." His gaze held hers. "Listen, I'll drive you home later if you want to have a beer or something. You've earned it."

"You're sure?" The thought of a cold one was tempting, particularly as the sun was setting and the first stars were going to come out any moment. With her belly starting to get full, she was feeling lazy and very chilled out.

"Of course. Enjoy yourself." He got up and disappeared for a minute, then came back with a bottle of beer and put it by her elbow.

The kids took a jar and decided to try catching fireflies, and the adults lounged on the deck, simply chatting about life. Lizzie sat back and took it all in, enjoying the idea of being included even if she didn't contribute much to the conversation. That was until Meggie piped up.

"Lizzie, we've been rude, only talking about ourselves. How are you liking the Cove so far?"

She smiled, turning the bottle around in her hands. "It's lovely here. I can't think of a nicer place to spend a summer. And Josh isn't *that* bad of a boss." She gave a half smile and everyone laughed.

"Josh said something about your mom being close to Springfield?"

She forced her face to relax. She tried not to think about the situation that much. Her last visit still stuck in her head, dragging her down. "Yes, that's right. She's in a care facility there. My dad looked after her as much as he could. I'm sure Josh told you she has Alzheimer's."

"Um . . . no, he didn't. I'm sorry to hear that. Oh my, that's so difficult."

Sounds of sympathy passed through the group. Lizzie met Josh's gaze. He looked apologetic, but she realized that despite her outpouring on the beach the night after her last visit, Josh had kept her confidence. She liked that about him. And for some odd reason, it didn't seem so difficult to talk about.

"It's been hard," she admitted. "Especially with my dad gone now, too." Attempting to lighten the mood, she smiled. "Which makes me want to say thank you again for inviting me tonight. I've missed this kind of thing the last few years. I had a—" Her throat tightened and she swallowed. "I had a happy childhood. It helps to remember that. And Charlie . . . well, she's my best friend. I like being closer to her, too."

Abby reached over and squeezed her hand. God, did the whole extended family have to be so damned generous? And speaking of Charlie, Lizzie really needed to have her over for lunch or take her shopping or something. Lizzie hadn't wanted to run to her friend's doorstep all summer, and lately she hadn't wanted to face questions about Josh, either. Charlie knew her better than anyone. She'd smell a lie a mile away.

"Anyway," Lizzie said, injecting a bit of brightness to her voice. "I didn't mean to be a mood killer. Let's talk about happier topics. Jess, when's your due date?"

Jess rubbed her huge tummy. "Soon," she grumbled. "Hopefully really soon. I've hit the 'oh my God I have a basketball in my stomach' stage. I can't get comfortable at night and I'm up nearly every hour to pee because he's sitting on my bladder." She put on a sad expression. "And I miss seeing my feet."

Everyone laughed. To demonstrate the point, Jess shifted in her chair. "I swear he's kicking field goals in there."

Lizzie saw Abby look at Tom and then Tom nod.

"Well, since Jess is due any day, this might be a good time to announce that there's going to be a little Arseneault running around next spring." Abby looked at everyone, her face beaming.

The deck went completely silent, and Lizzie saw Tom look at Josh and Josh look back, and something that wasn't quite happiness passed between the two. It wasn't anger, either. But it was definitely emotional, and Lizzie frowned.

"Well, congratulations!" Sarah went forward and gave Abby a huge hug. "I love spring babies! And yours and Jess's will be close together. And Charlie's, too. It's wonderful."

Abby squeezed Sarah back. "Thank you, Sarah."

The talk then morphed into a conversation about how Abby was feeling and when the baby was due and a million other things, and Lizzie sat back, her plate empty and a pang in her heart. She'd never have a big family like this. And Josh wasn't overly chatty right now, either. And then she remembered. Josh and Tom had history, and a history that centered around Josh's wife. Did Tom's news bring back memories or something?

Right now Josh was standing at the railing of the deck, looking down over the backyard and the smooth, black waters of the bay.

She got up and went to him, put a hand on his arm. "Josh? I'm getting a bit tired. Would you mind taking me home now?"

"Not at all." As she suspected, he almost looked relieved. "It's getting late anyway."

He turned from the railing and interrupted the conversation. "Hey, everyone. I'm going to run Lizzie home. She's had a long day."

Lizzie smiled brightly. "But thank you for dinner. Particularly since I was so late."

"You're welcome," Sarah answered, and Mark added, "Stop by anytime. Any friend of Josh's . . ."

Josh went forward and hugged Abby. "Congratulations, to both of you," he said, but there was a softness to his voice that told Lizzie the words were perhaps hard to say. When he released Abby, Tom was waiting.

Josh held out his hand. "So, you're gonna be a dad. This'll be fun to watch. Especially if karma has anything to do with it."

It seemed like everyone suddenly held their breath.

"You were a wicked terror when we were little. God has a way of repaying the favor."

Tom laughed. "Then just wait until it's your turn. He's going to have a riot with your kids."

The tension eased, and Lizzie picked up her bag and said a blanket good-bye to everyone.

Josh's pickup was parked out front, and it took only seconds for him to pull a U-turn and head to the edge of town and the road leading to Fiddler's Rock. The stars had come out, and Lizzie leaned back against the vinyl seat and relaxed her shoulders. Josh slowed once to let a raccoon scoot across the road, then kept on until they got to the cottage, the dark shape of the house silhouetted in front of the trees.

She turned on the seat, put her hand on her purse. "You want to come in and talk about it?"

His hands stayed on the steering wheel. "Talk about what?"

But his jaw had a stubborn set to it, and he stared straight ahead instead of at her.

"About why Abby and Tom's news isn't a cause for rejoicing. Because they seem pretty happy to me."

"They are. And I'm happy for them."

"You could have fooled me."

He looked at her then, but the wall shutting her out was still firmly in place.

"Come inside," she suggested gently. "I'll make some tea. Or pour you a whiskey."

"I should get back."

"To what? Your empty house? You're a stubborn cuss, I'll give you that. Must have served you well in the Army."

He lifted a solitary eyebrow. "At least in the Army people didn't nag."

She started laughing. "Fine. Suit yourself. I get it. I've wallowed in my bubble of misery lots of times. Have fun."

She clenched the leather strap of her bag, opened the door, and hopped down. Her steps crunched on the rock of the driveway as she made her way to the cottage door. The light wasn't on, so she reached into her purse, rummaging around for her keys. Josh's door opened and then closed again.

She'd found the keys and slipped the proper one into the lock when Josh's voice came across the clearing. "Whiskey, you say?"

Lizzie smiled to herself, opened the door, and waited for him.

CHAPTER 13

Josh questioned the wisdom in following her inside. All week he'd done a great job of keeping things platonic, because that was what he thought she wanted. And if he was truthful, part of him wanted that, too. Inside, she turned on a lamp, casting a soft, warm glow on the living room. "Make yourself comfortable," she suggested. "I'll get glasses. On the rocks, or do you want a mix?"

"Rocks works for me."

The cottage looked exactly the same as it had when Tom had lived here. Same rugged plaid-upholstered furniture, sturdy tables and shelves Tom had constructed himself in his workshop. Until today, Josh had been certain that he'd put his resentment toward Tom away for good. Josh didn't blame Tom anymore. He wasn't sure he ever had, though it had been easier than blaming himself or Erin. But tonight's announcement had brought certain memories rushing back and it had him on edge.

So whiskey. And Lizzie. Between the two, maybe he could forget. Or at least let it go.

He settled himself on one side of the sofa, crossed his right ankle over his knee. In no time Lizzie was back, two glasses in her hands. She handed him one and put the other on the coffee table. "I'll be back in a few minutes. I've been in work clothes all day."

"Sure," he responded, his mind following her to the bedroom, imagining her changing. He should probably stop fooling himself. He hadn't been able to stop thinking about her since that Sunday on the island. A man couldn't just forget something that memorable.

He sipped the whiskey, felt the welcome burn down the back of his throat, the flicker of it as it hit his stomach.

"There, that's better."

She'd barely been gone two minutes, but Josh's mouth went dry at the sight of her. It wasn't even remotely sexy, but a pair of plain black yoga pants and a snug V-neck T-shirt hugged her curves like a dream. Running—or whatever else she did for exercise—had made her butt high and tight, her waist spare, and the V-neck emphasized the delicious curve of her breasts. She held her own highball glass, the ice cubes clinking softly as she took the far end of the sofa, folding herself up in the corner with her legs crossed.

"Comfortable?" he asked dryly, tipping his glass for a sip.

She grinned. "Actually, I am. This is a really comfortable couch. If I'm not out on the deck enjoying the view, I'm usually here in the corner with a book or something."

He realized that sounded pretty lonely. He lived

alone, too, and the quiet, while welcome most of the time, could get a little *too* quiet. "What about Charlie? Do you spend a lot of time together?"

She shrugged, drank. "Some. But she's busy with her husband. I don't like to intrude."

"You're her best friend. It wouldn't be intruding. Especially with Charlie." He leaned back against the cushions. "She was pretty excited you were coming for the summer, you know."

Lizzie smiled again. "Okay, then let me put it this way. I'm not all that fond of third wheeling."

She looked a little too knowing as she said that. He regretted now ever telling her anything about Tom and Erin. He had probably been a bit transparent tonight.

When he didn't say anything, she put her glass down on a side table. "Josh?" His name was gentle on her lips. "Do you want to talk about it?"

"Talk about what?" He raised an eyebrow. Kept his expression deliberately bland.

She slid over on the couch and put her hand on his knee, the soft pressure warm and more welcoming than it should have been. "Not long ago you found me on the beach, upset because of my mom. I know what pain looks like, Josh, no matter how you try to hide it. And Abby and Tom's news hurt you tonight. I just don't know why. You mentioned once that you'd wanted children but that Erin hadn't. Does that have something to do with it?"

He debated telling her, but only Tom knew the most humiliating secret of Josh's marriage to the woman they'd both loved. And since they'd reconciled their friendship, Josh knew Tom would never laud it over him. Josh had hated his cousin for a long time, but he'd always known that Tom would never be cruel.

"Josh? Why don't you talk to me? I really do have a good ear."

"I don't need an ear." He handed her his glass. "Thanks for the drink, Lizzie, but I shouldn't finish it if I'm going to drive home."

He got up and got as far as the door to the kitchen when her voice stopped him, low and silky. "Do you want to go home?"

He hesitated. That was his first mistake. Considered what she was asking. That was his second. He should keep going, straight out the door, back to his house, and sleep on his thoughts so he could have a better head on his shoulders tomorrow. Sleeping with her when he was this upset simply wouldn't be smart.

Instead he could only think of the softness of her skin, how it was both sweet and salty, and how much he'd love to have her in his arms again.

He turned around. She was standing by the sofa, his glass still in her hand. She lifted it and tossed back the liquor. "There. Now you don't have to worry about the drink."

God almighty, she was a sexy little thing. He let out his breath and went back to where she was standing, close enough that she had to tip her chin way up to meet his gaze. "Are you asking me to stay, Lizzie?"

"Maybe. If you tell me what's eating at you."

He wrinkled his brow and stepped back. "Sex as a bargaining tool. I didn't think you had it in you."

"Not at all. I just think if you're going to take me to bed, the air should be clear. Because if you're with me, Josh, you're only with me. Not with whatever or whoever got you tied up in knots tonight."

He hated that she was right.

"It's not really something that promotes . . . you know."

" 'You know'?" She chuckled softly. Reached up and smoothed a piece of hair away from his temple. "What are you saying, Josh? That you spilling your guts is going to kill the fun boner?"

He couldn't help it; he snorted. It sounded so funny coming from her pert little mouth. She grinned wickedly and twirled the slight curl of hair around her finger. "Okay, I admit that I'm not sure what I'll do if you cry. But I think you need to get whatever it is off your chest."

He sighed.

She retrieved her glass from the table and handed it over. "You look like you could use this first," she suggested.

Josh took the glass and tossed down the rest of the alcohol, the mostly melted cubes tinkling back into the bottom. He took a deep breath, met her eyes, and decided he might as well just say it. Maybe—and he figured it was a very small chance—she was right and he'd feel better.

But damn. It was hard for a man to admit he hadn't been enough for his wife.

Lizzie watched as Josh tossed back the whiskey like it was water. He didn't even flinch as it had to burn its way down his esophagus like liquid fire. But the last ten minutes had told her two very important things. One, Josh was definitely holding something in, something that still had the power to hurt him, and she understood and empathized with it. And two, he still wanted her. After the cold shoulder throughout the week, all it had taken was her asking if he wanted to stay and he'd changed his mind about walking away.

Hot damn.

"Do you want another?"

He nodded and handed over the glass. "I'll take the next one slower," he answered with a sober nod.

She went to the kitchen for fresh ice and added a liberal splash of whiskey to each glass, then back to the living room. Josh was standing in front of the window, looking out over the dark, still waters of the inlet. She put her drink down, then went to him and put one hand on his back and handed over the drink with the other.

"Thanks," he said quietly.

"You're welcome."

"So," she said, standing beside him at the window. "You ready to tell me what's eating at you so much?"

He took a good-sized sip of the drink and swallowed. "You have to understand that what I'm about to tell you throws massive aspersions on my manhood."

"Aspersions?" She laughed, looking up at his profile. But halted when she could see he was mostly serious. "Okay. Try me. I'm guessing your manhood is just fine."

He took a deep breath. "So I thought Erin and I were trying to have a baby, but the whole time she was taking the pill behind my back."

Lizzie stared at him. "What? Were you not on the same page or what?"

He faced her and laughed bitterly. "Looking back, I don't think we were even in the same book. She knew I wanted a family, and she pretended to want to give it to me. It worked for a while, too. I thought we'd really turned a corner in our marriage. Like we could really be happy."

She wondered if he realized how much pain bled through what he thought was anger. If he blamed Erin or blamed himself. Considering what Lizzie knew of him so far and how he seemed to take responsibility for everyone in his family, she could guess that he placed a good portion of it squarely on his own shoulders.

"I'm sorry, Josh. That's a dirty trick, playing with your emotions like that." She reached over and touched his wrist. "How did you find out?"

He didn't move his arm away from her touch, but he didn't acknowledge it, either, and she wondered if he actually realized her fingers were on his wrist. He was back to staring out the window again, as if it were easier to say if he avoided eye contact.

"She was so determined to do one last deployment," he replied. "Then she told me she was going to be spending a weekend with friends. I checked her GPS when she got back, because I had a terrible feeling she'd been lying. She had. She'd come here, to Jewell Cove. To see Tom."

No wonder Josh had been so pissed at his cousin.

"Did they . . . ?" She left the question unfinished, knowing he'd understand anyway.

"Tom says no. And I believe him. We grew up together. And he was hurt as badly as I was, I think. But damn. At the time I didn't know if they had or hadn't been together. I didn't trust her not to lie about it, and Tom and I hadn't spoken in years. I couldn't be with her after that. From that day until the one when she left, I stayed on my side of the bed. All I could think was that if we slept together, and she got pregnant, I'd wonder if it was mine or his. I couldn't do that."

He turned away from the window and faced Lizzie. "A few weeks after she was deployed, I found the empty pack. Every month when she started her period we'd lament the fact that we hadn't been successful. I never realized she was such a good actress."

"You really wanted a family," Lizzie said softly.

"More than anything," he answered, and she heard the pain in his voice. "And she knew it. And the truth of the matter was, she wanted a family, too. Just not with me. She'd gone to see Tom that night to tell him she was going to leave me and that they could finally be together the way they should have been all along."

Lizzie swore. "Are you serious?" She'd met Tom. She liked Tom. But why on earth would anyone married to Josh be able to turn him away so easily? He was a good guy. Kind, compassionate, strong, funny, sexy—

Okay. This was not supposed to lead to a laundry list of his good points. She found him attractive on a lot of levels. Didn't mean *she* wanted to marry the guy—

"The whole time she was gone I didn't know what to do. I didn't want the marriage to end, but damn, I was tired of feeling like second choice. I thought maybe if she came back we could try some counseling or something. Instead she didn't come back at all. And the last thing I said—"

He stopped talking abruptly. His lips closed tight and Lizzie saw a muscle tic in his jaw.

"Josh," she said gently, rubbing his arm. "What did you say?"

"It doesn't matter."

Lizzie swallowed back a sigh. Josh had a lot of pride. She could relate to that. She wasn't proud of a lot of things she'd said and done over the last several months. But she didn't have the same regret as Josh. This was his wife. His marriage. And he could never have a do-over.

As he stared at the black water of the bay, Lizzie slid her arm off his arm and to his back, rubbing gently along his spine. "Josh, you put on a good face for everyone, don't you?"

He shrugged beneath her hand, but she persistently left it where it was. "What good would it do," he said bitterly, "to tell everyone the truth? She's gone. I don't want to be the guy who badmouths his dead wife. I might have been angry with her, I might have been hurt, but I never wanted her to die."

"Of course you didn't." Lizzie's heart melted, looking into his face, so closed against emotion. "And you don't want anyone to think badly of her, because what's the point, right? So you bottle all this inside and put on a smile for the world because Josh has to be the strong older brother and only son and town doctor and who knows what else."

"Be careful," he warned darkly, turning to face her, but she was glad of the spark of fire flickering in his eyes.

"You think I don't see it? Come on, Josh. We're more alike than you think. Russ Howard's daughter who can't make a mistake, who should look after her mother but keeps her in a home, who basically gets the boot from her job by her boss, who happens to be her ex? This is practically torture for a perfectionist like me."

He pulled away. "I know all that," he ground out. "You don't need to keep reminding me that being in Jewell Cove is nothing more than a punishment for you!"

"That's not what I meant!" Frustrated, Lizzie's voice lifted a little. "Just tell me what you said, Josh. I promise you won't go to hell or go up in flames or whatever it is you're afraid of. Just say it and get it off your chest for once."

"Fine." He reached out and cupped her chin, lifting it a little so she had no choice but to look right in his eyes. "I told her she'd better decide who she was coming home to, and if it wasn't me that she shouldn't bother coming home at all."

Despite her best intentions, Lizzie stepped back, away from his words, away from his touch. The pain and regret in his eyes seared her and she understood how much he must have hated himself all this time. What terrible, terrible last words to say to someone you loved. There was nothing Lizzie could say to make it better. It would just be platitudes. Of course he hadn't meant it *that* way. It didn't stop the remorse.

"See?" he accused. "You're shocked. And you hardly know me."

She knew him better than he realized, but she didn't say so. They were already treading on shaky ground.

"I'm shocked because those words don't sound like the person I've come to know these past weeks. And that tells me that you were hurt, and probably confused . . . and scared."

She wished she hadn't stepped back, and she made up for it by moving forward and putting her hand along his cheek. "I know what it's like to be scared, Josh. To be afraid of losing what's most important. Of not being good enough." She swallowed and admitted, "Of being afraid you'll never be good enough again."

"Yes," he said, looking her in the eyes. "But for me it was my heart."

"I don't understand."

"You're only talking about your job. But when you love someone, Lizzie, really love someone . . . you know what's important. And it's not a career or degree or a bank account balance or whatever. It comes down to who you are on the inside. What you think and how you treat people. And I'm not a very good person."

She absorbed the insult because she knew that he was hurting. She also recognized a difficult truth in his words. She'd cared for Ian. She'd never loved him, not like that. She'd never loved anyone that way.

"You're one of the best people I've ever met. Certainly better than me," she whispered, rubbing her thumb along Josh's bottom lip. "But I'm thinking we could be good together, Josh. Because we see each other so clearly."

He swallowed, his Adam's apple bobbing. "I don't know that I see you all that clearly at all. I think I know you and then you do something that doesn't follow."

She slid closer. "Like what, Josh?"

"Like I know you're focused on career and advancement, and you don't like small towns, and you prefer the city, and frankly, when you first got here you struck me as being a snob."

It might have actually hurt, except for the soft, husky quality of his voice. It rather reminded her of the scene in *Pride and Prejudice* where Darcy professed his love to Elizabeth despite her flaws, his face only a whisper away. The difference was they weren't even close to being in love. This was lust, pure and simple.

"And then you do other things, and I realize I was wrong about you." His breath caught a little.

She stood up on tiptoe and, feeling quite bold, gave his earlobe a nibble. "Is that so?"

His breath came out shaky. "Jesus, Lizzie."

She let her lips feather over the skin of his neck. "Things like what?" she asked.

"Things like the look on your face when you pull up a line of fish. The way you cry about your mother. The way . . ." He shuddered beneath her touch. "The way you look at me sometimes."

"How do I look at you, Josh?"

The heat seemed to have gone up ten degrees in the last two minutes. Lizzie touched the hollow of his throat with her tongue, tasting the warm saltiness of his skin.

"Like this."

Finally his unshakeable control seemed to snap. He took her hair in his hand and tugged at it, pulling her head back firmly but not painfully, so that her lips were tilted up instead of buried in the tantalizing skin of his neck. And he kissed her, a possessive, grand kiss that nearly took the knees out from beneath her and had her gasping for breath, holding on to his shoulders as his tongue swept into her mouth and he pulled her body against his.

Their hands were everywhere. Josh's gripped the hem of her T-shirt and he broke the kiss long enough to tug the garment over her head and drop it to the floor. His palm immediately covered her breast, the heat of him radiating through the black satin.

"Mmm," she hummed, hastily unbuttoning his shirt, wondering what he'd say if she said screw the time-consuming part and just ripped it open the way she wanted. Desire was pulsing through her now, hot and liberating. Finally she got rid of the last button and shoved the fabric over his shoulders. He moved his arms, awkwardly but efficiently, letting the shirt fall to the floor as she reached for the button and zipper of his cargo shorts.

And she might have had better progress if he hadn't shoved his hand down inside her yoga pants, making her call out with pleasure.

Somehow her pants and panties ended up around her feet and she stomped out of them, and his shorts quickly followed.

"As awesome as it would be to take you right here," he growled, "I think you'd better show me the way to the bedroom." He briefly grabbed his shorts and reached for his wallet, pulled out a condom, and met her gaze with a searing, knowing look. "After the island I didn't want to be caught unprepared again. I think we both knew this was inevitable."

It was probably the most foolish thing in the world to do. He'd unloaded a fair chunk of baggage tonight, and he was feeling like shit because his best friend was going to be a father. Was she taking advantage because for the first time in months she was feeling a need so intense that nothing else mattered?

"It's my turn to ask," she said softly, closing her eyes as his fingers slid over the curve of her bottom. "Are you sure, Josh? Because I want you to be sure."

His first answer was a kiss. Long, lazy, complete, with enough heat and intent to tell her that what had happened between them on the island was only a taste of what was to come.

"I'm sure. I want this, Lizzie. I want you. And that might be all I know for sure right now."

Her libido was speaking far louder than her common sense. "Then that's all I need to know," she replied, and she turned away from him and started down the tiny hall to the master bedroom.

And if he kept his eyes on her ass the whole way, all the better.

CHAPTER 14

His phone rang at fourteen minutes after four.

Lizzie rolled over, but Josh never so much as flinched. She smiled to herself briefly as she reached for his cell. The display said: "R&J Sullivan" and she immediately sat up in bed, holding the covers to her chest.

"Josh. Josh, wake up. It's your phone and it's Jess."

"Hmph," he mumbled.

The ringing stopped.

"Josh!" She gave him a nudge this time. "Josh, wake up. It's the middle of the night and Jess called. It has to be important."

He rolled to his back, scrubbed his hand over his face, and blinked a few times. "It's Jess?"

"I didn't want to answer, in case you didn't want her to know . . . you know. That we'd spent the night together."

More like Lizzie didn't want Jess to know. The last thing she needed was his family knowing what had gone on here tonight. Even minus the steamy details . . . of which there were many.

So many. Feminine muscles curled and contracted in remembrance.

He sat up, held out his hand. "Okay. Okay. God, I usually don't sleep that soundly. I'll call her back."

She put the phone in his hand and watched as he hit the button to call Jess back and waited for the phone to ring. She picked up after the first ring. Lizzie heard the tone, the click, and Jess's voice on the line in the utter quiet of the bedroom.

"Oh, thank God," Lizzie heard Jess say. "Josh, my water broke fifteen minutes ago. Rick's taking me to the hospital."

"Are you having contractions yet?"

"I thought they were just Braxton Hicks tonight at Sarah's. Best guess, according to Rick's watch, I'm seven minutes apart."

"You've got some time yet. And first ones tend to be a little slower, so don't panic. You go with Rick, and I'll meet you there, okay?"

"Okay." There was a beat of silence and then Lizzie heard Jess's voice once more. "Josh, I'm scared."

"Hell, Jess, you've been through far worse and at the end you're going to have a beautiful baby to hold in your arms. You just remember that. And I'll be there soon. Have I ever let you down?"

"Not once." Conversation broke off and Lizzie heard long, labored breaths through the phone. Josh simply waited until the contraction was over.

"Phew," Jess breathed. "Okay. We're off. Call Mom and Sarah, okay?"

"I will. See you soon."

He clicked off the phone. "Well. Looks like I'm off to the hospital."

"She called you first. Before your mom, or sister. Because you're a doctor?"

Josh shook his head. "No. A long time ago Jess was in a bad situation. I helped get her out of it. It's made us really close is all. When she's in a pinch, I get a call."

"That's sweet."

"She's my sister. Of course I look after her."

He slid out of bed and Lizzie got a quick glimpse of a beautiful tight butt before he pulled on his underwear. "Look, Lizzie, I'm sorry to run out without at least buying you breakfast."

"It's okay. Your family needs you."

He nodded. She'd half-hoped he'd ask her to go with him, but he didn't. And deep down she knew it was smart. Work and personal life completely separate, just the way she wanted, right? So why did it sting?

He had to go to the living room for his shirt, so Lizzie slid out from beneath the covers, shrugged on a light robe, and followed him. "Josh, hang tight a minute. You've hardly had any sleep. Let me at least make you a coffee for the road." She turned on the coffeemaker and snagged a pod of Italian roast to put in the dispenser. She only had one travel mug, and it was stainless steel emblazoned with the words "Trust Me, I'm a Doctor" on it. She put it beneath the dispenser and hit the button once the water was hot.

Josh appeared behind her, buttoning the last button of his shirt. "You didn't have to do that."

"I would have made you eggs, but I get the feeling time is of the essence. Go ahead and call Meggie and Sarah while it's brewing."

He did, saying he was just grabbing a coffee before

heading to the hospital, agreeing to meet the rest of
his family there. Lizzie heard Meggie agree to call
Abby . . . this was turning out to be a whole family
affair. And it would have warmed Lizzie's heart if she
didn't feel so left out.

Ridiculous.

She put the top on the coffee and handed it to him
as he was putting his phone in his pocket.

"Sorry about this," he apologized again.

"Don't be silly." She smiled. "Your sister is having
a baby. Big day. She needs her big brother. Go."

"I'll text you later with news, okay?"

"Of course. And I'll handle the office. We have
walk-in hours today."

"Right. Shit."

She swallowed tightly. Before drifting off to sleep,
she'd kind of imagined them getting up, having breakfast, going into the clinic together.

What on earth had she been thinking? What a crazy,
dumb idea. It was far too cozy a thought. Certainly not
what she wanted. Last night was what she'd wanted
for a while now, wasn't it? Hot, satisfying sex with
no strings, no repercussions at work?

"I got this," she said hoarsely, needing him to leave
now. "Go. Jess'll be looking for you."

"Thanks." He hesitated, then leaned forward and
gave her a quick kiss. "Thanks for last night. It was . . ."

"Yeah," she replied softly. "It was."

He flashed her a grin and then went to the door,
opened it, looked back for a flash of a moment, and
closed it behind him.

His truck started up, lights came on, and the beam
of light moved across the kitchen as he backed out of
the driveway and turned onto the road.

It was only then that Lizzie realized that she'd left her car at the clinic yesterday and that Josh had gone, taking her ride to work with him.

It was strange for Josh to be sitting in the waiting room rather than being in among the action. But Jess had her obstetrician, and Rick and Meggie were there to help her through. Josh had gone in briefly to kiss her forehead and tell her he was here, but then he'd gone to the waiting room with Sarah and Abby to wait. Tom, Abby explained, would be by later once there was news.

Tom.

The mess of feelings about Tom and Abby having a baby were now all twined up together with what had happened at Lizzie's. How the hell she and Josh had managed to go from his screwed-up relationship with Erin to making love still blew his mind, but he suspected that they'd both been looking for an excuse for a while. Ever since Lovers' Island, really. They'd started something that day that had been leading to last night.

He took a long sip of strong coffee, thanked Lizzie silently for the dark roast, and leaned back in his chair.

Tom had moved on. Why was it so hard for Josh? He knew, deep down, that it wasn't a case of who'd loved Erin more. Tom had loved Erin with all his heart. And he'd loved Josh, too. That knowledge was slightly uncomfortable. They'd been like brothers, and Tom had isolated himself rather than fight for Erin, rather than put himself in the middle of the marriage. It said a lot about the man Tom was. Said a lot about Josh, too, a lot that he wasn't very proud of.

He should have stepped aside.

But if he had, Tom wouldn't have Abby, and Josh also knew in his heart that Abby and Tom were meant to be together.

Damn, life could be complicated sometimes.

"Penny for your thoughts," Abby interrupted.

He turned his head and smiled at her. "I think you might need more than a penny."

She frowned and took the chair next to him. "Are you okay, Josh? I mean, with Tom and me? You left pretty soon after our announcement last night."

Josh swallowed the bitterness, focused on the good. "Of course I am. I'm happy for you two."

"He really wants you to be happy, too, you know. I think he still feels a little guilty sometimes. Like he doesn't deserve happiness until you find it, too." She smiled softly. "What a tangled web, huh?"

"You're not kidding." He put his hand on her shoulder. "It just brought back some memories, that's all. But I'm fine, Abby."

He thought back to how he'd dealt with his feelings and hoped he wasn't blushing.

"Lizzie got home all right?"

Damned heat crawled up his neck. He took another drink of coffee, wondering if the cup might camouflage his embarrassment. "Yeah. Safe and sound." And hot and naked. Just thinking about it made his body react. Meggie came down the hall, her eyes tired but twinkling. "I'm officially kicked out," she said, flopping into a seat. "Contractions are two minutes apart, and Jess is getting grouchy. Fast labor for a first one."

Josh chuckled. "You threw Rick to the wolves, did you?"

Meggie's eyes softened. "He's doing a fine job. I

swear, the two of them used to fight like cats and dogs. And now he's all 'sweetheart' and she's all 'honey' and he's holding her hand telling her how wonderful she is."

"That's lovely," Abby said wistfully.

Josh laughed. "Give it a while longer. He'll come out of there looking like he's been in a war zone and the peace treaty's just been announced. Battered, bruised, and happy."

There were a few windows to the waiting room and the gray dawn warmed to pinks and soft blues as the sun came up on another scorcher of a day. Sarah had brought a needlework project along and Josh noticed the needle moving slower and slower until she finally dozed off, her head resting against the pillar next to her chair. Meggie flipped through a magazine and Abby turned the pages of a book—it looked to be one of the ancient ones from the library at Foster House. All he had with him was his phone, and he was half-tempted to send Lizzie a text. But she'd probably gone back to bed, and besides, he wasn't really sure what to say.

She was his first since the end of his marriage. He imagined that would surprise her, and he knew for sure it hadn't been that long for her since her last lover. After all, she'd been with this Ian guy just this past spring.

Before Erin there had only been two others. It was pretty limited experience for a man over thirty. He figured it was better to keep that information to himself. Lizzie wasn't interested in anything serious, and hearing that sort of thing might scare her off big-time. Sex wasn't something he tended to do casually.

He wasn't looking for anything serious, either. He considered that for a bit. Maybe that was why it had been so good with Lizzie. So easy. No agenda other than being together and in the moment.

He picked up a magazine and started to flip blindly through the pages when his cell buzzed in his back pocket. He took it out and checked the screen and felt a little burst of pleasure when he saw a text from her.

Any news?

He put down the magazine and used both thumbs to type back:

Nothing yet. Shouldn't be long.

He hesitated and then typed:

Did you get any more sleep?

Not really. Went for a run on the beach. Don't worry about the clinic today.

Thanks. I'll check in later.

He put his phone down for a moment and deliberated. Realistically he should probably back right off where Lizzie was concerned. He reached for his coffee only to realize it had gone completely cold and put it back down on the table.

They were consenting adults. And last night . . . *damn*. Could he really just walk away from that entirely?

He picked up the phone again.

Hey, can I see you tonight?

The response seemed to take a long time coming, and he wondered if she'd left to do something or if she really didn't want to answer him.

I don't know, Josh. Can we talk about it later?

He really shouldn't feel let down by her response. Maybe it was just that she didn't want to talk about it in texts. It was easy to miss tone, nuance. He checked his watch. It was just after seven. Maybe she was getting ready for work. Maybe he was analyzing the shit out of the situation and he should just chill.

Of course. Will txt with news.

He felt like an idiot, but he added a smiling emoji to the end. God, what was he, sixteen?

And then he let out a breath and smiled to himself. Of course he wasn't. At sixteen the sex would never have been as good as it was last night.

It was another half hour before Rick came down the hall, looking utterly exhausted and completely thrilled. "It's a boy," he said proudly. He ran his hand through his hair. "Holy crap. I'm a dad."

Everyone got up and congratulated him with hugs and smiles. Josh shook his hand and asked after Jess.

"She was a real trooper," Rick said, pride filling his voice. "Apparently this was fast for a first birth, and he's over eight pounds. I always knew she was strong. But I had no idea."

Josh clapped him on the shoulder. "She has a good partner. Makes a big difference."

Indeed. Partnerships made the best marriages, to Josh's mind. Not that he'd really know. It wasn't from lack of trying . . . but looking back, he saw it seemed his marriage had been best when they weren't in the same country. What a sad statement.

Rick looked at Meggie. "Well, Grandma, Jess has asked for you. Once she's cleaned up a bit, you can all come for a visit."

Rick disappeared with Meggie, and Abby and Sarah decided to dash to the cafeteria for tea and a quick bite now that it was over. Josh went along simply for something to do and bought the girls their tea and an assortment of muffins to tide everyone over until they could have a proper breakfast. When they returned to the maternity unit, Jess had been moved into her room and the nurse walked them down the hall, past the nursery with babies, and up to a closed door.

She gave a tap on the door and opened it a crack.

"Some people here are awfully curious about a new baby boy. Should I let them in?"

Jess must have said yes, because the nurse opened the door for them to enter.

Josh had never seen his sister look so beautiful.

She looked tired and a little drawn, and her dark hair was damp around her face, curlier than ever. She didn't have on a smidge of makeup, but her face simply radiated a happiness and joy that no cosmetics could imitate. She'd changed into a pair of pajamas, and in the crook of her arm was a blanket-wrapped bundle. Her son. Josh got a lump in his throat. After all his baby sister had been through, it was incredible to see her so perfectly happy at this moment. No one he knew deserved it more.

Rick sat at the foot of the bed, beaming as most new fathers were bound to do. This was how it was supposed to be. A baby wanted and welcome and loved, and two parents who loved each other, too.

"So, do we have a name?" asked Sarah, stepping forward and putting her hot tea down on the rolling table that was currently pushed to the side. "Come on now, let his auntie have a turn. My first nephew! It's about time, Sis!"

Sarah gently took the bundle from Jess's arms and her face softened. "He's beautiful, Jess. A Collins through and through."

Abby laughed. "Don't discount the Foster blood in there, now." Josh watched as Abby reached over and took Rick's hand. "I think my cousin here had something to do with it."

Rick grinned. "Abby, you're beautiful, but I'm perfectly okay with our children looking just like their mother."

Which was the perfect answer, as all the women in the room melted.

Jess eased herself up a little. "In answer to your question, yes, we have a name." She looked at Rick. "We've decided on Liam Joshua Franklin Sullivan. A bit of a long handle, but I think he can handle it."

Josh stared at Jess, then looked over at Sarah and Meggie. Both had tears in their eyes. It was wonderful that Jess had included their father's name, particularly as he never lived to see any of his grandkids. "It's perfect," Josh said. "And I'm honored."

Rick nodded at Josh. "I know how much your help has meant to Jess over the years, and you're my best friend. We're the ones who're honored, Josh."

"Oh, for Pete's sake." Heads turned to Abby, who

was flapping her fingers in front of her face. "I don't know if it's hormones or what, but you all have got me crying now!"

There was another sniffle. "Me, too," Jess admitted.

Sarah was standing holding Liam, her hips moving to and fro in an automatic "mom" motion. "My hands are full, so don't make me cry. I can't wipe my nose."

They were all chuckling when the door opened again and Tom came through, dressed for work and carrying a teddy bear with a blue ribbon around its neck. Josh still felt a little awkward, so he reached for the chart at the foot of the bed and gave it a quick scan, just to keep occupied.

"Oh, now everyone's here!" Jess exclaimed. "Except Mark and the kids. But really. You guys . . ." She blinked again, quite quickly. "Thank you. Thank you all for sticking by me and for getting up in the middle of the night." She met Josh's gaze, a startled expression on her face. "Wait. Josh, don't you have patients to see?"

"Lizzie's covering for me this morning. Where else would I be but here?"

But what seemed odd was that it felt like Lizzie should be here, too. Probably just because he'd left her so abruptly this morning.

God, what would the people in this room say if they knew he'd left Lizzie's bed to come to the hospital? Plenty, he imagined. He knew they liked Lizzie, but would they still if they knew she and Josh had slept together? His mother certainly wouldn't understand how they could have a physical relationship knowing that it was strictly temporary. She was of the belief that sex should be part of a far deeper, more permanent relationship.

While it felt weird to be sneaking around at his age, he valued his privacy too much to make anything obvious. He'd already left his truck parked in front of Lizzie's cottage all night, which wasn't the best way of being discreet.

And he hadn't yet texted her with the news.

"Speaking of, I'll be back in a few minutes. I'm just going to check in with Robin and make sure everything's okay at the clinic."

He stepped outside and, in the quiet of the hall, pulled out his phone.

Baby Boy. 8 lbs 4 oz, 21 ½ inches long, Liam Joshua Franklin Sullivan.

The reply was swift.

Yay! Congrats, Uncle Josh! You must be thrilled. Fast work for Jess. Everything okay?

Everything is perfect. Clinic okay?

Once more the answer came back quickly.

I got this. Got some results back so need to go over tests later. Take a rain check on tonight?

He didn't want to push. And her tone seemed more easygoing now than it had earlier.

Of course. I'll check in later at the office.

Not necessary.

She, too, added a smiley face, just as he had earlier.

Take a day off and spend it with your family.
And give Jess and Rick my congrats.

And that was that.

He opened the door to Jess's room, but no one noticed him there. Meggie was holding Liam now, and Sarah was getting Jess some water and a muffin from the bag. Abby and Tom were standing together, Tom with one arm looped around his wife's waist, and Rick was sitting next to Jess, the picture of contentment. It was like everything fit into a perfect place and there was no room for Josh. He knew it wasn't true. But it felt true. He was the odd one out.

Today he really wasn't needed anywhere.

CHAPTER 15

After cabbing it to work, Lizzie spent the day keeping everything to a brutally efficient schedule. The last appointment of the day was slotted for three o'clock, and she managed to finish all the appointments by quarter to four and paperwork by four thirty, with a list of follow-up calls for Robin to make the next day and a stack of filing to go with it.

Lizzie had hit her second wind about 2:00 p.m. but now, with the work done, found herself at loose ends.

What she really wanted to do was drive to Josh's house, go inside, strip all his clothes off, and continue what they'd begun last night.

And that would be a big mistake. Engaging in an affair was risky enough. But she didn't have to be totally stupid about it. In the past Lizzie wouldn't have cared, but it was a different situation with Josh. Until this past year, she'd always kept her work and social life distinctly separate. Neither interfered with the other and it worked perfectly. And then Ian had come along, and for the first time she'd blurred the lines. It had been an unqualified disaster, and she didn't want to make the same mistakes. She had to look at the big picture.

The big picture said that Josh was a hot single doc who wasn't looking for anything permanent and she was temporary and definitely attracted. That part of it worked. What didn't work was that she was discovering she had feelings. Attachments. Like how she hadn't wanted him to get out of bed this morning. Like how it had hurt just a little that he didn't even consider asking her to go to the hospital with him. She wouldn't have, but the offer might have been nice.

This wasn't like her. Usually she welcomed the distance. Like when she was a kid and didn't like different foods touching each other on her plate. Compartmentalizing worked.

It was different in Jewell Cove. Everything seemed to blend together. Friends, neighbors, work, play . . . and, most of all, Josh. And that was very, very troubling. Josh Collins was getting under her skin.

What she really needed was a sounding board, so she picked up the phone and called Charlie. Lizzie hadn't spent a lot of time with her best friend lately, and it was time to remedy the situation. Charlie was thrilled with Lizzie's offer of pizza for dinner, particularly since Dave had taken on a moonlighting job for a few days, working on someone's boat up in Bar Harbor.

One Gino's special later, and Lizzie was on Charlie's doorstep.

The first thing Lizzie noticed was that Charlie had really expanded over the last few weeks. "Look at you! You're huge!" Lizzie said bluntly, but smiled from ear to ear. "How many weeks have you got left again?" It seemed like only yesterday she'd shown up to find

Charlie with a baby bump, and now she looked ready to pop.

Charlie laughed. "Nearly six. And I'm hitting that point where I feel like I am ready to move things along. It's like walking around with a basketball sitting on your bladder." Charlie waggled her fingers for the pizza box. "Come on in; we're starving."

Lizzie went in and slid off her sandals. "Hey, did you hear? Jess had a baby boy this morning. Over eight pounds and all ten fingers and toes. The family is over the moon."

"Oh yay!" Charlie's smile was wide. "And lucky Jess. I'm starting to understand how she's felt for the last month."

"I'm really sorry I haven't been around more," Lizzie apologized as she followed Charlie into the kitchen and put the pizza on the butcher block. "Work's kept me a bit busy, but I've been to see my mom, too, and I've been running on the beach a lot. Turns out I do okay with solitude. Who would have thought it?"

Charlie chuckled as she went for plates. "Lizzie darling, I think you're ready to hear something."

Lizzie finished opening the pizza box and faced her friend. "Oh?"

"Honey, you always had to go from one thing to another without stopping and you never really took time to be with yourself. I don't know why that is, but I think it's wonderful that you're actually comfortable enough with yourself now to enjoy your own company."

Lizzie sank down on one of the bar stools. "Cripes, Charlie. That's profound."

Charlie raised an eyebrow. "It happens now and again. I've probably just burned up my one remaining brain cell with that bit of insight." Charlie handed Lizzie a plate.

The pizza was still hot and Lizzie thought about what Charlie'd said as she slid a slice onto her plate. It was true, she supposed. She worked hard, and she'd played hard, too. She'd kept up a pretty active social life, but how meaningful had it really been? Not one of those friends had checked in with her since she'd left Springfield. Not one. And that might have stung a little except Lizzie realized she didn't really miss them, either. What did that say about her relationships?

Instead she found herself thinking about Josh. His smile, the way he kissed, how he looked steering the boat into the leaning dock at Lovers' Island and talked about searching for buried treasure. She was going to miss that when she left town.

Oh boy. She was in trouble, wasn't she? And wasn't that why she was here, after all? To have Charlie talk some sense into her?

"Charlie? I've done something really, really stupid."

Charlie plopped a piece of pizza on her plate, ripped off two pieces of paper towels in lieu of napkins, and handed Lizzie a soda from the fridge. "Oh, how bad can it be?" she joked. "What'd you do, sleep with Josh?"

Heat rushed up Lizzie's face.

"Oh shit. You did? Lizzie! When?" Pizza forgotten, Charlie sat on a stool and stared at her friend.

"Last night. Though we came close . . . once before."

"Last night? What . . . how?" Charlie popped the top on her soda and leaned in, her eyes twinkling. "Well. How was it?"

Lizzie couldn't help it; she laughed. "That's like four questions, Charlie. Pick one and I'll answer it. Maybe."

"Easy. First question: how was it?"

Lizzie looked down at her pizza, suddenly feeling a little bashful, which was not her style at all.

"Truthfully? It was amazing." She fought to keep the memories from surfacing again. They were more than a little X-rated and had been distracting her all day. She lifted her eyes and found Charlie studying her in the way she always did—with an honest eye.

"Honey," Charlie said softly. "Was it really that good?"

Lizzie felt unfamiliar emotions swamping her. "Don't. Don't talk in that tone of voice, okay? It makes me feel like I'm, I don't know, fragile or something."

Charlie sighed. "Okay, then I'll just ask. Are you falling in love with him?"

"Of course not," she denied quickly, and then her heart gave a strange lurch. No, it wasn't possible. She wasn't falling in love, for God's sake. She didn't *do* love. "It's just sex. I mean, I like him and everything. And last night when he found out that Abby's pregnant, the look on his face, I mean, he looked so conflicted. And he just kind of stands to the side, out of the way. And his family relies on him to hold things together, you know? They don't even realize they're doing it."

Charlie was smiling at her. "Liz. You know that old quote about 'the lady doth protest too much'?"

"I'm not in love with him," she insisted. Again, the weird thump in her chest. "I can't be, Charlie. I don't fall in love, you know that. I don't have time for love."

"Correction. You didn't have time for love. You always made sure you were too busy so you had a good excuse. But this summer you slowed down. Started to smell the roses. And the pheromones." Charlie lifted her slice of pizza and took a healthy bite of ham and pineapple.

"You just want that to be true," Lizzie argued. She picked up her pizza and started to eat, but a sense of panic had begun to swirl through her stomach. Love? What an idiotic notion. Love just got in the way. Love hurt.

More than that, love meant a commitment. Some people avoided commitment because they didn't want to be tied down, but Lizzie looked at it differently. When you committed yourself to someone, it was a promise. A promise to be there for them, to put them first.

And when you did that, you ran the risk of always letting them down. As much as she loved her father, as much as her parents had loved each other, Lizzie had seen the hurt in her mom's eyes when Russ had put his career first over family. In later years, when he'd slowed down, it had been better. And so Lizzie had learned from both the earlier days of the marriage and the later ones. And she was pretty sure what she was capable of. And what she wasn't.

"What are you really afraid of?" Charlie asked.

Lizzie put down her pizza. "I don't know. Failure? Russ Howard left big shoes to fill."

Charlie took a drink of soda. "That's always been your problem. Trying to be your dad. I don't know who made you feel like you had to, but they did you a huge disservice. The problem is you only want to be the best parts of your dad. Perfection doesn't exist, honey. Not even for him."

"Yeah, I think I've figured that out lately."

They were quiet for a few minutes, picking at their food. Charlie finally spoke. "So what are you going to do about Josh?"

Lizzie gave an amused huff. "Actually, I was kind of hoping you'd tell me what I should do."

Charlie shifted on the stool, ran her hand over the mound of her belly. Lizzie had never really considered children, but with Jess having her baby today, Abby announcing her pregnancy, and Charlie nearly ready to pop, marital and parental bliss seemed to surround her. She couldn't escape it if she tried.

"Liz," Charlie finally said, "Josh is a good guy. You could do a lot worse."

"But he's here, and I'm there, and the long-distance thing . . ."

"Then don't leave."

"And do what?" She pushed her plate aside, feeling slightly ill. "You have your job. The clinic doesn't need another doctor. Besides, I'm an ER doctor. This is fine for now, but honestly? Luke Pratt's case had me so fired up that I know where I belong. It's in an emergency room, Charlie. Not a family clinic in a small town."

"But if you were in love . . ."

Lizzie shook her head. "And then what? Be resentful because I'm unhappy in every other way? How well do you think a relationship could withstand that? Besides, I'm not in love with Josh. And he's not in love with me."

"So the other alternative then is an affair. A hot, steamy, summertime love affair with an end date."

It really was the only alternative, other than calling it quits altogether. And they'd already tried that and failed miserably. She supposed it had something to do with not really wanting to stay away from each other. . . .

"I need to lay out some ground rules, don't I?" Lizzie said glumly. Why couldn't sex or relationships or whatever this was be simple? Instead it had to be labeled as something and boundaries established and all sorts of other inconvenient categorizations.

"Probably," Charlie answered. "And Liz, there's still a good chance you could get hurt. I mean it, Josh is a really good guy. There aren't a lot of those around."

There were things Charlie didn't know, of course. And Josh had his demons. He wasn't perfect . . . but Lizzie kind of liked him better now that she knew he had a few flaws.

"I'm more worried that I'll be the one doing the hurting," Lizzie admitted. "I should probably sleep on it a while, huh?"

Charlie smiled. "Sweetie, overthinking is not your style. You jump in with both feet and you're passionate about it. You see what you want and you go for it. I've always admired that. Just be careful. I'm afraid one of these days that way of thinking is going to catch up with you and you're not going to be ready for it."

Lizzie thought back to the couple leaving the hospital without their baby. She thought about her mom, and her dad, and all the crap that had hit her in the past year.

It was time her life started on the upswing, and maybe her move to Jewell Cove had kick-started the process. It had certainly given her some perspective.

"Know what?" She sat up straighter and rolled her shoulders as an idea struck. "I think I hit that point the weekend I showed up in Jewell Cove and turned thirty. I need to let go of what's been holding me back."

"What do you mean?"

Now that the idea had popped into her head, it made perfect sense. She'd spent so much time holding on to what had been and burying herself in work so she wouldn't have to face letting go. That was where all her trouble had begun.

"Charlie, I need to put my parents' house on the market. It's not doing any good sitting there vacant, the way my dad left it. It's time I faced it and stopped wishing things were back the way they were. Life is different and it'll never be the same again. I need to let go. And yeah, maybe that's partially metaphorical, but it's true."

"Lizzie. Are you sure you're not just reacting to the situation and jumping from one thing into another? Maybe shifting your focus to the house is your way of avoiding dealing with Josh."

Her assessment stung a bit, but that was why Lizzie had come to Charlie. Charlie loved her and didn't try to sugarcoat her words. "Charlie, I'm positive." The more she spoke, the more she was certain. "I've been holding on too tight. If I want to move on, I need to make some decisions. I don't want to live in the house, Charlie. It should be with a family who can enjoy it. Make new memories."

Charlie reached over and patted her hand. "As long as you're sure."

"I'll ask Josh if I can have a few days. Meet a Realtor. Arrange to put stuff in storage."

"If you're determined, I can go help if you'd like."

Gratitude swept through Lizzie. "Really? It wouldn't be too much for you?"

Charlie laughed. "Listen, I'm glad I was able to take some time off work before the baby comes. But the nursery is ready, Dave is working, and I'm actually bored now and again. A few days with my best friend? Tell me, when am I going to get the opportunity for that after the baby's born? We'll drive down in your fancy car, pack up some stuff, list the house, go out to eat. A girls' weekend."

It occurred to Lizzie that her friendship with Charlie was the one relationship she trusted completely. What would she do without her best friend? They'd always been there for each other.

"We haven't had a real girls' weekend in months," Lizzie agreed. "I'd love to have you come. I don't even care if you do anything."

"Well, you won't have to face it alone. I guess that's something."

A new energy filled Lizzie. "It's more than something. Charlie, I know you had to drag me here for my birthday, but I'm glad you did. I did need the break. And this thing with Josh . . . a few days apart and some clear thinking will help. We both know it can't be a real thing. Maybe a summer fling is just what we both need to move on to the next stage in our lives."

"Sure, maybe," Charlie replied. Lizzie didn't think she sounded convinced, but it didn't matter. What mattered was feeling somewhat in charge of her life again. Making decisions. Moving forward.

When she left Charlie's an hour later, her stomach stuffed with pizza, her heart was also full. And while she didn't know what the future held, she knew how she was going to start making it better.

There was a Realtor's lockbox on the door and Lizzie leaned back, stretching out the kinks brought on from too much bending over. She'd pretty much managed a miracle in three short days.

Right now Charlie was folding clothing into boxes to be donated to a local homeless shelter. Lizzie had given her that job since it was low on the physical exertion scale and because stepping into her mom and dad's closets had brought back too many memories. It was the smells, really. Who knew they could last so long, the personal scents that were made up of years of living and loving and simply being in this house?

Lizzie was packing up the kitchen. She wasn't sure what she was going to do with all the household items, and soon a moving company was coming with a pod so she could store most of the boxes until a later date.

All the hard work had kept her mind off of Josh—well, mostly anyway.

Josh had been more than accommodating when she'd called asking for the time. All she'd had to say was that she'd decided it was time to sell the house and could she have a few days and he'd agreed. He'd even said it was only fair since she'd covered his butt during a family "thing," so it was no problem. No mention of their night together. No mention of anything at all.

It had almost been too easy. And it occurred to her that lately, when she got the things she wanted, she often wished they hadn't come so easily. Would Josh miss her when she was away? Or was he giving her space to figure out what she wanted? He probably was. She figured he was that smart.

Too smart for her in all likelihood.

But there wasn't time to think about it. Thirty minutes later a van from a charity came to collect some of the furniture. After that the pod arrived and Lizzie, along with a few burly men, set about loading it with the boxes she'd packed. In the middle of the chaos, a van from a local women's shelter showed up to collect the boxes of clothing.

There wasn't time for Lizzie to linger over items or get caught up in a lot of emotion, which was just how she wanted it. More than once she caught herself with a lump in her throat over simple things she hadn't thought of in years. Rather than dwell, she'd forced herself to carry on.

By 7:00 p.m. Lizzie and Charlie were tired and the house was very, very empty.

Lizzie leaned on the island in the kitchen and sighed. "It was so busy I didn't have time to be sentimental."

"Are you now?" Charlie braced her hands at her back and stretched.

"A little," Lizzie admitted. "It feels . . . final."

"I'm sorry, Lizzie. About your dad, and your mom . . . about all of it."

"I know. But it was the right thing to do. It feels good, even if it hurts."

Charlie nodded. "We should stop and see your mom tomorrow on the way home."

"I'd like that." She felt awkward and sad asking Charlie the next question, but of anyone in the world, she trusted Charlie the most. Especially with the truth.

"If we visit, will you do me a favor, Charlie? Will you watch my mom and give me your honest, medical opinion of her condition? I like to think I'm objective, but I know I'm not. And I'm the one who has to make decisions now. I don't have my dad taking point anymore." The burden weighed heavily. "Hell, the power of attorney all falls to me."

"Of course I will."

"Thanks." Relieved, she boosted herself away from the counter. "Let's get to the hotel. I booked us a nice room for tonight, and we'll order in room service, and watch a movie on pay-per-view. Like the old days, only a little more upscale."

"What? No microwave popcorn and dollar movie rentals?"

"Not this time. Lobster, steak . . . you name it, it's yours."

Lizzie locked the door behind her, leaving the porch light on. She wouldn't think about it anymore. The memories were hers to cherish, along with photographs and mementos. They were not for sale. All that was on the market was concrete and brick and wood and paint and all the other physical trappings of a home.

Not the love. Not the commitment, or the persistence to see it through, for better or for worse.

CHAPTER 16

Charlie woke the next morning with a throbbing headache, so rather than stop to see Rosemary, Lizzie took her straight back to Jewell Cove with strict orders to rest and put her feet up for a few days. Lizzie also made sure Charlie had a bottle of water the whole drive back to Maine, because she suspected Charlie was dehydrated. But the extra fluid meant more bathroom stops, and by the time Lizzie dropped Charlie at home it was two in the afternoon.

Lizzie couldn't help being concerned. Perhaps the weekend had been too strenuous for her. Charlie certainly wasn't her usual talkative self, and her smile was a little less bright as she said she thought she'd go inside for a nap.

"I'm sorry if I worked you too hard," Lizzie apologized.

"No, no! That's not it. I think I just tire out a little easier now. Besides, we did stay up late." Charlie sent a lopsided smile. "I've missed our midnight chats, Lizzie.

It was good, so don't worry. I'll have a nap and be right as rain."

"I hope so. When's your next checkup?"

"Wednesday. Don't worry, okay?"

"Okay." Lizzie leaned over and gave Charlie a quick hug. "Call me if you need me for anything."

"I will. And I'm sorry we didn't get to see your mom."

"I'll go up on my next day off. Don't worry."

Charlie took her overnight bag and went inside and Lizzie started up the car again. She was edgy. The work of the previous days had tired her out, but today she was at loose ends, trying to make sense of everything that had happened. Maybe she should have taken longer to go through the house. She wasn't certain the house was the cause of her restlessness, though. There were other things that were unresolved. Like the situation with Josh.

So where to now? She didn't want to go back to her cottage. All that waited for her there were loneliness and isolation. If anything, Lizzie wanted to feel alive and vital and active. In the past she'd make plans to go on a trip or zip lining or parasailing or on some other cockamamie scheme to give her an adrenaline rush. No such luck today.

But the sun was bright and the August heat soaked into her skin as she drove into town with the top down. She cruised down Main Street, searching for something, anything, to keep her occupied for another few hours. She wasn't really hungry, and none of the shops held much appeal, either. She could grab a suit and head for Fiddler's Beach, she supposed, but on a hot day like today it was bound to be crammed with tourists. What she'd really like was the breeze in her hair as she skimmed over the waves, leaving all her troubles behind.

When she saw a familiar blond head in the crowd on the docks, she braked and took a closer look.

The throng of people shifted and she saw him clearer now. Cutoff denim shorts, ratty T-shirt in army green, and his flip-flops. Her mouth watered just looking at him, and she smiled to herself as she pulled into the parking lot just above the docks, scanning for an open space. Last spring Charlie's description of Josh had been "a widowed army veteran." And he was. But oh, he was a lot more. She suspected Charlie had known exactly what she was doing when she asked Lizzie to cover her mat leave.

She got lucky and waited as a car pulled out of a space, and she pulled in. She could still see Josh, making his way to Sally's Dairy Shack, where the line was probably a dozen people deep. Anticipation curled down low in Lizzie's belly as she got out of the car and locked it, then adjusted the strap of her hobo bag on her shoulder.

He turned around just before she reached him, and a smile lit his face even though she couldn't really see his eyes because of his sunglasses.

"You're back," he said.

"Just. I dropped Charlie off at home and went looking for some trouble. And now I've found some."

His cheeks flushed and she was glad of it. "Trouble?"

She shrugged. "I just didn't feel like going back to the cottage yet. I need to . . . assimilate."

He nodded and they took a step forward as the line moved. "Rough few days, huh?"

"I've had better. Though it wasn't as bad as I

expected. Probably because I put off going through a lot of the personal things and put them in a pod instead."

"Rome wasn't built in a day. Putting the house up for sale was a huge step. Good for you, Lizzie."

Another step forward, closer to the order window.

"You've been there. You'd know."

"Yep." He nodded at her. "So. Trouble. What did you have in mind?"

About twenty things that she wouldn't dare say in public. He looked delectable today, like some tanned, blond surfer god built for fun. "Well, it looks like first thing on my agenda is ice cream."

"Wow. Living dangerously."

"I know. I might go really crazy and have a swirl cone today. Soft-serve is my favorite."

"And then what?"

She pushed her sunglasses to the top of her head. "A trip in the boat might be fun. Unless you don't have her out today."

"I just came back, actually. I took Matt and Suze out tubing in a nice little bay just north of here. Sarah picked them up at the wharf and I decided to grab an ice cream before heading home."

"Oh. Well, never mind."

They were nearly at the order window now. "We can still go out. I filled her with gas and there's lots of afternoon left."

"You don't mind?"

They'd reached the window and had to pause to give their order. "One regular swirl cone please," Lizzie said, and then Josh stepped up.

"Hey, Sally. I'll take a double scoop of your butter pecan."

Sally, who Lizzie guessed had to be in her sixties, raised an eyebrow at Josh. "Honey, you've been ordering the same flavor for as long as I can remember."

"Why mess with a good thing?" he asked, and Lizzie watched as he winked at the older woman. "Come on, Sal. You can't improve on perfection."

Sally laughed and grabbed a cone, went to the softserve machine, and looked over her shoulder at Lizzie. "You have to watch out for this one."

Lizzie grinned. "What, Josh? He's harmless."

Sally gave the cone a final flourish and handed it over to Lizzie. "He'd like you to think that, but I've known him since before his voice changed. Don't let that angelic look fool you."

"God, I'm standing right here," Josh complained, and Sally laughed.

Sally began scooping Josh's cone. "You know I'm right. And it's three fifty for the both of you."

"I'll get it," Lizzie said, reaching into her bag.

"Yeah, and then I'll owe you. No thanks." Josh took his cone from Sally and reached in his pocket.

But Lizzie handed Sally a five. "Thanks, Sally. For the cone and the warning. Well worth the cost."

Sally was laughing as she took the bill, and then Josh spoke up. "Hey. What is this?"

"Butter pecan on the bottom. New flavor on the top. Dulce de leche. Fancy way of saying 'caramel,' but I bet you like it."

He shook his head, but Lizzie grinned. It was clear who ruled the roost at the Dairy Shack and her name was Sally.

Lizzie and Josh wandered toward the docks, licking their cones along the way. "Are you really fooling me with your boy-next-door good looks?" Lizzie asked innocently.

"It's worked so far," he commented, and then she elbowed him in the arm and he laughed. It was a rich, full, easy sound that made her heart feel big.

"Now I know why you got a double scoop. You need to feed that giant ego of yours."

He chuckled beside her. "Damn, I missed you the last few days."

Lizzie stopped walking and stared at him. "Josh. You did?"

He met her gaze. "Yeah, I did. At the office, too. I like discussing cases with you. I like lots of things about you."

Her ice cream was melting quickly, and she had to either swipe at it with her tongue or have it running all down her fingers. She chose to lick, right around the base where the ice cream met the cone. When she looked up at Josh, his eyes were twinkling at her.

"Shut up," she said mildly. "I can only imagine what comments are swirling around in that brain of yours. Besides, you need to mind your own drip."

He didn't take his eyes off her as he licked the edges of his cone. And when he'd gotten the caramelly trickles under control, he winked at her and held out his hand.

"Come on. Let's take the *Constant* out for a spin. You can tell me about your trip and I'll fill you in on what's been going on here."

Now she understood the restless feeling she'd had when she'd driven into town today. She'd wanted to see him, get caught up on what had happened in her absence, see his smile, and hear his laugh. And feel his touch. Knowing exactly what she wanted, she put her

fingers in his and let him tug her along down the ramp
to where the *Constant* was tied.

Josh started the engine and eased the boat away from
the dock. Lizzie sat in the opposite seat, her handbag
tucked in by her feet. She looked tired. Tired but beautiful, with her hair falling around her shoulders and
wearing a pair of tight jeans and a yellow top that reminded him of sunshine and lemons.

He was glad to have her back. They'd have to talk
sometime about what had happened, but for now it was
good just to see her.

"So," he asked, calling to her over the top of the
sound of the motor and the waves, "where to, madam?"

She got up from her seat and stood next to him, the
wind blowing her hair off her face as she turned her
face up to the sky. Damn, she was something. Soft
where a woman needed to be soft but strong, too.

When she lowered her head and looked down into
his eyes, he already knew what she was going to say.

"Take me to Lovers' Island."

The trip seemed to take ten times as long as he
would have liked. Once she'd said the words, it didn't
matter that they were out on open water traveling fifty
miles an hour. Tension tightened between them, taut
with anticipation and possibility. He knew what she
meant by asking to go there, and smart or not, he was
willing to go along.

They skimmed over the waves and the shape of the
island appeared, hazy at first and then clearer until he
could see the outline of the dock, the view of it almost
like a type of foreplay. Lizzie came over, slid onto his
lap so that he had to look over her shoulder to see
where he was going. She twined her fingers through

the hair over his right ear and his breath shuddered through him. She was killing him here. . . .

Afraid of keeping up the speed when he was so distracted, he throttled down until they were barely moving. Particularly when Lizzie leaned forward and was scraping her teeth down the side of his neck.

He cursed under his breath and gripped the wheel for dear life.

"I can't dock like this," he growled, "and I don't want to start drifting and risk you getting sick. Three minutes, Liz. Three and I'll have us there."

She sucked his earlobe into her mouth and his eyes rolled back into his head. Lizzie Howard was going to be the end of him; he was sure of it.

"Three minutes," she whispered, and he ached with the feel of her hips pressed against his. "Three minutes and one second and I start taking my clothes off."

Holy hell.

She slid off his lap and back to her seat while he pushed the throttle. The boat hit the tops of the crests, skimming over the tops until he had to slow down to approach the dock. Even then he was more reckless than usual, coming in hot and without his usual care. "Make sure we don't bump," he commanded, and she obeyed, leaning over her side and keeping the side of the boat off the dock. He looked at his watch. Two minutes and thirty-five seconds. He'd gotten here with time to spare. Not that her clothes weren't going to come off . . . they were. But not here. Not yet.

He took precious seconds to reach into a storage bin and grab an emergency blanket. It was dull and slightly musty smelling, but he doubted either of them cared at this moment. Lizzie was already out of the boat waiting for him, and with his heart racing he hopped out, took her hand, and led her up the wharf to the path.

There was only one place to be right now. And that was at the very top of the island. At the top of the world, with the sea all around them and not another soul for miles and miles. God, he felt about eighteen again, and full of testosterone and invincibility and the rash innocence that he was untouchable by consequence. But just in case he was wrong, he dropped his hand to his back pocket briefly, making sure his wallet was still there. He'd taken three condoms with him the night he'd been at Lizzie's, and they'd used two. There was still one left.

At the summit they stopped. Up until this second, neither of them had spoken. It had been all about the urgency. But now, with them face-to-face, the moment had arrived. Josh unfolded the blanket and spread it out on the thin grass, not caring too much if it was even or not. "Go ahead," he said, his voice rough with impatience and desire. "Your three minutes are up."

Her eyes sparked as she reached for the hem of her shirt and pulled it over her head.

He swallowed tightly, clenching his hands at his sides. He would not be a barbarian. He'd remain in complete control. Even if the rest of his damned brain went into a complete meltdown.

Next went the bra, dropped on the corner of the blanket. Her pale breasts were exposed to the sun and he longed to touch them, kiss them. Was dying to just lose himself inside her. And still he waited.

Her jeans were more of a struggle because they were tight, but being the efficient type, she skimmed her panties down with them so that when she stepped free of the denim she was completely naked. There was something so basic, so elemental, about being naked in nature that felt Garden of Eden–ish to him. And still, he waited. Waited for her to say the words. Besides, despite the uncomfortableness of the situation, he was enjoying, savoring, the moment. The sight of her, the freedom of it, the confidence. Damn, she was beautiful.

"What are you waiting for?" she asked.

There it was. He stripped off his T-shirt and tossed it on top of her pile of clothing. Then he reached for his wallet, took out the condom, and tossed it to her, then unbuttoned his shorts, slipped both them and his underwear off, and they joined the other articles. Now he and Lizzie were both stark naked with no sound but the waves on the rocks below and the wind whistling through the grass and shrubs.

The only two people in the world, with everything left behind them.

Josh stepped forward and took her in his arms, reveling in the feel of her skin pressed against his—breasts, pelvis, thighs, toes. Her arms looped around his neck as they kissed, long and deep.

"I wasn't sure you wanted this again," he uttered, filling his hand with her breast, watching with pleasure as she tipped her head back.

"Wanting it was never the problem," she replied, the last word coming out on a sweet breath.

Their coming together was urgent and yet not rushed. Josh lost himself in the feel of her surrounding him, made sure she reached her own measure of satisfaction before letting himself go. Gulls screamed overhead, Lizzie's cries echoing on the wind with them, and Josh covered her mouth with his as he found his own release. Nothing had ever been this wild, this sweet, this satisfying. His heart pounded and his ribs rose and fell with his breathing as he braced himself on his elbows and looked down into her face.

He was falling in love with her. He hadn't wanted to, and God knew she didn't want that from him, either. But it was there just the same. When they were together something just clicked into place. He'd thought he'd be able to keep it light. Noncommittal. But he really should have known better. He wasn't built that way. It went beyond attraction. It went beyond their differences—those were still there and they'd be foolish to ignore them. But deep down, right in the heart of things, he understood her. And he got the feeling that she understood him, too.

But he wouldn't say the words. Not now, perhaps not ever. Because if he'd learned anything from his marriage, it was that sometimes love simply wasn't enough.

"Josh?"

He blinked. Kissed her lightly and slid out of her body. But when he looked down, momentary panic froze his chest.

"What is it?" she asked, rising up to her elbows.

"The condom broke," he said tightly. "Shit. Lizzie, I'm sorry."

She looked up at him. "Not your fault. Don't freak out." She slid up the blanket and pushed her hair away from her face. "I can always Plan B it."

Of course she could. And probably should. Neither of them wanted her to get pregnant, did they? And yet the straightforward way she said it left a bitter taste in his mouth. She wasn't Erin, for God's sake, and he knew that. And Erin had deliberately let him believe she wanted his babies when she hadn't at all. Still, it stung that once again his genetic material was unquestionably undesirable.

Five minutes ago he'd been thinking he was falling in love with Lizzie and now he was faced with the knowledge that he still had way too much baggage to bring to a relationship.

"We kind of let our hormones get away with us, didn't we?" he asked, trying to ease the mood a little. He reached for his shorts and handed over her jeans and panties.

"I needed the outlet," she admitted, squirming into her panties and then reaching for her bra. She flashed him a smile, but it wasn't the intimate, slightly emotional smile of earlier. "Josh, really, it's going to be okay. We're not going to end up accidental parents or something."

"I know," he answered. "I just . . ." But he didn't know what he wanted to say. He didn't want to bring his past failures into the conversation.

She'd fastened her bra and pulled her shirt back on. "We probably should talk about what's happening between us. What this is going to look like, you know?"

He laughed a little. "It looks like we're a couple of horny teenagers."

She smiled, just a little bit, but some of the tension eased. "I know. Ever since that first day on the beach, I can't stop thinking about it. But it's physical, right? And I think we should make definite rules so that neither of us gets hurt down the road."

Ah, the rules. Rules according to Lizzie, no doubt. But he'd hear her out, because he wasn't at all comfortable with the direction his thoughts had gone this afternoon.

"Okay. What's the first rule?" he asked. He grabbed his shirt from the blanket and pulled it over his head.

"Rule number one: either of us can call it off at any time, no hard feelings."

"Ouch."

She frowned. "Josh, we both know I'm not staying in Jewell Cove. Charlie's going to want her job back. Therefore, this is a short-term thing. If it gets to be too much, I think we both need to know we can exit gracefully without a lot of drama."

This was sounding more like a business negotiation than a relationship. Maybe he should be happy about that.

Then why wasn't he?

"Okay," he agreed. "There's an opt-out feature. Got it."

"Rule number two." She ticked it off on her finger. "Our physical relationship can't bleed over into our working relationship. We have to be discreet."

"It doesn't get more discreet than an island in the middle of the ocean," he replied, starting to get annoyed at her rules. So far it was sex without consequences. Well, other than the broken rubber. And that annoyed him as well.

"Right," she agreed.

"And what about number three?" he asked.

"Number three?"

He regarded her steadily. "Sure, isn't there a number three to round things out?"

"Oh. Well, um . . ." She seemed momentarily flustered, and then she smiled at him again. "Let's leave number three open. Either of us has the right to institute a new rule as we feel is necessary."

Wow, this whole thing was sucking the romance out of the situation at a really quick rate. "So what you're saying is, we're having a secret fling that'll be over the minute Charlie's mat leave is done and we're going to amicably go our separate ways."

"Exactly!"

He started to laugh. "Do you really think that's possible? We're people. I mean, this sounds perfect in theory . . ." Actually, it didn't sound all that perfect at all. It sounded cold, calculated. Sexual satisfaction without any emotion or feeling. "But I'm not sure of the practicality of it."

"Loads of people have done friends with benefits before."

He leaned forward a little. "I'm not loads of people, Lizzie. I care about you. I couldn't make love to you otherwise."

Her face changed. He couldn't really say how, except that it was like a mask fell over her expression, shutting him out.

"You don't like me calling it 'making love,' do you?"

"Come on, Josh. It's not. It's sex. It's scratching an itch. We both know that."

He felt like his heart was in his throat when he responded, "What if it's not?"

She scrambled up from the blanket. "Don't be ridiculous. Of course that's all this is. Jeez, Josh."

When he got up, she took the opportunity to snatch the blanket up from the ground and start folding it.

"Would it be so bad?" he asked, his insides trembling. Did she think she was the only one who was scared? "Caring for someone?"

She held the blanket close to her chest. "I do care for you." For a moment her face softened. "Please don't think I don't. But you're talking about love. And that's impossible."

Right. Because he was so goddamned unlovable, though he really didn't understand why. Or maybe he just kept picking the wrong kind of woman. He should have listened to the voice in his head that said right from the beginning that Lizzie was too big for this small town. All he'd really wanted was a family of his own, the chance to practice medicine, and a little downtime on the water. A simple life. And the women he got involved with all wanted more.

He was tired of not being good enough.

"We should go," he said.

There was quiet for a few minutes, an awkward silence as they both absorbed what those three words meant. A refusal of her offer.

She looked down at a spot by his foot and her cheeks stained pink. "Um, shouldn't we, uh, dispose of that somehow?"

"I guess."

"There's not exactly a trash can nearby."

He wanted to laugh at her tart expression. The whole thing felt ridiculously surreal. "Can't we just throw it into the grass or something?"

At any other moment it would have been funny. Instead it was just uncomfortable. Lizzie reached into her bag. "Gross. Here," she said, digging around and coming up with a small paper bag from the pharmacy. "Put it in here until we can get to a garbage can."

He picked up the condom by his fingertips and dropped it into the bag. "Just like we were never here, huh?"

She sighed. "Josh—"

"No, I get it. And I even understand your rules,

Lizzie." He took a breath. "But I can't abide by them. It's not who I am. I thought it was for a little while. I honestly thought I could do this. Being with you was exciting and a rush. But I care for you. And if I'm going to be with someone . . . I think I really have to be with her, you know?" He looked at her, felt the first stabs of regret. "I don't know how to do sex for fun. I tried, but I guess I'm just not built that way."

"I don't have anything more to offer you." She met his gaze. "It wouldn't be fair of me to pretend I do."

He could appreciate that she was being brutally honest, but it didn't mean he had to like it. "You sell yourself short, but that's your problem, not mine," he replied. "You won't have to worry about being discreet from now on, okay? We'll dial it back, keep it strictly professional. No hard feelings."

"If that's what you want."

What he wanted was some emotion out of her. Something that said she was sorry their brief affair was over. That this wasn't so damned . . . easy for her. He thought of the night he found her crying on the beach. Mess and all, that was the Lizzie he really liked. But she didn't want to let herself be vulnerable, he realized. And when she was, she acted like she did today. By taking charge, taking risks. Not by letting someone in.

Someday she would have to, but he could tell that wasn't today. And he wasn't that man.

"Let's go," he suggested, turning his back. She picked up the blanket and clutched it to her chest and then started toward the path as if nothing had ever happened.

Frustrated, Josh kicked out at a rock, sending it tumbling. But when he did, his eyes lit on something odd.

"Lizzie, wait!" he called out.

She paused at the top of the path, but he turned away and knelt down to examine what he'd uncovered. The rock rolled down the slope, bouncing on a ridge and tumbling over the edge to the gully below.

"What is it?" she asked.

He reached down and rubbed at the dirt. There was a string there, old and dirty, and he dug around it, uncovering a lump of brown hide. He carefully pulled it out of the ground, weighted it in his palm.

"A drawstring pouch," he said, their argument forgotten. "A leather one, though the material's in pretty bad shape."

She dropped the blanket and came over. "Really? What's in it?"

Gingerly he undid the string and poured the contents of the bag into his palm.

CHAPTER 17

Temporarily forgetting the tension between her and Josh, Lizzie stared at the items as they tumbled into his hand. Coins, more than a dozen of them, and an ornate locket. All hidden under a silly rock. Or lost there.

"Those look old," she said, leaning over to peer into his hand.

"They *are* old," he confirmed. "Holy shit. Do you know what these are?" He touched the coins with his finger. "I think these are real gold, Lizzie. And silver. They're probably worth a fortune. I think this is part of the treasure."

She squatted down beside him. "Do you really think a treasure exists, Josh? Really? I mean, these could be worthless." His eyes were huge and she felt an unwanted tenderness wash over her. She could well imagine him as a blond, curly-haired boy searching for this very thing, with this exact rapt expression on his face.

"They're old. Even if they're not gold or anything, the age alone means they'd be worth something to a collector." He picked up the locket, the chain dangling over the edge of his hand. "Look at this. What do you suppose it's made of?"

The front of the locket was made from material different from anything she'd ever seen. Behind a glass crystal was a wispy pattern of delicate leaves like a fern or flower and tiny seed pearls adorning the bottom. "I have no idea. But it's beautiful."

He turned it over. "There are pictures inside." He moved it closer to his face as he opened it. "Interesting. Look at that and tell me what you see."

She took the pendant and examined the photo. "A big man, with black hair, and the moustache gives him quite a roguish look." She gave a laugh. "You know, he kind of reminds me of Tom a little bit."

"I think so, too. I think this might be Charles Arseneault."

"And the woman?"

Josh met Lizzie's gaze. "It has to be Constance Arnold. The woman he gave everything up for, the woman he married."

"Is Summer related to her? Do you think the pouch was hers? Why would she have such a thing here, in the middle of nowhere?"

"The stories have always said that she was instrumental in transporting slaves to Canada. If they used this island as a rendezvous, she could have been here, easily."

"I don't know about the coins, but this is definitely gold," Lizzie said, reaching out and touching the locket as it lay in his palm.

"We searched this island for years and found nothing," Josh said, standing. "To find it today . . ."

He didn't have to finish the sentence. Charles and

Constance had loved each other. A love big enough that they'd made sacrifices and taken risks, if the stories were indeed true. It certainly made what was between Josh and Lizzie look like a farce.

"What are you going to do with it?" Lizzie asked, dropping her hand. She took a step back. While their argument seemed forgotten, she couldn't gracefully exit. There was still the walk back to the dock and the boat ride back to Jewell Cove to endure.

"I'm going to take it back, have someone who's actually qualified look at it and appraise it." He poured the contents back into the pouch and pulled the string tight. "Then I'll see. I'm not even sure what ownership rules apply here."

"Right," she said weakly.

"We should probably head back anyway."

She nodded, turned away, and picked up the blanket again. For some strange reason there was a stinging behind her eyes. This was not how she'd imagined today ending. When she'd seen Josh on the waterfront, a little escape had seemed like the perfect outlet. But instead of it relieving her tension, now it just made her feel empty.

They picked their way down to the shore again, back to the dock where the boat was tied. Before they got on, though, Lizzie stopped Josh with a hand on his arm.

"Josh, I'm really sorry. I didn't mean for us to fight. I didn't mean to make things more difficult. I thought we needed to be honest is all." She swallowed thickly, more upset than she expected to be. "I'm sorry, too, that we're not on the same page. But it's better to know now than later, when we could both get hurt."

Her attempt to ease the situation didn't work,

though. Josh moved his arm from beneath her touch and lifted his hand, cupping her jaw in the curve of his palm. "Lizzie," he said softly, "who said I'm not hurt?"

"Josh," she choked out. God, the last thing she wanted to do was hurt him.

"It's okay," he answered, sliding his fingers off her skin. "I'll get over it. I was just kidding myself anyway. You've never made any secret of the fact that you aren't a small-town girl. You're a city girl who likes a city pace and you're going back to where you belong. I've learned my lesson."

He got into the boat, solicitously held out a hand to help her in, and then, once she was seated, started it up, backed away from the dock. It was only seconds until they were headed back to Jewell Cove, skimming over the chop as evening clouds began to move in, a precursor to the rain forecast for the next day. The sound of the motor filled the air, eliminating the need to talk. A good thing, too. She knew what he meant. He'd been comparing her to Erin and determining that he wouldn't make the same mistake twice. She didn't want to be hurt, but she was.

Twenty minutes later the wharf was in sight and Lizzie reached down and retrieved her bag, clutching the handle in her hands until her knuckles went white. Once they docked she'd be walking away from Josh. She should have known it was a mistake to start anything with him. *Hell, should have?* She had known. And ignored it. At least Josh wouldn't fire her. He needed her to cover in Charlie's absence, and Lizzie knew him well enough now to know he'd maintain a professional veneer for the next few months until Charlie returned to work.

He didn't even tie the boat, just pulled up slowly,

eased it next to the dock, and held it steady while Lizzie got out.

She looked down at him once her feet were on the solid surface. "Josh, are we okay? I don't want things to be awkward at work, you know?"

He looked up at her. "We're fine. No hard feelings, Lizzie. We want different things. Like you said, better to figure it out now."

His eyes were utterly sincere, but there was a tightness in his jaw. She *had* hurt him, hadn't she? Without meaning to. And all he'd been was supportive since she moved here.

Once again, she felt as though she'd screwed up everything.

"I'll see you at the clinic then," she answered, mustering up a smile.

"Sure will," he replied, and sent her a smile. But not the intimate one she'd gotten used to, or the one with the edge that said he was dying to touch her again. This was unfailingly polite and made her feel like crap.

He pulled away, leaving her standing there on the dock feeling like an idiot.

Finally she turned her back and walked up the pier, to the lot where her car was parked. And as she drove back to the cottage at Fiddler's Rock, she figured she would have been better off going zip lining after all.

Over the following days Lizzie formed a pattern of existence.

She worked her shifts according to the schedule posted, saw patients, wrote prescriptions, smiled when it was required, spoke to Josh when necessary, and was the model of professionalism at the clinic. She checked in with Charlie every other day, often taking a treat or something she'd picked up for the baby: brownies, a stuffed toy, a rattle, fresh lemonade. On the opposite days she called to check up on her mom, sometimes talking to her and other times talking with the staff.

Lizzie and Charlie made the drive the following Sunday. Charlie was feeling better, still tired, and Lizzie had checked her blood pressure and found it higher than she would have liked, so she was keeping a close eye.

But a day out would be good, particularly one where they could drive with the top down and relax with each other.

Right now they were past Portland and almost to the state line when Charlie rolled her head against the seat back, looking at Lizzie from behind oversized sunglasses. "Okay, chick. I've been waiting for days for you to say something about Josh and you're closed up tighter than a clam. Either you two are being incredibly discreet or that whole situation blew up. Which is it?"

A strange emotion clutched at Lizzie's heart for just a second. "It blew up. Actually, I blew it up. But it's okay, Charlie. Really."

"Uh-huh." Charlie still stared at her. "You trying to convince me or you?"

Lizzie concentrated on the road. "I didn't bring you along for the third degree."

"Fair enough."

And in typical Charlie fashion, she shut up.

It drove Lizzie crazy. It was just like the first day she'd been in Jewell Cove, sitting on Charlie's deck, such a mess about her dad and her leave of absence and everything else that she wanted to talk and was scared to. And Charlie had simply waited. Just like she was doing now, her face turned up toward the sun, her hand resting on her swollen belly.

"I hate it when you do that."

Charlie never cracked a smile. "Do what?"

"That whole silent treatment thing."

Still, Charlie kept her head against the back of the seat and let the light bathe her face. "Liz, you said you don't want to talk about it. So I'm not. You're a big girl. It's none of my business."

"Argh!" Lizzie's fingers tightened on the wheel. "You know I can see through everything you're saying or doing, right?"

Finally Charlie smiled. "Of course. Just like I know it's driving you insane."

To demonstrate the point, she went quiet once more.

"Fine," Lizzie finally said, setting the cruise control. "I put it out there. The ground rules, like we talked about that weekend we packed up the house."

"What happened?" Charlie looked over at her again. Lizzie couldn't see her eyes, but she could tell Charlie was intrigued.

"He turned me down flat."

Lizzie didn't feel the need to mention that they'd had mind-blowing sex at the summit of Lovers' Island first. It turned out there were a few things she didn't share with her best friend.

"Turned you down? Are you serious?" Finally Charlie's head came away from the back of the seat.

The rejection still stung, and at first Lizzie had thought it was just her pride talking. But it wasn't all that. And it wasn't just the knowledge that she'd hurt Josh, either, though she felt terrible about that. She was hurting, too. She missed him. Missed joking with him, talking to him, knowing he was there if she needed to vent. She kept going back to that night on the beach when he'd held her in his arms. That scene stayed in the forefront of her memory far more than their sexual encounters.

It hadn't been just sex for her, either. She'd merely told herself that.

So she looked over at Charlie for a moment, then fixed her eyes back on the road again. "It's better now, anyway," she replied. "It wasn't just fun. We were starting to get emotionally involved. Josh is a keeper, Charlie. I'd only be wasting his time. He wants the white picket fence and wife and kids and that's just not what I want."

"Are you sure?"

"What?"

Traffic was light and Lizzie put on her signal and pulled out to pass a car, then smoothly pulled back into her lane again.

"Liz, up until this week, you've been happier in Jewell Cove than I've seen you in a long time. But I think you're scared. I think you want to be your father and you're afraid you might be. It's hard to be married to two loves. One of them inevitably becomes a mistress—the one you see when you can make time. I loved your parents, Lizzie, and I loved being in your home. But your mom was a mistress a lot of the time."

"I know," Lizzie whispered.

"And if you were honest with Josh, and with yourself, then maybe you did the right thing. But I'm not convinced you've been honest with yourself. Because that would mean turning things on their head and you've had a lot of that already this year."

"You really should have specialized in psych, you know that?" But Lizzie's tone was teasing. Charlie had a way about her, a way of getting to the heart of things without making Lizzie completely defensive.

"I see a lot of patients come through my door. I get to study people a lot, see what makes them tick. What stresses them out and makes them happy."

"Sometimes I think I do a lot of stuff to prove that I'm happy whether I am or not," Lizzie admitted.

"Well, at any rate, I'm sorry about you and Josh, though I understand it. Is everything okay at the office?"

"Perfect," Lizzie responded, and Charlie laughed. "I sounded a little snippy there, didn't I?" Lizzie asked.

"If I know Josh, he's the model of efficiency and professionalism. He can hide his feelings quite well, too, you know."

Except he'd let Lizzie in, she realized. He'd told her things about his marriage, about his life, that she was sure he hadn't shared freely elsewhere. And that made her feel even worse.

They arrived at the home just after lunch. Lizzie had picked up some yarn at Treasures, just as she'd promised during her last visit. She also brought a few treats from the bakery, not knowing what might tempt her mom this time and hedging her bets. And then she prayed it was a good day.

It was not.

There were moments of lucidity, but Rosemary was easily agitated and even the acceptance of the yarn was underwhelming. Rosemary kept looking for her purse since she seemed to think she owed Lizzie money, which Lizzie took just to appease her mom's agitation and then put back when she wasn't looking. Charlie's eyes were soft with sympathy as they sat for tea and sweets. Lizzie didn't even mention putting the house up for sale. On a good day maybe, but today she didn't want to upset her mom any more than she already was.

By three o'clock Lizzie was exhausted.

They were back in the car and driving home when Lizzie let out a huge breath. "Damn. I should be visiting more often. At least every week."

"Why aren't you? Is it the long drive?"

"It's not that long. I don't know. I think I'm scared of what I'll find each time."

Charlie reached over and patted her thigh. "Sweetie, I can't imagine what that's like. But maybe if you visit more often, the changes won't seem as drastic. I don't know what the answer is."

"You see the difference, don't you?"

Charlie pushed her sunglasses to the top of her head. "Unfortunately, yes. I know today wasn't a good day, but she's not as steady as she used to be, either. She's in the right place. If you tried to look after her at home, you'd constantly be worried about falls and accidents and you'd have to hire help. And then you'd exhaust yourself at night when you had to do it alone."

What Charlie was saying made sense. "I just wish I didn't feel so guilty. Every time I leave her I feel like the worst daughter in the world."

Charlie knit her brows. "Now you stop that. You are not the worst daughter. You're giving her the kind of care she needs, for her sake, not yours. And I'm sure if you asked, her doctor would approve her going out for a day with you. You could spend some time together outside the facility."

Another good idea. What if she brought her mom to Jewell Cove for a day? They could visit the wharf, eat lunch on the deck overlooking the ocean, maybe even stop by a shop or two and pick out something nice and pretty she could put in her room. Or go to Treasures for more yarn.

"What about your mom, Charlie?" Lizzie changed the subject. "Are your parents going to visit when the baby is born?"

Charlie laughed. "Oh, they'll come up for a few days, I suppose. Probably stay at the inn, since the motel won't quite meet their standards. I don't think they're as thrilled about being grandparents as I'd like. But then, I didn't expect it, either. I'm happy, and that's what matters. Their expectations don't bother me anymore."

"I wish I could get to that Zen place," Lizzie lamented. Problem was, she didn't really know anymore what would make her happy. Until she figured that out, she felt all over the map. The one thing she kept clinging to was going back to her job in Springfield and picking up where she'd left off. She wasn't sure that was possible, though.

They were half an hour outside Jewell Cove when Charlie's face brightened. "Oh my gosh, I forgot to ask you. Have you heard anything about the stuff Josh found out at Aquteg Island? Apparently he found a locket and coins or something."

Lizzie felt her face heat. "I heard," she answered, not wanting to elaborate. "Any news about what he's going to do with it?"

"It's all hearsay. Dave heard it from Rick, who was down at the waterfront, but apparently the coins are real and he gets to keep them. He took the locket to Abby and Tom, to see if it belongs to Tom's family. Abby's found a lot of photos at Foster House, and Tom's family probably have some, too. I guess the locket has a picture of a man who might be Charles Arseneault. Isn't it exciting? I haven't been here long and even I know the story of the rumored treasure out there. People will be going crazy now looking for more."

The idea of the island crawling with treasure hunters made Lizzie feel a little bit ill. She'd started to think of it as her and Josh's little paradise, wild and untouched. Which wasn't accurate at all, but lately none of her feelings seemed logical.

"What's he going to do with it?" Lizzie hadn't asked Josh any questions. Asking about the leather bag and its contents would only remind them of that afternoon, and she was trying to avoid that as much as possible.

"No one knows. He could sell the coins and make a killing, I'm guessing. Though Josh doesn't strike me as someone who cares too much about being rich."

No, he didn't. Josh was just . . . Josh. Lizzie had often heard the saying "enough is as good as a feast," and that definitely applied to him. She flashed back to a memory of him splashing into the water, diving under, and coming up with his eyes twinkling. Perhaps Josh had had enough heartache in his life that he focused on appreciating the simple things.

Charlie winced and let out a breath. Lizzie frowned as she glanced over. "You okay?"

"Just Braxton Hicks. I've been having them for a few weeks now. They're just uncomfortable. Twingy."

"You've got a plan if you go into labor, though, right?"

Charlie nodded. "Dave's got his cell on him at all times now. My hospital bag is all packed. First babies take a while anyway, Liz. We'll have time to get there."

"You call me if you need anything, though, okay?"

"I know. And if my feet puff up like mad or I get a blinding headache I'll call you. I know my BP is up."

"You're patronizing me, but I don't care as long as you mean it."

Charlie smiled. "I love you, Liz."

"Well, right back at you."

Dave was waiting for them, standing on the front step when Charlie arrived. Lizzie watched as Charlie got out of the car, an awkward motion due to her advanced pregnancy, with a bright smile for her husband. Dave was so big that when he hugged her she all but disappeared in his arms, and Lizzie felt that stupid pang again in her chest.

She was jealous. Not that she begrudged her best friend one iota of happiness. But no one had ever looked at Lizzie like that.

Except once. At the top of the island, there'd been a moment when Josh had gazed into her eyes and it had been like lightning. *Boom! Crash!* In that brief moment, no one else in the world existed.

And she'd thrown it away.

CHAPTER 18

After looking for the treasure on Aquteg Island for the whole of his life, it seemed, now Josh didn't want anything to do with it.

He sat at his kitchen table and stared at the leather bag. When he looked at the pouch all he could see was Lizzie's face as she picked up the blanket to fold it, her hair blowing in the wind and a stubborn expression on her face. And he second-guessed himself constantly. He'd said he wasn't "built that way," but the truth was he missed her. Seeing her every day at work was nothing short of torture. His brain was thinking just fine, but his body hadn't gotten the message, because every time they passed in the narrow corridor all he wanted to do was press her against the wall and kiss her senseless.

But he didn't. He watched her go by with her tidy hair and starchy white coat and told himself it was for the best.

Ian Martin, one of the town's lawyers, had looked into the matter and it turned out that the coins, which were genuine, belonged to Josh. He didn't care about their worth, but he knew someone who did. Or rather something. The Jewell Cove Historical Society. They'd been trying to set up a permanent home for years and had lobbied hard for Foster House when Abby had inherited it. Right now they made their home in a smaller house on Schooner Street, just one block off Main. It was a hundred and fifty years old and always needed renovating and restoration. Josh figured that he'd give them half the coins for their collection and the other half he'd let an agent auction for him and he'd give them the money to make some changes to the house. It only made sense. He certainly didn't need the money.

The locket, on the other hand, was a different matter. After he went through the faded photos from the Arseneaults and at Foster House, not to mention the few the historical society had, it had been easy to identify the man in the photo as Charles Arseneault. They also appeared to confirm that the woman in the opposite photo was his wife, Constance Arnold.

Josh felt Tom was more entitled to the locket than he was, so he gave his cousin a call and they made plans to meet at Josh's on Friday night, as long as the weather held out. The forecast model showed a tropical storm forming in the Atlantic, and if the path was right Friday night and Saturday could get messy.

Which made him think of Lizzie at the cottage all alone. If the storm strengthened to a hurricane, she'd need to do some prep.

And then he reminded himself that she was a grown-up, competent woman. And that Tom was the landlord of the cottage and he'd see to any preparations that needed doing.

Lizzie had made it perfectly clear that she didn't need Josh . . . at all.

Lizzie hopped in her car and put the bag containing her supper on the passenger seat. The spicy scent of Pasta Pomodoro filled the air, and she'd splurged on a salad and order of tiramisu. It had been a hell of a day. First of all, seeing Josh for eight solid hours was enough to try any woman's willpower. Then she'd had the world's grumpiest senior citizen in with a case of gout, a chain-smoker with emphysema wondering why he was having more trouble breathing, a fifty-something woman on the wrong side of menopause, and, to end the day, a four-and-a-half-year-old little girl who was deathly afraid of needles needing her immunizations before she started school.

Every day had its difficult patients, but today it seemed like they all ended up in Lizzie's exam room at once. To top it off, there was no need to worry about the broken condom. She'd gotten her period, and she was grouchy and crampy and ready for the day to be over.

She was really, really looking forward to some of Gino's spicy sauce, pasta, and a big glass of a Montepulciano she was fond of.

When she finally turned into the drive of the cottage, her appetite suddenly took a nosedive. There was no mistaking the Mercedes in the driveway. It was Ian Fortnam's. What in the world was he doing here?

She pulled in beside his car and turned off the ignition. Nerves twisted around in her stomach. Sure, she'd been thinking more and more about Springfield lately and her job there, but she was utterly unprepared to find Ian at her home.

Correction: at the cottage. It wasn't her home. She bit down on her lip. Even if it felt very much as if it were.

She got out of the car, noticed his was empty. But when she shut her car door, he appeared around the corner of her deck. "Lizzie!" he called, smiling and waving.

"Ian. What a surprise." Wasn't it, just. She pasted on a smile and reconciled herself to the fact that dinner would have to wait. She had to find out what he wanted first. He looked exactly the same as she remembered. Khaki pants, perfectly pressed; button-down shirt, expensive; reddish-brown hair, precisely cut and with a hint of product to keep it in place.

"This place is great. So rustic and . . . isolated."

She frowned. It was, but did he have to make it sound so unappealing? "It's very peaceful," she replied. "Especially in the mornings, when I run on the beach."

She went to the front door. "Hang on a minute. I'll let you in through the patio doors."

She dumped her bags on the counter and went straight to the doors, flipping the latch and sliding them open. "Come on in. I didn't know you were coming or I wouldn't have stopped on the way home from the clinic."

He gave a cursory look at the cottage. "Wow. This is really roughing it for you."

She forced a smile. "You think? I mean, it's simple, but it's got all the amenities and a gorgeous claw-foot tub. I've been very comfortable this summer. Plus the breeze off the ocean is fabulous."

"Yes, you do have quite a view. I was enjoying it as I waited for you to come home."

"Can I get you something to drink, Ian? Then we can go out on the deck and you can tell me what brought you all the way to Jewell Cove."

"A gin and tonic if you've got it."

Lizzie blinked. *Right.* G&T was Ian's preferred drink, and in her condo she'd always had some on hand in the liquor cabinet. "I'm afraid I don't," she apologized. "But I can offer you a glass of wine or a beer. And I think I have a few sodas in the fridge."

Ian's eyebrows rose. "I guess I'll have a soda. I'm not much of a beer man."

She went to the kitchen, aware that Ian was behind her.

"Wow, there's not much room in here."

She shrugged, more annoyed by the second. "There's just me, and you know I've never been much of a cook. I don't need a big kitchen."

Which reminded her that her pasta was still on the counter and she was damned hungry. What was he doing here that he couldn't say with a phone call, anyway?

She took out a can of soda and handed it to him, then took the bottle of open pinot grigio and poured herself a glass. She was dying to ask him why he was here but wanted to be patient. Cool.

In control. Resigned, she put her food in the fridge.

"Shall we sit on the deck?" she asked. "It's nice out there, and I've been inside most of the day."

"Sure," he answered, and she led the way back outside. From the way he was looking at the cottage, she could tell it wasn't quite up to his standards. Maybe it *was* a bit rustic, but it was cozy. She'd thought so from the beginning.

They settled into a pair of chairs and Lizzie let out a sigh. This was her favorite time of day, really. At the end of the summer the sun was mellow, the ocean beautiful, and the breeze fresh.

"Tired?" Ian asked, tipping up his can. She realized she hadn't even bothered to offer him a glass with ice. She wondered why she cared so little. Ian was her boss. Or had been, until her leave of absence. He was the one in the position of making things right again. He might have news of the lawsuit. And right now she was more concerned with her pasta and empty stomach. It made no sense, because with things being awkward between her and Josh her position at the hospital was more important than ever.

"Not really tired," Lizzie replied, taking a sip of the crisp wine. "Just chilling out. My schedule's a dream here, really." She chuckled a little. "I just had some crotchety patients today. I earned my wine."

"I never thought I'd see you at a family practice. Especially not in a small town."

"Life is full of surprises," she answered dryly. "I had to do something. I didn't have a job, Ian. I wasn't about to sit in my condo and take up basket weaving or macramé or something." *Bam.* If he thought she was going to avoid the subject, he was sorely mistaken. It was what it was and she wouldn't pretend otherwise.

"About that . . . ," Ian started the subject, then halted a little.

"Is that why you drove all the way out here, Ian? What is it? Do I not have a job to go back to? Is it something to do with the lawsuit? Because you haven't called once all summer. Not that I expected you to, but finding you on my doorstep is a bit of a surprise."

He put his soda can down on a small table, then turned his chair so he was facing her. "It's good news, actually. The hospital is settling the suit. You don't need to worry about that."

It surprised her that she didn't really react to his news. Truthfully, she hadn't been worried—much. She'd spent far more time wondering about the family affected than any civil litigation. She wondered, as she looked into Ian's handsome face, if he ever felt the same sort of qualms or fits of conscience.

"I made a mistake, Ian. It cost that family their baby. I really wasn't thinking too much about a lawsuit."

"Of course." His eyes softened. "I understand that, Lizzie. You've got a good heart. You always did."

"Is that why you came? To tell me about the lawsuit, tell me what a good person I am?"

His gaze held hers. "Partly. I understand you're angry with me. I hope you believe me when I say I was trying to do what was best. It wasn't all in the interest of the hospital. I'm worried about you, too."

"I was angry at first," she admitted. "But I did need the break. I was on the verge of burnout. I stopped resenting you for that part of it a while ago."

It was true, she realized. It bugged her that Ian had been right, because she didn't like to be wrong. She wasn't blind to her faults. But her time here hadn't been so bad. Jewell Cove was a nice town with nice people.

And Josh. It seemed hugely inappropriate that she would think of him while sitting with Ian, but she couldn't help it. The two of them were doctors but as different as rain is from sun.

She knew which she preferred, and it made her uneasy. She'd left Ian behind without too much difficulty. Josh was going to be a lot harder to forget.

"I'm glad," Ian replied, relief evident in his voice.

"Look, Lizzie, I wanted to see how you're doing, if the time off has been good for you. I can see it was. You've got that sparkle back in your eyes and you look rested. I'm so glad."

"My schedule isn't quite as demanding as I'm used to."

He chuckled. "I bet. Are you longing to get back to the craziness of the ER? I can't picture you really being happy here. Nice for a vacation, but it's not you in the long term. You're not happy unless you're in the middle of the action, with something new to challenge you every day. Ingrown toenails must get a little boring after a while."

It bugged her that Ian would presume to tell her about herself. He'd only known her a few years.

What bothered her more was knowing that he was right. That he was describing the old Lizzie to a T. Hadn't she thought the exact same thing when she'd arrived?

"Are you offering me my job back, Ian?"

"I am. It's not the same without you, Lizzie. I know you took this job out of spite, that you were unhappy with me. But that's all over now. We can move past it, can't we?"

She stared at him, unsure of what to say, wondering if she should actually say anything at all. What was he saying? That he wanted her back as well?

"You mean the leave of absence thing, right?" She sat back in her chair a bit, considering, doing a lot of tongue biting because she didn't want to say anything rash.

"That," he said softly. "And other things as well. I've missed you."

She hadn't missed him. Not that way. "Ian," she said, wanting to be clear but tactful, too, "we got together because we had things in common and, well, it was convenient. But I'm not in that place anymore. Those reasons aren't enough for me."

His smile faded. "They used to be. And it was more than that, Lizzie. I cared for you. I still do."

"And that's why you didn't call me all summer?"

He blushed a little.

"I didn't call you, either." She vaguely remembered a rumor at the hospital about Ian seeing someone new just before Lizzie left. Not for a second did she think that had anything to do with her leaving. Ian did have some integrity, after all. "You were with someone else for a while. Didn't that work out?"

The blush deepened, an unflattering shade next to his reddish hair. "It didn't, no." He swallowed and looked at her. "She wasn't you."

Lizzie had the odd feeling that she should be happy. That Ian was here, offering her not only her job but also a second chance at romance. She knew for sure she didn't want the relationship, and she had no idea how she felt about the job. How was that possible when only weeks ago she'd been furious at being let go?

He put his hand on hers and twined their fingers together. "Lizzie, we can work things out, can't we? We're the same sort of people with the same goals and dreams. I know what makes you tick. I want to try again. I want to go back to how things used to be."

Lizzie pulled her hand away. She couldn't stop thinking about Josh, the way he looked at her that day on the island when they'd made love. She didn't want to, but she suspected that he was now the man who'd set the bar for her, and right now Ian wasn't coming remotely close to measuring up. She was starting to see herself a little more clearly thanks to Josh.

"Things won't be like they used to be because I'm not like I used to be," she said quietly. "I've changed, Ian. And I don't feel that way about you anymore. I want someone who can blow my mind, who can surprise me. Who can make my life exciting and an adventure. We have too much in common. I don't want to be the woman on your arm because we fit or could be this great power couple." She blinked against a sudden stinging in her eyes. "You know what I want, Ian? I want a grand passion. I want to be swept off my feet. And it might not always be comfortable and it might not be easy, but that's okay. You and I would never have that kind of relationship. And it's not fair to you for me to pretend. I need to be honest with you from the start."

Quiet descended on them, uncomfortable and heavy. Ian stared out over the bay, hurt written on every feature. Lizzie waited, and as the seconds ticked on she wished he'd say something so they could move forward.

Finally he sighed. "Okay," he said quietly. "Okay. I get it. Ouch, but I get it."

Her face relaxed slightly. "Thank you, Ian. I wasn't trying to hurt you. It's just . . . it's really over, that's all."

"And the job?" he asked. "Are you still coming back? We could really use you. It wasn't long ago that you were the best doctor in the department. You're young and ambitious and smart and your career is just beginning."

Funny, her dad had said the same thing on her first

day on staff at the hospital. He'd been so happy and proud and she'd been happy, too, seeing that light in his eye. His approval and encouragement had meant so much.

What would he think of the woman sitting here today? Would he feel disappointment? Pride? Did any of it matter? He was gone. Really, really gone.

She missed the pace and challenge of working in an emergency department. But she wasn't sure she fit in in Springfield anymore, either.

"Can I have some time to think about it?" she asked. "I'm here covering Charlie's mat leave, and she hasn't even delivered yet."

"Surely it wouldn't be hard to find a replacement for a few months." He chuckled. "I'm not sure why this place needs two doctors anyway."

She didn't like the way he said it. As if Jewell Cove were barely worth mentioning.

"I can't just up and leave. Besides, she's my best friend. I want to be here when her baby's born."

"So come back and visit." He frowned. "Besides, what about your mom? Don't you hate being so far away from her?"

It was a direct hit to Lizzie's conscience, but it also made it easier for her to step back. "I've been visiting, don't worry. My mother isn't any of your concern. You were the one who forced me out. If I need some time to think about your offer, I'm going to take it."

He finished his drink and put down his can. "I see."

"Did you think I would leap at the chance to return?"

He raised an eyebrow. "Actually, yes. I think I did. You're different than I remember, Lizzie. If I didn't know better, I'd say this town has gotten to you."

If Josh or Charlie or even Jess or Sarah had said such a thing, it would have been a compliment. Lizzie knew Ian didn't mean it that way. God, had she been this snobby when she'd arrived? No wonder Josh had been cool at first.

She stood. "I'll think about it, Ian. That's all I can promise right now."

Ian stood, too, but she'd underestimated his persistence. "Is there a place in town I could book for the night? I'd like to take you to breakfast in the morning. We could talk some more."

Lizzie was at a loss for words for a minute. He'd planned on staying in Jewell Cove overnight? And he hadn't booked a room, which meant . . .

He'd been planning to stay here. *Presumptuous much?*

"There's a motel on the main drag into town, but it's a little, um, plain for your standards. There's an inn a few streets up from the harbor that would probably be okay. It's a busy time of year, though."

She didn't offer to let him stay at the cottage—certainly not in her room, and not in the spare room, either.

"I'll try there," he replied. The strain between them multiplied as Ian accepted the cue that it was time for him to leave. "Breakfast tomorrow, though, before I have to head back?"

It was awkward, but really, she didn't have bad feelings. Breakfast was no biggie. "There's a café called 'Breezes' that serves a great breakfast. Let's meet at nine?"

"Nine, then. And think about what I said, okay? You're a big asset to the department. I'd like to see you return." His gaze met hers. "Regardless of our personal status."

"I will," she said, leading the way to the door.

When he was gone she took out the container of pasta she'd brought home. She'd been hungry then, but she wasn't anymore. Now she didn't know what she felt. It was all so confusing, jumbled up together. The problem, she realized, was that she no longer knew what she wanted. She knew she wanted to be back in an emergency room, but she didn't know how or where. That it might not be in Springfield was something she hadn't considered.

So she put the dish down and changed into shorts and a T-shirt. Nothing felt as good as running on Fiddler's Beach when her mind got working overtime. Maybe then she would have a few answers. And her appetite back.

CHAPTER 19

Breezes was doing a bustling business the next morning. Lizzie'd slept poorly and then missed her alarm, and now she was late. Ian was waiting at a table when she walked in, and she smiled and asked Linda for a coffee refill on the way by the counter, giving the waitress her stainless travel mug. Ian, as usual, was dressed impeccably, in entirely appropriate business casual, his pants precisely creased and his shirt without a single wrinkle.

"Sorry I'm late," Lizzie said, sitting across from him. "Did you find a place all right?"

He nodded, his finger hooked through the handle of his coffee mug. "The inn is surprisingly nice," he offered. "I got the last room, and it was a little small, but the bed was comfortable and it's very quaint."

The backhanded compliment irked her. "I'm glad it met with your approval," she replied, relieved when Linda arrived with her coffee and a pair of menus.

"Here you go, Doc," Linda said, putting down the mug. "You want me to bring a carafe over and leave it?"

"That'd be great, Linda, thanks." Lizzie smiled at Ian. "I'm afraid my love of caffeine is a matter of public record now."

Ian's smile was small and he looked at the single-page breakfast menu. "Do you eat here often?" he asked.

She shrugged. "Well, there's here, the Italian place, and the Rusty Fern, which is the local pub. The clinic's only a hop, skip, and a jump away, so the café is perfect for a quick bite."

He scanned the menu. "I was kind of hoping for some eggs Florentine or something. The menu's kind of plain, isn't it?"

"Try the blueberry pancakes with the maple ham. They're local and delicious."

He frowned. "I don't usually eat that many carbs for breakfast."

Lizzie put down her menu. "Ian, I get it. You think I'm wasting my time here. It's not fancy or high-class or whatever you're used to. I was the same way at first, but really, this is not the armpit of the universe."

He looked taken aback. "I never said it was."

"I like it here." She'd thought long and hard last night, and while she hadn't come to any big conclusions, she'd mulled over her decisions the last few years and why she'd made them.

What she'd come up with had caused her to toss and turn a good portion of the night.

How many of her decisions had been made because of what was expected of her? Had they been what she really wanted? Or had she been trying to be the person she thought others wanted her to be?

That she wasn't sure hinted at the answer. And it was damned scary to think about. Who was she if not that person?

Her whole identity had been wrapped up in two things. Being a doctor and being Russ Howard's daughter. Living up to his reputation. Wanting him to be proud.

And then she thought of Charlie, who'd found the courage to ignore familial expectations and instead had found so much happiness.

God, she was so confused. Worst of all, she realized that the only person to burden her with those expectations was herself.

Ian was watching her curiously. "Lizzie, are you all right?"

"I'm fine. It's just been a lot to think about, Ian. Let's order, okay? I think better on a full stomach." She tried a smile and knew it fell flat. He wanted an answer, and she wasn't going to be able to give him one today.

She ordered a ham and mushroom omelet with a fruit bowl while Ian pursed his lips and finally decided on oatmeal with maple sugar and berries. Linda disappeared again just as the door opened and a line of people came through. A glance outside showed a bus of tourists disembarking for a midmorning coffee break. Linda was going to have her hands full.

"Lizzie? I asked you if you'd made any decision about the job."

She looked at Ian. Really looked at him. He was good-looking, successful, smart. The hospital had become her home away from home. She'd enjoyed the staff, the work. But she wasn't ready to go back yet. She'd made a commitment and she had to honor it, at least for a while longer. "I'm sorry, Ian, but I haven't. I told you I'd think about it, and I will. But I promised Charlie that I would be here for when she had her baby, and I made a promise to Dr. Collins, too. I can't just ditch them because you say it's all over and I can come back."

He balled up his paper napkin. "For heaven's sake, Lizzie. This is your career we're talking about. If Charlie is your friend she'll understand. And haven't you had enough of playing doctor at a rinky-dink family practice? Come on. You can't tell me you find it stimulating enough for you."

The noise in the café grew louder as the crowd increased. Lizzie's patience was fraying. "Charlie's my best friend and she shouldn't have to understand. And as far as this practice, the ER isn't all glamour, either. Know what? It's been nice in a way, because it's not just about patching people up to move them on. It's getting to know people, having them trust you with their care." She leaned forward. "The mayor had a heart attack a while back. And while the emergency got my adrenaline up again, I've enjoyed the weeks since, too, working with his cardiologist, watching his progress. I don't usually get to see that part of it. When I say I need time to think about it, I'm not just putting you off. I really do want to think about it, because my next move is an important one. I won't be rushed. And if that doesn't work for your time line, so be it."

She finished, sat back, and took a restorative drink of coffee.

"Lizzie! Hi!"

Lizzie turned her head to see Sarah heading in her direction. "Oh, hi, Sarah." She could see the woman's gaze fall on Ian, so Lizzie instantly performed introductions. "Sarah, this is Ian. Ian, Sarah. Sarah is the sister of the doctor I'm working with. And Sarah, Ian's my old boss."

Ian held out his hand and shook Sarah's, getting out

of his chair about halfway before sitting down again. "Yes, I'm just in town trying to convince Lizzie how much we need her back."

Lizzie looked into Sarah's eyes. "He stayed at the inn last night. Said it was quite comfortable."

"Well, this is the best breakfast in town." Sarah smiled brightly, not knowing of course that Ian already had disparaged the variety, or lack of it. "Enjoy yourselves." She looked at Lizzie again and then her smile turned quizzical. "Hey, I've seen that mug before." She was looking at Lizzie's stainless one that said, "Trust Me, I'm a Doctor." "I think Josh had one just like it at the hospital when Jess had her baby."

Lizzie's heart froze. *Right.* The morning after they'd slept together. She'd made him the coffee before he left, and he'd returned the mug to the office. Leave it to the ever-diligent Sarah to notice. Great timing, too.

Lizzie couldn't think of something to say, and the beat of silence was all it took for Sarah to catch on. Her eyes widened and her smile was a little more forced. "Um, anyway, I was going to grab something to eat, but with this crowd I'll just head home. I'll see you around. Nice meeting you, Ian."

"Likewise."

When she was gone silence fell once more while conversations erupted all around them.

"Josh?" Ian finally asked.

"He borrowed my mug one day. His other sister was in labor and he went to the hospital."

"You're not looking at me. Don't tell me you've started an affair with the other doctor in town."

"Frankly, what I do in my personal life is none of your business. Not anymore."

He cursed. "What the hell, Lizzie? You call this

getting your life back on track? You know, the case with that baby . . . I can understand that. Everyone misses something now and again. Everyone makes mistakes. But since then your life decisions have been so . . . ugh, I don't even know what." He threw his napkin on the table in disgust.

Lizzie didn't need any more time to think. The carefully planned career she'd envisioned didn't exist and she didn't even feel that bad about it. Maybe she'd regret it later, but she straightened her spine and looked at him.

"You know, I don't think I need more time. I'm sorry, Ian, but I won't be returning. You can feel free to hire someone in my position if you're short-staffed."

His mouth dropped open. "Lizzie. Don't be stupid."

Was that really what he thought? She wondered how she could ever have found him attractive or thought they'd had so much in common. She'd changed. No, not changed. It felt like she was finally waking up to the person she wanted to be. She didn't know if that person wanted to be in Jewell Cove or make a fresh start somewhere else; there was a lot of soul-searching to do. But cutting ties felt good.

"No, this is good. I can't have a do-over, but I can make a fresh start. I really don't think it would work, Ian. I can't imagine taking orders from you anymore."

The volume in the little restaurant had reached a fever pitch, and Lizzie looked over to find a very frazzled Linda trying to manage everything with only one other waitress. "Breakfast is on me, so enjoy it. And good luck, Ian."

He reached out and stopped her with a hand. "Lizzie, you're making a mistake."

She pulled her hand away. "Just add it to my list,

then," she replied. She left him sitting there and went to the counter.

Linda looked up. "I'm sorry, Lizzie. We didn't find out about the bus until the last minute. I know it's taking a long time—"

"Don't worry about it. You can cancel my order, and I'll pay for my guest's now."

"You're sure?"

"Oh," Lizzie said, "I'm positive. Thanks, Linda. I'll see you later."

Lizzie shouldered her bag, clutched her travel mug, and left him behind.

Josh stuck the brush in the bucket and took it out again, dripping with water and soap, and scrubbed along the side of the *Constant* with hard strokes.

His lawn was mowed and the garbage at the curb for pickup and he'd been dying to find something to do. So washing his boat was it. With the storm tracking northward, there was a good chance Maine would suffer a direct hit by the weekend. And even if it didn't, the hurricane would make for some dangerous surge. He'd want to keep his boat out of the water in any case.

Besides, the physical labor kept him from getting angry.

But when a car door slammed and he looked up to find Lizzie standing at the end of his driveway, he knew it would take a lot more than scrubbing at some fiberglass to get rid of his edginess.

She came down the short paved drive carrying a white bakery box in her hands. *Peace offering?* he wondered. Because he knew who'd been in town and knew they'd had breakfast together this morning.

And he hated that it bothered him so much.

"You took the boat out of the water," she observed, smiling at him as she approached.

"Storm's coming. Last thing I want is her smashed up against the dock. Lots of people taking theirs out in the next day or so."

Lizzie's smile flickered a bit at his sharp tone. "The latest forecast says we're in for it."

"Not the first time," he said. He knew he was being curt but couldn't seem to help it. She didn't want him. He wasn't good enough, was he? And barely any time after she walked away, her old fling was in town. She hadn't wasted any time.

"I brought you some cinnamon rolls," she said, holding out the box.

They were his favorite. It irked him that she knew it.

He didn't take them. "Are they to cushion the bad news?"

"Bad news?" She pulled her hands back in, retracted the offer, holding them now while her face took on an entirely too-innocent, confused look.

He dipped his brush again and scrubbed with renewed vigor. "I know who was in town, Lizzie. When are you leaving?"

"What?"

He looked over his shoulder at her. "That is why you're here, isn't it?"

She didn't answer.

He put down the brush, measured his breath. He'd been thinking about her all afternoon, ever since Sarah had gone home. He knew his sister meant well, but she'd poked her nose into his business again and he wished she hadn't. That stupid travel mug, an insignif-icant detail, but Sarah picked up on it. Knew it was

Lizzie's, knew he'd shown up at the hospital at four thirty in the morning with it in his hand. Sarah had said with all the looks he and Lizzie had been sending each other over the summer, she figured he'd spent the night.

And she was concerned because she'd seen Lizzie with her old boss and it had sure looked like they were more than coworkers. Good old Sarah, looking out for her big brother Josh.

He'd kept his cool, thanked her for the concern but insisted it was nothing, and sent her on her way so he could stew about it in peace.

Hours later he was still stewing.

He couldn't look at Lizzie, not yet. "Did he offer you your job back?"

"Yes," she said quietly.

"Does he want you back?"

A pause. "Yes," she replied.

"And when do you leave? I'll have to advertise for another replacement."

She came forward and put the bakery box down on the ground, a few feet away from him. "I never said I was leaving."

He finally faced her, hoping to God he wasn't giving himself away by doing so. That day on the island, when they'd argued, he'd known their brief . . . whatever was over. He'd known today was coming. But it still hurt. He'd wanted to believe in her. He'd cared. He'd started to feel things he hadn't felt before.

But he'd be damned if he'd be the second stringer, the alternate in whatever game she was playing.

"Come on, Lizzie. Of course you are. All you've wanted since you got here was to get your job back. I know you're bored to tears. And you sure as hell aren't staying here for me." It hurt to say, so he turned away again. "Don't worry about it. I'll find someone else for a few months."

"That's it?" she asked. "That's what you're going to say to me today?"

He swallowed, hard. "Was there something else?"

Lizzie gave a short, sharp laugh. "Listen, I know Sarah must have come by to see you. I'm guessing she knows about us. She probably also misinterpreted what she saw. I just wanted to explain."

Josh clenched his teeth. "What's to explain? When did he get here?" Josh wasn't even sure why he asked. The last thing he wanted was to talk about Ian what's-his-name.

"He was waiting for me when I got home last night. Then he stayed at the inn and we met for breakfast. I told him I needed time to think."

Josh let out a short laugh. "Sweetheart, we both know that him staying at the inn means nothing. It's just appearances. And you're always very conscious of that, aren't you?"

She looked as if he'd struck her. "You're being a bastard."

"Self-preservation, sweetheart."

"Stop calling me that. I don't like it the way you're saying it."

So much energy and resentment was coiled up inside him. "Listen, we both knew going into this that it was a limited-time thing. No commitments. No falling in love crap. You made that pretty clear out on the island the other day. So if you want to go back to Springfield, just go."

She didn't reply, and eventually he turned around to face her. Tears shimmered in her eyes and her bottom lip quivered.

It cut into the very heart of him, seeing her cry like that. The urge to apologize and take her in his arms was so strong. But he couldn't. He couldn't willingly let himself go all-in with a woman who wasn't going to do the same. Not again.

So he stood his ground, watched her cry, felt like the world's biggest asshole.

"Is that all you have to say to me?"

"We covered this before, remember? You were the one with the rules. The opt-out and the secrecy. I'm pretty sure none of that's changed. You just thought you were going to be the one to opt out and it bugs you that you're not."

He was surprised to see her cheeks turn a brilliant pink. "You're sure, aren't you? Because you're so sure about everything," she snapped at him, and two tears spilled over her lashes and down her cheeks. "You have all the answers, don't you, Josh? I finally understand that even if I told you you were wrong, you wouldn't believe me. You made your mind up about me the day I came to town."

"That's not entirely true. I saw sides of you that were different. Sides that I . . . liked a lot." He caught himself, but she noticed the hesitation and somehow it only seemed to make her angrier.

"I could say I never should have come here, but that would be a lie." Her words were sharp stabs in the quiet evening. "I needed these few months to see my life clearly. I'm staying until after Charlie has her baby. After that I'll go, if that's what you want."

"What I want?" He gave a bitter laugh. "Do you

know what I want, Lizzie? Peace. I am so tired of all the drama. So tired of games and subtext and trying to be what everyone expects me to be. I should never have married Erin, but I did. I should have seen the writing on the wall. I am so tired of having to smile all the time and be the mature one who sets an example for everyone else. I feel that pressure. What I want is a partner who loves me as much as I love her. Who is committed one hundred percent. Someone I can trust completely. What I don't want is a good time sneaking around pretending to be someone I'm not. I'm done doing that."

She lifted her chin. "Know what, Josh? I think I could stand in front of you offering all those things and you wouldn't see it. Because you don't actually believe that sort of devotion exists for you. The problem isn't that there isn't a woman out there for you, but that you won't be able to recognize her when you see her." Another tear trembled on the edge of her lashes. "The problem isn't me. It's that you'll never let yourself trust anyone again. You'll never let yourself be that vulnerable again. And that's a pretty lonely existence."

He felt like he'd been punched in the solar plexus.

"Until you're willing to open your heart, you're going to be unhappy. Believe me, I know." She took a breath. "Enjoy the rolls."

She turned on her heel and walked away. The night was cool but muggy, yet she seemed to be hugging her arms around herself and her head was down and her stride wasn't the confident, efficient one he was used to seeing.

The top was up on her car, too, and she got inside and shut the door and he couldn't see her anymore.

After she drove away, he picked up the bakery box

and in a fit of frustration threw it toward his garage. Chunks of cinnamon sugar pastry went flying, landing all over his driveway. "Goddammit," he muttered, leaning against the side of his boat. He wiped his hand over his face.

Lizzie had come here to explain and he hadn't let her. Instead he'd just ranted all his frustrations that had been bubbling throughout the day. Sarah's meddling had gotten to him. It wouldn't surprise him if he also got calls from Jess and Meggie tonight, checking up on him, asking what was going on.

He wasn't up to that, and Lizzie was working the clinic tomorrow. He picked up the scattered rolls and put them in the compost, then put away his cleaning supplies and put the cover on the boat. When that was done he checked the gas in his generator just in case they lost power when the hurricane hit. There wasn't much else to do for now, though, and rather than sit home and feel sorry for himself, he decided to take himself down to the Rusty Fern to see if he could find a dart game and a few drinks. Anything to distract him from what a jerk he'd been.

CHAPTER 20

Lizzie would rather do anything else than go to the office and see patients, but it was her scheduled day and so she got there fifteen minutes before the first appointment, put on the coffee, greeted Robin when she arrived, and took several deep breaths trying to calm the anxiety bubbling around in her stomach.

She had to talk to Charlie. Charlie was the only one who'd understand at this point, and Lizzie had some decisions to make.

Robin stuck her head in Lizzie's office carrying a cup of black coffee. "Thought you could use this before we start."

"That smells heavenly. Thank you, Robin."

Robin looked at her closely. "More makeup than usual today. Everything all right?"

Lizzie forced a smile. "Of course it is. Why do you ask?" She could fake it, right? People didn't need to know that she had gone home last night and cried over stupid Josh Collins.

"Well, news at the café this morning is that Bryce

had to pick up Josh at the Fern last night and take him home. I wondered if you knew anything about that."

Lizzie had been about to take a drink of her coffee, but she stopped with the cup an inch from her lips. "Josh was drunk?"

"As a skunk, apparently. Showed up around nine thirty and started hitting the rye. I have to say, I think that's the first time I've heard of Josh getting hammered since he moved back."

He'd really been upset then. Over her? Or just the situation in general? Everyone had a breaking point. God, she knew that right enough.

"I didn't know. Is he okay?"

Robin shrugged. "Probably sleeping off a wicked hangover this morning. Glad you were on the schedule is all I can say." She hesitated. "For a while I thought that maybe you and Josh . . ." Robin looked a little embarrassed but carried on. "Anyway, with you being a little worse for wear, well, I guess I'm saying that if you need to talk, let me know."

Lizzie was touched. Robin cracked jokes, but she wasn't gossipy and she didn't tend to stick her nose too deeply in people's business. "Thanks, Robin, but I'm fine. Really."

Robin nodded and moved back to the door. "First appointment is in room two. Whenever you're ready."

Lizzie sighed and took a drink of coffee, her mind working double time. Josh had gone out and gotten three sheets to the wind last night? That didn't sound like him at all. It was bad enough that his cousin the police chief had picked him up and taken him home. That sort of behavior was so unlike Josh that she was worried. He thought she didn't understand, but she did. More than he could imagine. She knew exactly what it was like to be faced with expectations every day. Why else did she cut loose away from the office? She supposed, thinking about it, that her trips and adventures over the years had been her form of rebellion.

Josh's escape was being out on the water.

On the heels of the worry came anger. If he'd let her explain, things might have been very different last night. But the moment she'd set foot on his property she'd known there was no sense trying to get through to him. He had his mind made up.

Well, one of them had to keep the practice running today. She left her half cup of coffee on her desk, popped a mint into her mouth, and headed for the first appointment of the day.

At lunchtime she went out for a walk in the early September sun, stopped at the market, and picked up a turkey sandwich, which she ate sitting on a bench in the square.

She sipped at her diet soda and closed her eyes, letting the sun soak into her face. She paid attention to her senses, the way the breeze fluttered on her skin, the salty tang in the air from the ocean, the sound of voices and traffic and the leaves on the trees and a short horn blast from a boat either coming in or leaving the cove. When she opened her eyes she was staring up at the statue of Edward Jewell, the town's namesake, and she thought of Josh, and the bag they'd found, and how they'd never even talked about it even though it had to be terribly exciting for him. He'd been looking for evidence of a treasure since he was a boy.

She was tied to this town. It was utterly unexpected, but there it was. Jewell Cove felt like a home. Or at least the closest thing she'd had to a home since she'd grown up and her mom had started getting sick.

And other than Charlie, Lizzie doubted anyone would care whether she came or went.

She packed up the remnants of her lunch and walked back to the office. Inside, Luke Pratt was waiting for his appointment and he greeted her with a bright smile, calling her his "favorite doc." Robin had brewed a fresh pot of coffee and, as Lizzie was tucking her purse away, brought her a mug full of steaming brew.

Reminders of how she'd become part of the community seemed to be everywhere. Luke made her laugh; one of the old ladies from the church group thanked her and called her "dear" and said she was feeling much better since starting her new blood pressure medication. And Lizzie had the distinct pleasure of letting a young woman know she was pregnant, almost exactly one year after her wedding day.

It wasn't exciting and her heart wasn't pounding with adrenaline and excitement, but now, faced with the prospect of leaving town, Lizzie was starting to appreciate it a little bit more.

But how could she stay? After last night, she knew working with Josh would be nearly impossible. And would she really be content doing this forever?

She met Charlie at her house after work. Dave had made dinner, and Lizzie sat down to a lovely meal of grilled chicken and salad. Once they'd eaten, Dave told Charlie to put her feet up and he'd clean up while she and Lizzie visited.

Lizzie watched him disappear into the house carrying their plates and then looked over at Charlie. "You're a lucky woman, you know that?"

Charlie smiled softly. "I know. Ever since I mentioned having to watch my blood pressure, he's been a sweetheart. I'm so ready for this baby to arrive, Liz.

And I've got another few weeks to go. I'll go crazy by then."

"Short trip," Lizzie joked, and Charlie laughed. Lizzie got a warm fuzzy feeling seeing her best friend so happy, though she was a bit concerned with Charlie's color. Her feet continued to swell, too, and Lizzie couldn't help but ask, "When was the last time you checked your BP?"

"This morning. It's okay. Not as low as I'd like, but okay."

"Don't try to tough it out," Lizzie advised. "If it spikes, you get yourself to the hospital, you hear?"

"Yes, Mom," she replied. "And tonight isn't about me. I'm going to sit here like the beached whale I am. I want to know what's going on with you. I heard today that Josh got so drunk at the pub that Bryce had to come and take him home."

"Yeah."

"You know anything about that?"

"I might."

Charlie huffed. "Are you going to make me pull it out of you?"

Lizzie shook her head. "No. I'm just not sure where to start."

In her typical way, Charlie simply waited.

"Okay," Lizzie said, shifting in her chair and crossing her legs lotus-style on the wide seat. "Here's the deal. Ian came to see me the day before yesterday."

"Ian?" Charlie sat up a little straighter. "You mean your ex-boss, ex-boyfriend, Ian?"

"The one and only," Lizzie answered. "And he offered me my old position back."

Charlie's eyes were sharp. "As a doctor or as a girlfriend?"

"Both."

Charlie rolled her eyes and Lizzie laughed. This was why she loved Charlie. She managed to put things into perfect perspective.

"And you said . . ."

Lizzie let out a long breath. "Well, definitely no to the girlfriend. I mean, he hasn't called once since I left. I can't put my finger on why, but I got the impression that he'd maybe been seeing someone and wasn't anymore. You know, looking to hook up again."

"Nice."

"Right?" Lizzie laughed. "The job thing was a harder decision. I told him I needed time to think."

"He wants you back now, doesn't he?"

"At first I told him I definitely wouldn't leave until after your baby is born. I promised to be here for that."

Worry pulled at Charlie's face. "At first. Does that mean you changed your mind?"

"Yeah, I did."

Charlie looked away. "When do you leave?"

"I'm not."

Charlie's head snapped back quickly, her gaze meeting Lizzie with surprise. "What do you mean, you're not?"

"I'm not going back to Springfield. There've been a few viewings of the house and it'll sell. I won't have any trouble selling my condo, either."

Charlie's face lit up. "You're staying here?"

"I don't know, Charlie. Even if I decided to leave emergency medicine behind, I can't work with Josh. Things totally blew up there. He wouldn't even let me explain. The things he said—"

Lizzie broke off, a lump in her throat. "I can't believe I'm going to admit this. I cried a lot last night.

Over him. I never cry over guys. Josh is . . . was . . . different. I should have followed my own rule. It only gets messy when you mix work with your personal life."

"Oh, honey. Do you think you love him?"

The lump grew larger, more painful. "I don't know. I might. I don't ever remember feeling this way. I'm angry, but I'm sad and hurt and confused. . . ."

Charlie laughed. "That sounds about right. When Dave and I were trying to figure things out, I was a wreck. I didn't know what I wanted."

"Yes, exactly." Lizzie nodded. "And I think I need to figure out what I want before I can put that on anyone else. Right now it's mostly cluing in to what I don't want."

Charlie's hand rubbed in circles on her belly and she shifted a little, getting comfortable. "You don't want your old job back, then."

"Not there. Part of the reason the stress got to me is because I felt like I had to live up to my dad's reputation. I put a lot of extra pressure on myself. His daughter wouldn't make careless mistakes, you know? And I felt like I'd let him down, and a lot of other people down, too, who'd believed in me. Add that into seeing the family grieve and I lost my edge."

"I knew your dad. He would have been proud of you no matter what. Liz, you put so much pressure on yourself to be everything. No one can live up to that."

"I know. I think I have to take a step back and make my own way. As Lizzie Howard and not Russ Howard's daughter. I don't know where I'm going to end up, but that's how I want to move forward."

"There's no hope for you and Josh?"

"I don't know. He says he's over his ex, but he has

issues he hasn't resolved yet. We started something up thinking it would be fun. A fling. But Josh isn't a fling type and I don't think he's ready for something serious. His mind is closed where I'm concerned."

"I'm sorry."

"Me, too, actually. I mean, the idea of a real relationship has me scared to death. But it hurts to let him go, Charlie."

Tears were threatening again. "Oh, for Pete's sake, what's wrong with me?"

Charlie reached over and patted her hand. "You let someone in, sweetie. And then they shut you out. It hurts."

"Damn right it does," she agreed.

They sat for a few more minutes.

"I really got used to having you around more. I'm going to miss you if you leave."

"Josh said he'd find someone to take over the rest of your leave. No worries there."

"Maybe you can find something closer."

"Maybe." Liz's heart was heavy as she added, "I have my mom to think about, too. I need to be close to wherever she is. I'm the only family she has now. I don't really know where to begin, you know?"

"Of course I do." Charlie's eyes were dark with concern. "Are you sure you can't talk to Josh? Work things out?"

"He has to be willing to listen," Lizzie said. "I'm not blameless. I sent him mixed signals all summer. I got scared after we slept together and came up with those stupid rules and basically told him it was a friends with benefits thing."

"Josh isn't an FWB type."

"Exactly. And I told him I didn't have anything

more to offer. I still thought I'd be leaving to go back to Springfield. God, what a mess I am."

"Then take time and figure it out. Find your joy, Liz. You've gone cliff diving and bungee jumping and zip lining and Lord knows what else. Be just as fearless with your life. Take a chance. Find what you want to do and step off the edge into the unknown. Go after what makes you happy and the rest will fall into place."

"That's good advice." She smiled at Charlie. "You know you're my sister from another mother, right?"

"Of course I am. Which is why this baby here is going to call you 'Auntie Liz.'"

"I can't wait to meet him or her."

"Her," Charlie whispered. "I wasn't supposed to know, but I saw the sonogram results. We're having a girl."

It was so damned perfect that Lizzie nearly started crying again.

Charlie's eyes misted over, too. "Do you want to stay over, Liz? You can have the spare room. We can stay up and drink hot cocoa and talk, like we used to do."

She nodded. "I'd like that a lot."

The evening was cooling, so they got up and went inside where it was warm. Dave had washed the dishes and hung the tea towel on the oven door handle. He was sitting in front of the television, watching a baseball game and putting together what looked to be a mobile for the baby's room.

"You're sure I'm not intruding?"

"Don't be silly. Of course not."

Charlie gave Lizzie something to sleep in and before long they were ensconced in Lizzie's room with mugs of hot chocolate and a plate of cookies and a stern admonishment from Charlie to not worry about crumbs. They talked and laughed and Lizzie felt the baby move and they cried a little for things they'd lost and those they'd gained, too. And when the moon rose, Charlie fell asleep instead of going to her own bed with her husband and Lizzie crawled beneath the covers and watched her best friend, her heart mostly full.

But there was still one empty space. And Lizzie suspected it was Josh-sized. She wasn't sure what to do with it. The only thing she knew for sure was that she had to keep moving forward.

CHAPTER 21

The storm had been named Nancy and by Friday afternoon Florida and the Carolinas were starting to feel the effects.

In Jewell Cove, the day was sunny and warm, slightly muggier than usual thanks to the tropical air pushing north. At first glance it seemed ridiculous that a huge weather event was on its way. But the sea was already sending a warning, rougher than normal, and boats were being either taken out of the water or secured as much as possible. The public beach was closed and hurricane warning flags whipped in the breeze. Not a sharp, stormy wind, but an ominous hush of chaos to come.

Lizzie had experienced big storms before, but never right on the coast. Even with the wind and waves, she stood on her back deck on Friday afternoon and got the strange sensation that the atmosphere was holding its breath. Nancy was a Category 2 storm but expected to be downgraded to a Cat 1 by the time it reached landfall in Maine, then onward to a direct hit on the Fundy coast in New Brunswick and Nova Scotia. Everyone said it was going to get wild.

They'd closed the clinic to walk-in hours for the afternoon, and Lizzie had gone home to look after storm prep. The deck looked bare with the two small planters she'd bought and the small table and chairs set sitting in the living room. The barbecue she'd moved to a sheltered corner and secured to the deck railing with bungee cords pulled tight.

She didn't have a generator, though Tom had offered to bring a small one by so she could run lights and water. She'd told him to keep it in case someone needed it in an emergency. Instead she checked the batteries in her flashlights, charged her phone, had a bath, and then filled the tub again with water.

At eleven thirty she closed her book and gave the forecast one last check and unease settled in her stomach. She'd thought she'd be okay, but now the idea of waiting out the storm all by herself made her nervous. She thought about calling Charlie and seeing if she could stay there, but it was so late she was sure Charlie and Dave were asleep. She'd just wait to see what morning held. If it wasn't too bad, maybe she'd lock up the cottage and head over.

Light rain started around four. Lizzie heard it and tried to go back to sleep, but it was no use. By six the wind picked up and Lizzie got out of bed and stood at the patio doors, watching the water. It was gray and harsh with angry whitecaps. The leaves on the trees tossed and snapped, but Lizzie knew that this was only the beginning. It would get much worse before it finally pushed through.

She made a cup of coffee and cooked eggs and toast while she still had power. And it was a good thing, because she'd just run the water in the sink to clean up her mess when there was a flicker, then a second flicker, and then nothing.

She sighed, washed her plate and pan, and went to the bedroom to get dressed.

She was just coming out when there was a pounding on the front door. It took her all of five seconds to get there and open it, but in that short amount of time Josh was soaked. He wore a slicker and boots and she stepped aside, letting him in out of the weather. "It's seven o'clock, you lunatic!"

It was a silly thing to say, but the truth was she was so glad to see him it was ridiculous. They'd barely spoken since that night in his driveway.

"Hello to you, too. Your power out?"

She nodded. "Yeah, about fifteen minutes ago. What are you doing out here?"

His gaze locked with hers. "I suppose I'm an idiot. But I was worried about you out here alone. Wanted to make sure you'd battened down the hatches and had everything you need. Wasn't sure you'd been through one of these before."

She was touched. She didn't want to be, but she was, particularly after the way they'd left things. "I'm fine, Josh, but I appreciate you coming by. I even had coffee before the power went out." She smiled at him. Despite all the hard feelings and yes, even the heartache, she didn't want things to be nasty between them. She cared about him, probably too much. Enough that it made her heart hurt to see him. Lizzie, who always kept perspective when it came to relationships and matters of the heart, had broken the number-one rule: the opt-out. She couldn't opt out now. It wasn't a matter of being together or not. He'd found a place in her heart and he was there to stay.

Damn.

"Did Tom bring by a generator?"

"Hmmm? Oh no. I told him to save it. If the storm is as bad as they say, there could be others who need it a lot worse than me, you know?"

"That's good of you."

"I've occasionally rethought that position. Particularly when the wind started to come up."

As if to answer her comment, a gust rattled the house, making her jump.

His jacket dripped onto the floor. "You want to come in for a bit?" she asked. "Not like there's anything to do, but I can offer you some still-warm coffee. The pot's probably still hot."

"I'll take it."

"Hang your jacket up to dry, then."

She poured them each a cup as he took off his jacket, and they went into the cramped living room. The storm raged outside the windows as they each sat on an end of the sofa and sipped. "You did some prep. Good thing. Your patio stuff would have been in the bay later today if you hadn't."

"The barbecue's lashed to the railings and the tub's full of water. I figure I can live on protein bars for a while if I have to."

"It seems kind of isolated out here, though, doesn't it?"

"Yeah. I didn't count on that." She took another drink; the coffee was cooling rapidly. "Did you really come out here to check up on me?"

He nodded. "I've got a couple of jugs of water and some oil lamps out in the truck. If the power stays off a long time, it's good to have some light." He shrugged. "At least it's not a winter nor'easter, where you have to worry about heat and pipes freezing and getting snowed in."

She wasn't so sure. Being snowed in . . . particularly with Josh . . . held a certain allure. He'd shut her down the other night. But her feelings hadn't been shut off so easily.

"It was nice of you, Josh, considering. I know you're not happy with me right now."

He was quiet for a few moments. "It's not you I'm not happy with. It's me. I like to pretend that everything is in the past and it doesn't affect me anymore, but clearly it does."

"It's understandable," she replied.

"No, it's not. I snapped at you and then I went out and made an ass of myself. Some pillar of the community, huh?"

She straightened her spine. "So what? You're human." She shrugged. "Know what, Josh? It can be hard living up to such a stellar example. Believe me, I know. Sometimes it's nice to know that 'perfect' people mess up once in a while. I don't think one transgression will tarnish your reputation too badly."

She took a sip of coffee and sent him a wry look. "Besides, all you have to do is pop one of those dimples at the little old ladies and you're back in their good graces. Mention that your bender was over a woman and you'll get all the 'poor Joshes' you can handle."

"Don't even," he remarked. A little of the tension between them eased, but not all. The last words they'd really spoken—other than necessary updates at work, which they tried to avoid—had been filled with anger and resentment.

"Lizzie," he said quietly, so quietly she wasn't sure he'd spoken at all. The storm was spooling up now, the trees bending in the wind and spray from the cove misting the windows. It was funny how she'd never noticed the everyday hum of electricity before, but in the absence of it the air felt empty and expectant, punctuated by gusts that made the little house tremble.

She looked over at him.

"Liz, the other night . . . I was angry. And maybe a little scared. I think you came to explain and I didn't give you a chance. All I could see was the past repeating itself. You told me the score from the beginning. I was the one who tried to change the rules."

Oh God. He really had no idea how she felt. "Oh, Josh," she said as a strange relief filled her. "I guess it's not surprising that you feel that way. I did a good job fooling both of us with those damned rules."

"Both of us?"

She put her mug down on the coffee table, turned on the sofa, and tucked her leg beneath her. "Yes, both of us. I was scared, too. I'm still scared. Those rules, they were my way of trying to protect myself."

"From getting hurt."

"In a way, yes. That night at your house, I came to tell you that I'd seen Ian. I wanted you to hear it from me and not anyone else. But then Sarah saw us—she's the one who told you, right?"

"It wasn't her fault. She just worries about me. Obsessively." He rolled his eyes. "I know she just doesn't want to see me hurt again. She was there when I was at my worst after Erin died. She saw it all. I understand it, even if her meddling drives me crazy."

"And she told you I'd had breakfast with Ian."

"And that you looked cozy. And that you'd made a point of saying he'd stayed at the inn."

"He did stay at the inn." She held Josh's gaze steadily. "He came to see me, acted as if the last four months hadn't happened. I couldn't believe it. The gall, you know? He offered me my job back. And the girl-friend position, too, which is quite hysterical when I think about it. As if. So I told him I needed to think and I sent him to the inn and we made plans to meet for breakfast. I don't want Ian. I haven't for some time and I was never in love with him. He just . . . checked what I thought were the right boxes. And so did my job. They—both of them—were what I thought I was supposed to do. Mostly to live up to my dad's legacy. When Ian left the café that day, I'd turned down both positions. That's what I was coming to tell you."

His lips had dropped open. "You're not going back to Springfield?"

She shook her head. "I don't fit there anymore. I need to find my own place and make my own way rather than trying to be Dr. Howard Junior. Does that make sense?"

"Yes," he said, "it does. I'm sorry I bit your head off."

"I wanted to tell you, but you didn't want to hear it. And you wouldn't have believed me. I understand why, Josh. I know you came second with Erin and how that made you feel. I know that sometimes I remind you of her and that hurts."

"You were honest with me, Liz. Always, even when I didn't want to hear it."

She was so relieved they were talking again. She'd missed that so much. "Josh, you deserve to be first in someone's life. And that won't happen until you believe that it can be true. I don't know how you're going to find your way to trusting again, but I hope you do."

"I know you're right. I knew it the other night, too. I felt so shitty about how I treated you that I figured I'd fix everything with some rye and Coke. And then a few more and the next thing I knew I was cursing all women and they called Bryce to come get me and take me home."

Her heart softened even more. "I'll stay until you can find someone else. I want to spend some time with Charlie anyway. And if we can find a way to getting along, to . . . being friends, maybe, I could stay until the maternity leave is over. I need to figure out what to do next anyway. Where I want to work, and if that means being close to my mom or moving her somewhere else to be near me. I don't like being hours away from her now. I need her close by. And she needs me for whatever time she has left."

"Stay," he said softly. "We'll make it work."

And then their gazes held and that damnable chemistry flared to life again. Only it was something more. Not just attraction but something bigger. Fuller. Something scary and amazing and it didn't take words or actions. It was just there between them, holding them both captive. It wasn't staying because they could be civil. It was *stay. With me*. She didn't need to hear the words to know it was true.

She'd gone and fallen for him. It had happened by degrees all summer, she admitted to herself, with first the stargazing, then crying on his shoulder, the kisses, swimming, making love . . . all of it. But the thing that toppled her over the edge was right now, sitting in the middle of a hurricane, Mother Nature throwing a tantrum outside while inside he quietly apologized and asked Lizzie to forgive him.

"Josh," she whispered, twisting her fingers together. "I need to apologize, too. For those stupid rules I asked you to agree to, for being so difficult and sending so many mixed signals."

"It's okay. I knew all along you were going through a lot."

"I was lying to myself, acting like we didn't matter. That it was just a fling. What you said on the island that day wasn't just about you. You said you weren't built to do friends with benefits. And the thing is, I am. Or rather, I was. It never presented a big problem, until this summer. Until you, Josh. I couldn't separate my feelings anymore, and that scared me to death. So I kept putting up walls. Making rules. And then I kept breaking them."

"Scared," he repeated, and she nodded slowly.

"Scared. Of my feelings for you. Of falling for you when doing so would mess up all my careful plans. Scared of letting you in and then—"

She looked down as her eyes suddenly began to sting. "Scared of letting myself love you only to lose you later. I don't know how much more loss I can stand this year. I lost my confidence, and I lost my dad, and I'm losing my mom by degrees. My heart is not an infinite resource, you know?"

She blinked hard, willing the stinging to go away.

And then he put a finger beneath her chin, raising it so she was looking at him again.

"You used the word 'love.'"

"I know. And it scares me shitless."

He laughed suddenly, an emotion-packed sound that reached in and grabbed her heart.

"If it helps, I'm as scared as you are."

She smiled at him. "It does, actually."

"Then will you come over here and kiss me?"

She slid across the sofa until she was next to him. Her heart was pounding so hard she could hear it in her ears, and her stomach was a mess of nerves, but the most delicious kind. She raised her hand, placed it along his cheek, feeling the rough stubble there. He closed his eyes as she moved her fingertips, and she traced a fingernail over his bottom lip.

It was soft and she rose up on her knee and leaned in the last bit of the way to put her mouth on his.

The kiss was tender, sweet, unrushed. It was a get-to-know-you kiss and a welcome-back kiss and a starting-over kiss all wrapped up in one. Josh lifted his arm and circled it around her, pulling her down against his chest, and she lay on top of him, feeling like they had all the time in the world.

His hand slid beneath her sweatshirt and grazed the soft skin of her waist, up over her ribs, making her arch toward him a little more, seeking his touch. But then it went away again and his hand curled around her neck, shifting her slightly until the kiss was broken and their foreheads were pressed together.

"Liz," he said. "Are you saying that you want to stay in Jewell Cove?"

She swallowed. "I don't know. Let's just take one thing at a time, okay?" She smiled against his lips. "I've spent years planning every aspect of my career. I think I'd like to wing it for a while. Live in the moment. Enjoy what's right in front of me."

They were kissing again when there was a sharp

crack and a crash. They jumped off the couch, startled by the loud noise, and Lizzie rushed to the window to look outside.

"It's not out back," she said. "And the grill is still on the deck."

Josh went to the kitchen window. "It's out here!" he called to her. "One of the big pine trees at the end of the driveway."

She went to his side and looked out. Sure enough, the howling wind had taken out an ancient pine, and the tree now blocked the end of the drive. Lizzie stared at the huge root system left behind and wondered at the amount of force it would take for such a thing to occur. It was awesome in the truest sense of the word.

Josh was thinking a bit differently. "Looks like I'm stranded right along with you," he observed.

"I can think of worse fates," she joked, putting her hand on his arm.

They were nearly in each other's arms again when Lizzie's phone buzzed.

"It's Charlie," Lizzie said, opening the message. "Shit. She's in labor." Josh's eyes met hers, clearly worried. "She says the road into town is closed because of trees down and they can't get through to the hospital."

Lizzie bit her lip, her gaze turning to the window where the fallen tree was barely visible in the sheets of rain. Charlie needed a doctor, and as Lizzie looked at Josh she knew he understood exactly what she was thinking.

"I'll go," he said. "I've got the slicker. It's only a mile or so."

"It's closer to two miles, in one-hundred-mile-an-hour winds and this rain." She ran her hand through her hair. "You're not going by yourself. I've got a rain-coat somewhere. We'll go together."

"You need to stay where it's safe." He was already texting Charlie, but Lizzie shook her head. No way was he going alone. And if Charlie did end up delivering the baby at home, Lizzie needed to be there, especially if she was this close.

"I promised her I would be there for the birth of her baby. I'm going with you, Josh. Give me two minutes."

Two minutes was all it took for her to grab a rain-coat from her closet. She didn't have boots, so she put on sneakers—the best she could do under the circumstances. Josh was dressed and pulling his hood over his head, tying the strings tightly beneath his chin, and she did the same.

With a big breath, they opened the door, stepped out into the madness, and Lizzie shut it tight and locked it again.

The wind hit them hard, nearly knocking Lizzie off her feet as the rain bit at her face. "You sure you want to do this?" Josh called out.

"I'm sure!" she called back.

"Watch for trees," he advised. "And let's do this as quickly as we can."

Keeping up a fast pace was impossible as they got hit with gust after gust of wind. The sound was wild and eerie; there were no cars on the road or people anywhere. With the power outage the houses were all dark. It felt otherworldly, and Lizzie grabbed Josh's hand as they trudged along the road toward Charlie and Dave's house.

It took them almost forty minutes to make the trek through the storm. There were several trees down and the rain came in sheets, soaking through Lizzie's pants and shoes. When they reached the lane to the cottage, Lizzie let go of his hand and ran to the front door, her sneakers squidging all the way. Josh hustled up behind her just as she was pounding on the door.

Dave opened it, looking harried and very relieved.

"The cavalry's here!" Lizzie announced, stepping inside. Josh went in behind her, and they took off their shoes as Dave shut the door behind them. "Where is she, Dave?"

"In the living room, foolish girl. She was cold and wanted to be near the fireplace. God, it's good to see you guys. How the hell did you get here?"

Josh answered, "We walked from Lizzie's. There's a tree down at her place or else we would have brought the truck."

"I'll go to Charlie. Dave, I'm soaked from the waist down. Do you think you could find me a pair of Charlie's sweats or scrubs and some thick socks?"

"Of course."

A moan came from the living room and Lizzie rushed away.

She found Charlie sitting on one of the loungers from the deck, and Lizzie started laughing. "Oh my God, this is perfect!"

Charlie's forehead glistened with sweat and some of her hair stuck to her face, but she was sitting up just as she would be in a hospital bed. "Glad you find it funny. I wanted to have my baby in a nice comfortable maternity ward, with, you know, electricity and stuff."

"I've got the generator running, baby," Dave said, coming into the room with the wad of clothes in his hands.

"Oh, thank you," Lizzie said, taking the clothes. Her sweatshirt was still dry, but her pants and feet were soaked through. "Charlie, you breathe through the contraction. Josh, maybe you can get Charlie's bag from Dave and take some vitals while I change. Then we'll get down to business."

Dave and Josh disappeared into the bedroom while Lizzie stripped down to her panties and pulled on soft, warm sweatpants and some sort of fuzzy purple socks that were ugly as sin but blessedly warm.

"That feels good. It's wicked nasty out there," Lizzie said, tossing her wet clothes on the small hearth in front of the fireplace.

"You sound like a real Mainer," Charlie gasped.

"What can I say, this place grows on you." Lizzie pulled up a kitchen chair and sat next to Charlie, noting the time on her watch. "Breathe, honey. Nice big breaths. Have you been timing your contractions?"

Charlie sent Lizzie a dark look as she breathed out. "Of course I've been timing them."

"How far apart?"

"Four minutes. Give or take. Though that one felt closer."

Lizzie glanced at her watch again.

"I'm going to have to check you, okay?"

Charlie's face was red and damp with a sheen of sweat as she recovered from the contraction. "Okay. I'd rather it was you than Josh."

Lizzie laughed again. "I bet. Listen, don't worry about a thing, okay? One little baby and three doctors? This is going to be smooth sailing."

Josh and Dave returned, but Lizzie didn't think about seniority or anything else. She just took charge. "Dave, you find a way to boil some water or dig out some alcohol so we can sterilize those scissors, and Josh, you find something we can use for a clamp for the cord, okay? And I'm going to need some towels. Has your water broken yet, Charlie?"

"Not yet," she answered.

"Okay then. I want a garbage bag, too, Dave, and a pile of towels."

Lizzie rooted around in Charlie's bag and found a pair of sterile gloves. "Okay, Charlie. Let's see how far along you are."

Another contraction came, though, and Lizzie glanced at her watch. Barely two and a half minutes and things were speeding up. The contractions were getting closer together, and as Charlie breathed Lizzie could tell that her friend couldn't speak through the pain. She was still panting when Dave returned with a bag and towels, and when Charlie saw him she shot him a glare. "This is all your fault," she groaned, leaning back and closing her eyes.

He drew back as if burned.

"Don't worry," Josh said, coming into the room with a basin and a bottle of alcohol. "She's just in transition."

"Just in transition? *Just* in transition?" Charlie growled, opening her eyes to include him in her wrath.

"And this is why men don't have babies," Lizzie soothed. "Okay, guys, you stay up there for a moment while I have a look."

She knelt in front of the lounger and eased the garbage bag under Charlie's bottom, then layered a couple of soft towels before pulling the sheet down. "There. Now let's get your underwear off, sweetie." Charlie was already covered with a light blanket— apparently the feeling cold bit was true.

Lizzie's exam was brief and she was glad she and Josh hadn't taken any longer arriving. "This isn't going to be long at all. Are you ready to be a mom? You're doing so great." She pulled down the blanket and looked at her best friend. "You can do this. You're nearly there."

Dave sat on the chair Lizzie had abandoned and took Charlie's hand. "I'm here, honey. I'm so proud of you."

Lizzie looked up at Josh, who was taking the stethoscope out of Charlie's bag.

"I love you, Dave." In between contractions now, Charlie's voice softened and Dave touched his lips to hers. Josh needed to listen to the baby, but Lizzie could tell that he didn't want to interrupt the moment.

Another contraction built and Charlie leaned her head forward, holding Dave's hand, breathing in rhythm until Lizzie realized they were all matching her breath for breath.

Josh moved in and had a listen as Charlie rested for the short time between contractions. He met Lizzie's gaze and frowned. "The heart rate's a little slow."

"She's progressing well, though." Unease began to trickle through Lizzie at the suggestion that something might not be 100 percent right. "Do you want me to try to move things along?"

"What's the heart rate?" Charlie asked, still slightly out of breath.

Josh put a reassuring hand on her shoulder. "Not low enough for you to worry about. You put on your mom hat and leave the doctoring to us, okay? We just need you to do your job, which is going to be to push. Very soon, I hope." Josh looked down at Charlie. "We got this, Charlie. I promise."

Again with the skitter down Lizzie's spine.

Outside, the hurricane raged, shaking the cottage with its fury, whipping branches off trees and churning the ocean into a dark-gray froth. But inside they were only focused on Charlie and her labor. During the next contraction her water broke, and Lizzie and Josh worked to take away the wet towels and replace them with new, soft ones. At the next check Lizzie gave Charlie the all clear. "If you feel like pushing, go ahead. Just let your body do the work, okay, honey?"

Dave uttered words of encouragement, but it was four more contractions before the urge to push overtook her.

"She's crowning!" Lizzie exclaimed, beaming at Charlie. Lizzie focused on the baby, on Charlie, tried to ignore the small voice in her head that told her not to get too comfortable. Not to miss anything. The last baby she'd delivered—

No, she couldn't think like that. That was an entirely different situation with an accident and a preemie and—

"Lizzie," Josh's voice interrupted her thoughts. "Hey."

She looked up, dazed. And she could tell Josh knew where her thoughts had gone.

"I'm fine. I've got it."

The baby crowned. Josh was at Lizzie's shoulder, Dave was at Charlie's head, stroking her hair, and things were heating up.

And then Lizzie saw the cord and her heart stopped a little.

The umbilical cord was wrapped around the baby's neck. In her head, Lizzie knew this wasn't a big deal. It was common enough. But that, with the decreased heart rate earlier and her general sense of unease, made Lizzie freeze. What if she was missing something?

"You've got this," Josh said in her ear.

She swallowed. "Charlie honey, don't push for a minute, okay?"

"Easy for you to say!" Charlie grunted and bore down.

"Don't push!" Lizzie commanded, trying not to panic. It was just a cord.

Josh put his hand on her shoulder. "I can step in, but you need to do this. You *can* do it. Just ease the cord over the baby's head." His voice was warm and low so as not to alarm Charlie any further.

Lizzie's eyes blurred with tears and Josh came around, wiped them with his thumbs, and kissed her forehead. "You've got this," he repeated. "Nice and easy, loosen the cord and slip it over. It's only wrapped around once."

With his voice soft and encouraging in her ear, she loosened the cord. The baby turned a little, in preparation for birthing the shoulders, and Lizzie let out a breath.

"Okay, Charlie. Next contraction you give 'em hell."

There was a groan and a yell, and then the baby slid into Lizzie's waiting hands. Josh was there with a pink towel and Lizzie laughed with joy as the baby's first cries filled the room. They bundled her as best they could with the cord still attached and placed her on Charlie's tummy.

"Congratulations, Mom and Dad," Lizzie said, weeping now. "A beautiful, healthy baby girl."

Josh's hands squeezed Lizzie's shoulders. "Told you so," he said in her ear.

"Yes, you did," she replied, tilting her head to rest on his hand for a second. "Thank you, Josh."

He gave her a final squeeze, then took over clamping and helping Dave cut the cord. Lizzie attended to Charlie, and Dave took over the task of a first bath with some of the water he'd heated when Lizzie and Josh had arrived. When both mom and baby were cleaned up, Lizzie helped Charlie settle the baby at her breast.

The sight was so emotional that Lizzie escaped to the kitchen, giving Charlie and Dave some privacy. Josh went with her, and when they were around the corner he simply took her in his arms and held her tight.

She put her arms around his back and held on.

"Josh?"

"Hmmm?"

She tilted her head up to look at him. "I think I love you, Josh."

"Just think?"

"It's a big step for me." She smiled, somehow both tired and energized.

"In that case, I think I love you, too."

She wouldn't weep again. She wouldn't. But the words made her want to.

"For a while I was so afraid. And then you were there and I knew you trusted me."

"I knew what you were thinking. But we all make mistakes, Charlie. And we can't let those mistakes freeze us up and make us afraid to try again."

"You're not just talking about the baby."

"Smart girl. The truth is, if Erin hadn't died, we would have divorced. Our marriage wasn't meant to be. And if that's true, surely that means there's someone else out there for me who is the right one. I can't let myself be afraid and miss the best thing to ever happen to me."

"You're saying that the problem isn't trust but loving the wrong person all along?"

"Maybe. Or maybe the point is, it doesn't matter. Trust, faith . . . it all means something intangible. It's based on something more than hard evidence. And maybe what it is for me is love. Either way, I'm ready to try again."

"Me, too," she whispered. "Except . . ."

He pulled away a bit. "Except what?"

She wanted to do this right. Be sure, not screw it up. "Josh, I've always planned my career step-by-step. And then I let my impulsive side take over my personal life to make up for it. Both crashed and burned. I went looking for adventure, but what I really wanted was something to make me feel alive. You do that for me, Josh. When I look at you. When I touch you. I don't want to ruin that. I just . . . I need you to agree to one more rule."

"Oh great. Another one of Lizzie's rules." His tone was joking, but she could see the shadow of worry in his eyes. "What is it?"

"Be patient with me. I want to do things right. Just be patient with me and be beside me as I figure that out, okay?"

"That's it?"

"That's it."

"I think you'll find I can be very patient . . . about some things," Josh said. Then he dipped his head and kissed her. Hard. Possessively. So passionately that it curled her purple-covered toes.

"Are they kissing?" came a yell from the living room, and Lizzie and Josh broke apart. Josh's face flamed red as they saw Dave standing in the doorway with a smirk on his face.

"Oh yeah!" he called back. "Big-time."

"Woo hoo!"

Lizzie laughed. And then Josh pulled her close and she knew somehow they'd figure it all out.

CHAPTER 22

Two months later

Lizzie huddled into her thick sweater, watching as Josh zipped his fleece up to the top, guarding against the bitter wind off the ocean. The boat ride to Lovers' Island had been a cold one, and in early November the beach felt barren and wild. They'd spent an hour scouring the peak of the island where they'd found the leather pouch but had come up empty. Not that they'd really expected to find anything. Still, Josh's eyes lit up when the mythical treasure was mentioned, even though he hadn't kept a bit of the initial find to himself. The historical society was benefiting greatly from the coins. The rest of the treasure, if there was any, remained a mystery.

Josh and Lizzie both wanted to go to the beach before heading back to Jewell Cove, though. Lizzie stopped, spread her arms wide as if to embrace the wind, and closed her eyes. She was 100 percent enjoying her new adventure—being head over heels in love with the man beside her.

Her eyes were still closed when she felt him there, his body blocking the wind, his lips on hers as his arms pulled her against him. She responded by looping her arms around his neck and kissing him back until they were both out of breath.

"Remember our first trip here?" he asked, his lips close to her ear.

"Of course." She grinned up at him, remembering the day very clearly. "You were very naughty."

"I was falling in love with you even then," he answered, taking her gloved hand in his.

"Me, too." She'd been too afraid, too stubborn, to admit it.

True to his word, Josh had been patient with her while she sorted out what she wanted to do. He'd been free with his affection but reserved in his demands, and she loved him all the more for it. Never in her life had anyone accepted her in this way. The freedom of it had made her decisions easier in the end. She'd waited until today to tell him, hoping he'd be happy with her choices. She'd made them for herself, but also with her and Josh's relationship in mind, and she was quite excited.

"Let's sit over here," she suggested, pointing to a spot where the sand met rock. They found a natural seat in the granite and perched on it, sheltered a little from the cold wind.

"You're a little crazy for wanting to come out here this time of year," Josh teased. "It's freezing. And I'm sure you don't want to strip to your underwear and go for a dip."

"I'm not into hypothermia," she replied. "But I did want to come here for a reason, Josh. I have news."

"Good news?" His eyebrows went up, and she saw a shadow of apprehension. Bless him, he had given her so much freedom, but she knew he had insecurities.

"I think it's good news. I hope you will, too." She spun on the rock so that her legs were over his and his arm was around her. "I've been offered a job in Brunswick, in the emergency room there."

Josh's face lightened. "But that's so close! Commutable distance for sure."

She nodded. "And my hours wouldn't be heavy, either. No more sixty-hour weeks for this chick." She leaned against his shoulder. "I love emergency medicine, but I thought it was time I had a life, too."

"I like that idea," Josh replied.

"Me, too. Since the best parts of my life right now happen to be in Jewell Cove, it made sense to look for something nearby."

"Congratulations," he said, squeezing her close and giving her a kiss. "I'm happy for you. For us, too."

"So you're okay with it? I haven't accepted yet."

"It's your decision, Liz. But yeah, it's incredibly workable. I'm more than okay with it."

"I was thinking, too," she said, "that it would be nice to have my mom closer. I found a few living facilities in the area that specialize in memory loss patients." She met his gaze. "I was wondering if you'd go with me and check a few of them out."

"Of course I will," he said warmly. "I'd be honored, honey."

She'd taken him to meet her mom a few weeks earlier, and it had been a good day for Rosemary. She'd taken to Josh right away, calling him a "handsome young man" and telling him stories of Lizzie when she was a girl. It had been so lovely and yet bittersweet. It always amazed Lizzie how her mom could remember things from the past like that but forget something that had happened only minutes before. Still, it had been important to have her approval.

And for the first time Lizzie had included someone else in her decisions, and that felt good. Like . . . . a partnership. Entirely new but wonderful just the same.

"Thank you, Josh. For being patient with me while I decided what I wanted my life to look like."

"It's the first of your rules that was easy to follow. At least until now." He grinned and touched the tip of her nose with a finger. "There was one thing I wondered, though, Lizzie. And I don't mean to rush you, but—"

He reached into his pocket. "I want to give you this. But only if you're ready for it."

He held out a key.

"To my house, to use as you wish. As often as you wish. And when you're ready, to use every day."

"You're asking me to move in with you?"

He nodded. "But only when you're ready. In the meantime, you can come and go." He smiled at her. "Hell, you already have a toothbrush in my bathroom."

She did, because she'd been spending more and more nights there lately. The cottage was great, but it had always been a temporary spot for her. If she was truly going to settle in Jewell Cove, she needed to have a home.

A physical home. Because she'd already found a home for her heart.

"I know you don't like to overly plan your personal life, but I thought I'd put it out there anyway." Josh put the key in her palm and closed her fingers over it. It was warm from his jacket pocket.

"I find I'm not so scared of planning these days," she mused, squeezing the key tightly. Josh was inviting her into his life. Perhaps it was time she really invited him into hers.

She shifted so that she was sitting on his lap, her arm around his shoulders and her temple against his cheek. "I love you, Josh. And I'd be happy to accept your key, on one condition."

"Oh God. You and your conditions . . ." But there was no apprehension in his voice this time, and she smiled to herself. He trusted her, she realized. Trust that had been so hard for him to give, but he'd given it to her along with the key. What an incredible gift.

"I'll take it, if you make an honest woman out of me."

Josh leaned back so he could see her fully. She loved the shock on his face. He hadn't expected that, but it felt right. And one thing hadn't changed about Lizzie: when something felt right, she made the decision and went for it. Just like she had the day Charlie had asked her to move to Jewell Cove. It had been the best impulsive decision of her life.

"An honest woman . . . are you talking about marriage?"

"If you're interested in marrying again. I know the first time didn't go so well—"

"Wait." He stared at her. "Lizzie. Are you saying you would marry me if I asked you?"

"Why don't you try it and find out?"

He didn't miss a beat. "Will you marry me, Lizzie Howard?"

"Yes."

"Just like that. No conditions or rules?"

"Just like that. But there are rules, Josh."

He groaned.

She cupped his face in her hands. "Rules like for better or worse. Richer or poorer, and all that jazz." She felt her heart constrict as she threw caution to the wind and went all the way. "And there are children to consider. I think I'd like to have a few." Emotion rushed over her as she said the words. She knew what kids meant to Josh. The idea of being mother to his was so big and so perfect she wasn't sure what to do with all the feelings.

He pulled her close. "Easiest rules in the world to follow," he murmured.

Lizzie snuggled deeper into his arms, listened to the breakers on the sand, and for the first time in her life felt like she was exactly where she belonged.

Home.